'Sharp, confident writing, as dark and twisty as the Brighton Lanes' Peter James

'Hays' impressive debut is a complex, twisty, disorienting tale that truly keeps readers guessing until the very end' Karen Dionne

'A cracker of a debut! I couldn't put it down' Paula Daly

'The writing shines from every page of this twisted tale … debuts don't come sharper than this' Ruth Dugdall

'Superb, up-to-the-minute thriller and an amazing crime debut. Prepare to be seriously disturbed' Paul Finch

'This chilling, claustrophobic tale set in Brighton introduces an original, fresh new voice in crime fiction' Cal Moriarty

'Wonderfully layered and gripping, I had to take breaks just to catch my breath' Jendella Benson

'A fresh and raw thrill-ride through Brighton's underbelly. What an enjoyable read!' Lilja Sigurðardóttir

'This truly is a cracking debut, and I can hardly believe it is Ms Hay's first. I see a long career' Louise Beech

'I am not often short of words to sum up a book, but I think I cannot do this debut by L. V. Hay enough justice. A mind-blowing debut thriller that I cannot recommend highly enough' Atticus Finch

'An intense, pacy, psychological debut. The author's background in scriptwriting shines through' Mari Hannah

'From the cover to the title to the set-up to the ending, L. V. Hay's *The Other Twin* will wrong-foot you in ALL the best ways' Caz Frear

'Hay's writing is sharp and smart, filled with insights about sibling rivalry, sisterly love and the lies that bind families together. This is an exceptional debut – original, daring, well written and emotionally truthful' Paul Burston

'Uncovering the truth propels her into a world of deception. An unsettling whirlwind of a novel with a startlingly dark core. 5 Stars' *The Sun*

'With twists and turns in every corner, prepare to be surprised by this psychological mystery' *Closer*

'Well written, engrossing and brilliantly unique, this is a fab debut' *Heat*

'Like Peter James before her, Hay utilises the Brighton setting to create a claustrophobic and complex read that will have you questioning and guessing from start to finish. *The Other Twin* is a killer crime-thriller that you won't be able to put down' *Culture Fly*

'*The Other Twin* is slick and compulsive. Lucy V Hay's writing is fluid and to the point, sometimes frantic, and often chilling' Random Things through My Letterbox

'This is so much more than your standard psychological thriller. It is a breath of fresh air! I loved the nest of lies and deceit this story was built upon. A great, brilliantly written, confident mystery and I can't wait to read more from L. V. Hay' Damp Pebbles

'This book, these characters, and this story will stay with me forever. I am gobsmacked. Totally. Utterly. Gobsmacked … It is phenomenal. It is pure and unadulterated perfection on paper' Emma the Little Bookworm

'Filled with highly descriptive prose, an amazing sense of place and authentic dialogue. The characters are strong, believable, diverse and suitably flawed' Off The Shelf Books

'It's an excellent psychological thriller from an extremely talented writer with a storyline that had me holding my breath' Novel Gossip

'Outstanding. Superb. Epic. Compelling from the first moment, this story will drag you into its grip and refuse to let you go until the very end' Books of All Kinds

'Packed full of tension, emotion and diversity, it is like a breath of fresh air … the complexity of this book will haunt me for some time. Absolutely stunning!' Ali the Dragon Slayer

'I loved how unexpected the truth turned out to be. It was staring me in the eyes and I simply didn't recognise it, understand it, see it … This is a great debut' The Belgian Reviewer

'*The Other Twin* is set to be seismic! From the narrative, to the characterisation, the myriad aspects of this novel conspire in creating a masterpiece!' Ronnie Turner

'The writing – the pace, the characterisation, the vivid sense of place, the dialogue – is superb. The book is fresh, wholly original, and very current, with characters who are stunning in their complexity' Being Anne

'I was flabbergasted that it was the author's debut, as the intense level of complexity stunned me beyond belief. To be able to show such fine-tuned roller-coaster moments in a debut novel, really is something to be proud of' The Writing Garnet

'If you like your psychological thrillers dark, compelling, twisted, thought-provoking and emotional with a real sense of the here and now then you are going to LOVE *The Other Twin*!' Chapter in My Life

'Engaging, addictive and fast-paced – and it's also heart-breaking and emotionally compelling' Crime By the Book

'This book was rich with some superb characters. The twists were riveting and really added suspense. Would I recommend it? HELL YEAH, I would! If you are looking for an emotive, sexy, sinister, dark and twisted read … you'll find it in *The Other Twin*' Crime Book Junkie

'A distinctively different modern psychological thriller, and a cracking read' Blue Book Balloon

'A terrifying mirror reflecting a portrait of our society cut through by magnificent and emotional writing that frees the truth and the truths about life' Chocolate 'N' Waffles

'With a maze of lies and secrets at every turn but also love and acceptance … it was easy for me to fall under this book's spell!' Rae Reads

'A truly brilliant novel that surprises the reader at every turn. Hay is a magnificent writer who enchants the reader' Segnalibro

'A gripping, fast-paced and breath-taking book about fighting for the truth' Have Books Will Read

'I found myself completely drawn in by the way Hay mingled the urgent suspense of a psychological thriller with the deep emotion of a domestic drama' The Suspense Is Thrilling Me

'I absolutely love it when an author messes with my head so hard I feel like I am stuck in a revolving door for hours on end. It's simply unbelievable when you realise this is the author's debut and it promises incredible things for the future' Novel Deelights

'There is a great sense of place captured here and the author has managed to bring the location to life for the reader … gripping and fascinating' Reflections of a Reader

'A very dark and mysterious book' Els Book World

'Beautifully written and hugely layered, this storyline slowly peels back like an onion until the core of the story is revealed and the tears can finally be shed. Dealing with relevant, contemporary issues, Lucy Hay has created a contemporary thriller with a heart of darkness. A terrific read!' Live and Deadly

'The plot has so many twists and turns as secrets and lies are revealed turning the characters and their lives upside down. A brilliant debut!' Book Literati

'This is one very clever, well-written story that fans of psychological thrillers are going to love' Chelle's Book Reviews

'Tension builds and the novel gets twistier the more you read. The underlying issues and themes in the book make for a very timely, insightful novel that more than delivers' The Book Trail

'A whirlwind of secrets and emotional turmoil. It's an invigorating read and one with plenty of surprises lurking in the shadows' Cheryl MM Book Blog

'The novel certainly packs a real punch. The characters are well formed and get under your skin so that you can't help but become involved in the story in a visceral sort of way. *The Other Twin* has an eerily realistic edge to it' Jaffa Reads Too

'Lucy Hay leads the reader down a dark, gritty and heart-thumping road. It has a mature and extremely well-written style and is creatively clever' Love Books Group

'An engrossing and addictive read with a distinctive style. A thought-provoking and perceptive psychological thriller for the social-media age' My Chestnut Reading Tree

'A very well-written story that really drags you in by the scruff of the neck. It is like nothing I've ever read before!' It's All About The Books

'A very complex and confidently written debut and the subject gives it an edgy and relevant feel' My Reading Corner

'Modern, edgy and unique. Lucy Hay has created a fresh and inclusive mystery!' Anne Bonny Book Reviews

'There is a dark and twisted mystery at the heart. It is also a story of family, of separation and of loss. The ending is poignant and moving, the sense of acceptance and overall freedom that emanates from the page is a truly beautiful thing' Jen Meds Book Reviews

'A brilliantly crafted thriller that takes the reader on a journey in and around Brighton and tackles many current themes. *The Other Twin* is packed with tension' The Last Word Book Review

'Brilliantly extraordinary! *The Other Twin* not only doesn't sit in a particular genre, it takes a hammer and smashes down the barriers between genres' The Book Magnet

'This is a many-layered puzzle of a book!' Sal's World of Books

'Took my breath away. I lost count of the times I thought I knew what happened only to be proven wrong a few pages later. A fascinating read' Steph's Book Blog

'This is an astonishing story, not only for how the characters are written but how this difficult story is told with delicacy and sweetness … kept me glued till the last page' Varietats

'Lucy Hay entwines character with modern issues without making the narrative contrived or clichéd. The result is a beautifully crafted book which keeps you on the edge of your seat and delivers a breathless, satisfying read' Books, Life and Everything

'*The Other Twin* is one of the books that I will always bring up in conversations with friends. Truly one of the best books, if not THE best, I have read so far this year!' The P Turners Book Blog

'*The Other Twin* has it all; sex, secrets and social media all set in a claustrophobic version of Brighton that oozes intrigue and suspense. L. V. Hay takes us on the journey confidently and eloquently. This is an accomplished psychological thriller with an original and highly memorable ending' The Word's Shortlist

'I enjoyed reading *The Other Twin* as I am a sucker for a deep, dark secret … It also had a touch of glamour, which one doesn't often see in British thrillers, and which was a nice contrast to the darker side of the writing' Retreat West

'There's plenty of darkness and intrigue in a book set among the social-media generation. With revelations and deceptions around every corner – all delivered by the characters and never forced by the plot – it's a gripping yarn!' Crime Thriller Hound

ABOUT THE AUTHOR

Lucy V. Hay is a novelist, script editor and blogger who helps writers via her Bang2write consultancy. She is the associate producer of Brit Thrillers *Deviation* (2012) and *Assassin* (2015), both starring Danny Dyer. Lucy is also head reader for the London Screenwriters' Festival. She has written three non-fiction books: *Writing & Selling Thriller Screenplays,* its follow-up, *Drama Screenplays*, and, most recently, *Writing Diverse Characters For Fiction, TV & Film*. She is also the author of 'The Intersection Series' of Young Adult novels.

Her debut adult novel, *The Other Twin*, has attracted widespread praise.

She lives in Devon with her husband, three children, five cats and five African land snails. Follow Lucy on Twitter *@LucyVHayAuthor*; on Facebook: *facebook.com/LucyHayB2W*; and her website: *lucyvhayauthor.com*.

Do No Harm

L. V. HAY

**ORENDA
BOOKS**

Orenda Books
16 Carson Road
West Dulwich
London SE21 8HU
www.orendabooks.co.uk

First published in the United Kingdom by Orenda Books 2018
Copyright © L. V. Hay 2018

A catalogue record for this book is available from the British Library.

ISBN 978-1-912374-21-2
eISBN 978-1-912374-22-9

Typeset in Garamond by MacGuru Ltd
Printed and bound in Denmark by Nørhaven, Viborg

For sales and distribution, please contact *info@orendabooks.co.uk*

To all of those who think love has to hurt:
it doesn't.

Let go, walk away and don't look back.

—L. V. Hay

PART ONE

May–June

'*Appear weak when you are strong, and strong when you are weak.*'
—Sun Tzu

I'm early.

I regard the hotel in the wing mirror of my car. I see my own reflection – my nostrils flaring as I take in the venue. If you'd listened to me, you could have had so much more than this. Modern build on an industrial estate? Ugh.

Behind me I can see the gawdy, fluorescent signs for a chain cinema, a bowling alley, various fast-food restaurants, one of which offers an 'all you can eat' buffet bonanza. It's what the Staceys and Chads like to call an 'entertainment park', though I cannot for one second imagine what's so entertaining about these places. Give me a low-key, low-lit restaurant with a ludicrously expensive wine list any day.

Oh no, this is no good. If it had been up to me, I would have found you somewhere far more flash to celebrate your nuptials. But that ship has sailed. For now.

I might be down, as they say – but I'm not out.

A group of people appear behind my car. I watch their reflections. They're in frocks and suits – two couples, the women tottering on high heels, holding on to their men's elbows. They must be going to your wedding.

Then behind them, a tired-looking family: the man is in a shirt and tie, an incongruous pink cloth over one shoulder. He carries a sleeping baby girl in a flowery dress with an overly large bow on the back. The woman wears a trouser suit, the jacket just a smidge too small across her bust. Two little boys in bow ties run ahead of her; she holds her arms out to them as if she's shepherding geese.

A woman in a purple beautician's tabard stops next to the wedding party. She smiles and laughs, beckoning them with her. She's diminutive and young-looking, orange panstick caked on her pale skin. There will be a subterranean salon somewhere in the hotel's depths. The smell of stale sweat will be masked by scented candles, vanilla or patchouli, but the tang of human musk will persist. You can scrub the masseuse tables, the floors, the jacuzzi; you can launder the towels, spray liberal amounts of deodorant and air freshener, strip away our clothes, our pretensions. But it's always there. Flesh – animal, predatory. Demanding domination, submission.

It's what we all are, underneath it all.

I look at my watch. In just one and a half hours you will be married. I suppose I ought to have prepared myself for this day. I felt sure you would wander – as you claimed you needed to – then return, certain you could do no better. I guess I never thought you would leave me so finally, splashing about in your wake.

I'm such a fool.

I check for a concierge or at least a doorman: none. My view into the hotel is unobstructed from my parking space; I can see directly into the reception area through its oversized front window. The rest of the wedding party has stalled next to the big booth in the hallway. The beautician has left them.

The front desk is unmanned. Typical. Two of the men in the group are having some sort of row. One of the women makes a gesture towards the little boys, a clear: Won't anyone think of the children?

The boys have not even noticed though. They've taken off their posh shoes and now race each other across reception, sliding in their socks across the floor. I note the hotel at least attempts to look a cut above. The reception desk is probably oak, the flooring marble, perhaps. But behind front of house, the hotel's owners will have cut back, I'm sure. The carpet on the stairs will reveal its wear, despite the obligatory busy pattern; there will be black scuffmarks on the skirting boards. I can see the curtains on the hall windows sway in the breeze, no lead weights to hold them down. This is three stars at best.

You deserve so much better than this pathetic outfit.

A sharp pain pierces through my chest. Caught unawares, I suck in my breath. The wave makes its way down into my stomach, where it recedes to a dull ache. This has all happened too quickly; I've barely had any time to adjust. But that's got to be a good a thing, surely? Marry in haste, repent at leisure, as they say. But no matter. This marriage will never make it out of the starting blocks. I will see to that.

Repent you will.

One

'I've got it!'

The door to the bridal suite opened and my best mate, Triss, practically fell through it, holding up a plastic bottle. Her face was triumphant, her pale skin flushed almost as red as her hair. She threw her car keys down on the nightstand. 'You would not believe the high street! It's jammed to f—!'

'Ssssh!' I jumped in, before Triss could swear. My six-year-old son, Denny, sat cross-legged on the bed as my stylist brushed and attempted to part his hair. In his hands was my iPad. He did not look up at Triss, but I was aware he was listening. Before I knew it, he'd be telling his mates the new profanity he'd learned over the weekend. Or worse still, he'd repeat it to his dad – my ex, Maxwell.

Triss grinned at me, handing over the bottle of hair relaxant I'd sent her back into town to get. She'd been gone much longer than I expected. I wasn't sure we'd have time to straighten my hair now from its usual, tight curls. Glum, I regarded my reflection in the mirror. If only I hadn't forgotten my hair-products bag! I still wasn't sure how I'd managed that; I was sure I had left it next to the door so I would see it on my way out. Oh, well.

'I think you should go full Solange Knowles, anyway,' Triss declared, reading my expression. She joined me in the mirror and framed both her pale hands around my Afro. She was careful not to shove her hands in it; she knew I hated that. 'If I had hair this awesome, I would wear it as big as possible.'

'You have gorgeous hair!' I said. It was true; Triss's flowing locks were like a Thracian goddess's. She would not look out of place in an old Renaissance painting, or lounging on a giant seashell.

But my best friend just folded her arms and gave me a look. Nearly thirty years of friendship meant I could decode it in an instant. We were polar opposites in so many ways: she was white, I was black; she was tall, I was short; I was a mum, whereas she wouldn't have kids even if she was the last woman on earth and it meant the human race would go extinct. We worked in the same school, but she was a mathematician, while I specialised in language. Yet we were bound together from childhood – like sisters.

So, like a true sister, I couldn't resist: 'You're right, we're both hideous.'

Triss gave that foghorn laugh of hers and swatted me on the arm. She peeled off her T-shirt and denim cut-offs, kicking her flip-flops across the room. One of them hit Denny on the head.

'Oi!' he yelped.

'Sorry, squirt, was an accident!' Triss stood at the wardrobe, pulling a slip off its hanger. She turned and winked at Denny '… Or was it??'

Denny laughed and threw the flip-flop back at her.

☉

'You can't come in!'

I heard Triss's indignant voice in the front room of the bridal suite. A smile came unbidden to my lips, painted an uncharacteristic fuschia. Triss had guarded the bridal suite all morning. She'd taken her maid-of-honour duties so seriously she'd downloaded a checklist from the internet. It had included lots of ridiculous drinking games for the hen party. My stomach flopped over at the fragmented memory of sambuca shots and young men in sailor hats gyrating, whipped cream squirted on their hairless, oiled chests. Ugh.

In the bathroom, I was perched awkwardly on the closed lid of the toilet. The hair and make-up artist had told me to 'stay right there'. I hadn't caught her name. She, too, was the result of Triss's googling, since we hadn't had much time to put the wedding together.

Whatever her name was, she was a formidable woman. She leaned over me, sweeping foundation and powder across my cheekbones and muttering.

I could hear Triss's voice continuing outside the bathroom: 'It's bad luck, Sebastian! Go back to your room!'

I looked in the only mirror in the lacklustre bridal suite. My make-up was done – 'Minimal, I think,' the artist declared, as if it were *her* idea – and we had settled on leaving my hair as it was, clipping some of it back behind my ear. Denny had piped up with the brilliant idea of pinning one of the spare buttonholes in it too. I now matched the bouquets, as if this had been the plan all along. My boy had a great eye.

'We done?' I said now, as I moved towards the door.

I smoothed my dress down. It was off the peg and not white – I had done this before, after all – but it was beautiful. I'd explained to Triss I didn't want the hoo-ha of last time: all pins and measurements and the sucking in of teeth and waists. So she had taken me shopping one lunchtime at various upmarket boutiques. I'd never been comfortable showing off. At my first wedding, I had felt less princess and more walking iceberg. As my dear old dad would have said had he lived to see it, 'You could sink the *Titanic* all over again with that, girl!'

This time, I'd eventually settled on a green silk gown with gold beading, tapered in a fishtail style. It was probably supposed to be a cocktail dress but, in Triss's words, it was 'understated', and it went well with my dark skin and brown eyes. We'd chosen it then barely made it back in time for afternoon registration. I'd arrived to the wide, nine-year-old eyes of class E6, their curiosity about my lateness palpable underneath their unison sing-song greeting: 'Good *afternoon*, Mrs Stevens.'

I regarded the sparkling rock on my finger as I opened the bathroom door: I wouldn't be Mrs Stevens for much longer. Good riddance. I'd had so much hope before I'd married Maxwell and observed all the silly rules and traditions of my wedding day. And it had still gone wrong…

'Hey.'

Triss clucked in disapproval as I appeared in the bedroom. She was still only wearing her slip; her maid-of-honour dress lay on the bed. She grabbed the empty bouquets box and attempted to hold it in front of me, like a shield.

But she was too late. Sebastian had turned towards me. Bright-blue eyes and sandy hair, he was a classically good-looking white boy, with chiselled cheekbones and a strong jaw. He wasn't tall; he met me nose-to-nose at about five eight, but he was pleasingly broad in the shoulder. I noted his floppy, neglected fringe was gone. Like so many grooms, he'd gone for a short back and sides for the occasion. A smile froze on his face as he drank me in.

'Wow. Just … wow. You look amazing, Lily.'

I grinned and did a twirl for him.

'Of course she does!' The make-up artist followed me out of the bathroom. 'I've been slaving over her get-up for an hour!'

'All right, love, don't make it sound like you've had nothing to work with! God!' Triss was loyal to a fault sometimes.

As Triss paid the hair and make-up artist, Sebastian took the opportunity to give me a chaste peck on my overglossed lips. I laughed as he tried to wipe his mouth surreptitiously with the back of his hand.

'Ready?' I said.

Sebastian grinned and nodded. He was already in his suit, though he was missing his tie, jacket and top hat. His waistcoat was petrol green and he'd rolled up his sleeves, exposing his forearms. I didn't know what it was about a guy's forearms – they always made me shiver with anticipation. I leaned in to give him another kiss, but we were interrupted.

'Yuk!' Denny fell backwards on the bed, pretending to gag and thrashing his skinny legs. He was all arms and elbows and knees. It made the fact he was named for my father even more ridiculous: Dennis Okenodo had been a veritable giant, with big, meaty hands and broad shoulders.

'All right, mate, you ready to be best man?' Sebastian laughed.

Denny sat up and shrugged, nonchalant. Like Sebastian, he was wearing a petrol-green waistcoat, though he had his jacket on, plus a bow tie at his collar, held on by elastic.

'So … everything been okay in here?' Something about Sebastian's calm but studied expression set my inner alarm bells ringing.

'What's happened?' I lowered my voice, so Denny couldn't hear.

'Nothing's happened; everything's fine.'

But Sebastian's answer had come too quickly. I gave him a little frown. 'Is it … really?' I said quietly.

My fiancé's shoulders slumped. I turned my back and signalled for Sebastian to do the same, in case Denny had learned to lip-read. Kids changed so fast, you could get left behind if you were complacent.

'Tell me the truth.'

Sebastian sighed. 'I think I saw Maxwell's car.'

'Driving past the hotel?'

'No, in the car park.'

I groaned inwardly. This was the last thing we needed. I'd wanted today to go off without a hitch, but if Maxwell showed up, things could quickly get messy. Flamboyant, destructive, incapable of processing what he didn't want to hear, Maxwell was a human whirlwind of a man. I knew this only too well, because I'd been married to him for nearly six miserable years and had Denny with him.

'But he stayed in his car?' Confusion whirled through me: was this some kind of creepy vigil? Or was he planning to show up at the wedding? Forced to consider the two choices, I'd have preferred the former.

Sebastian nodded. 'I showed the guy on reception a picture of him on my phone. Y'know, just to be safe.'

'That was a good idea.' I breathed out, trying to calm my skittering heartbeat.

Seated at the dressing table, Triss grabbed a hairbrush and waved it in the air. 'Well, he needn't think he's going to cause any trouble, else I'll shove this up his arse.'

I glanced at Denny – apparently he was too absorbed in the iPad to notice what we were discussing.

'It'll be fine.' Sebastian's tone was measured, deliberate.

I almost expected him to grab my wrist and pat the back of my hand, as if I'd had an attack of the vapours. He was so old-fashioned sometimes.

He pecked me on the cheek and, as he turned to leave, he threw over his shoulder, 'I like your hair like that.'

'Told you.' Denny said. He had been listening all along.

Two

Shit, shit, shit. This was so typical of Maxwell. Why couldn't he just leave them alone?

Sebastian parted the curtains on the hotel landing as he went down the stairs. He'd patrolled the landing every twenty minutes for the last two hours and, sure enough, Maxwell's boy-toy car was still below. He'd parked at the back of the large car park at first, but had crept forwards every half hour or so. It couldn't be coincidence. Lily's ex knew they were getting married today; he was supposed to be picking Denny up after the reception.

Irritated now on top of being nervous, Sebastian tramped down the stairs towards reception. His stomach lurched. He'd not been able to eat a thing at breakfast, sipping on stewed black coffee instead. Was it normal to feel so nervous before one's wedding? He had no clue – he'd never done it before. And he'd never really thought about it either. He'd not been against it, it was just that, until nine months ago – and Lily – marriage had been something other people did.

Sebastian arrived in reception. The space around the large desk was deserted but for a black silhouette in the window. Despite the sound of his footsteps on the marble floor, she did not look his way.

'Mum.'

Sebastian's mother turned and smiled. There was a faux look of surprise on her face, as if she'd chanced upon him here, rather than received an actual invitation to her only child's nuptials. As she rose from her chair, Sebastian was shocked momentarily at how long it took her to rise, how frail she seemed.

'Darling.' Fran air-kissed both his cheeks then grabbed him by the shoulders, holding him at arm's length. 'Let's take a look at you.'

Sebastian waited, impatient, as she adjusted his tie and his jacket collar. She nodded at last; he passed muster, it seemed.

'Handsome, as ever!' she said.

Sebastian cast his own eyes over his mother's outfit. She was dressed almost head to toe in black, the only colour the red of her lips, nails and handbag.

Sebastian's uncharitable side rose up – his frustrations with Maxwell showing as he spoke. 'You look like you're going to a funeral.'

Fran's smile faltered. 'Don't, darling. This is a happy occasion.'

Shame flooded through Sebastian. He was being an arse. It wasn't his mother's fault Maxwell was loitering outside. 'Sorry, Mum. Just feeling a bit stressed.'

'Is everything okay?'

'Why wouldn't it be?'

'Just asking, darling. I have done this myself, you know. A million years ago now, but I do remember.' Fran sighed, and as she did so, a sharp cough exploded from her mouth, seeming to take her by surprise. She put an embroidered handkerchief to her mouth. A volley of three or four more coughs followed, her shoulders shaking.

Sebastian guided Fran to a leather settee. 'That's a nasty cough, Mum.'

'Oh, just a touch of summer flu.' Fran smiled, patting him on the arm. 'I bet Lily looks lovely in her dress. But then, she'd know how to make the best of herself, I expect … having done this before.'

Sebastian felt irritation wash over him again. He didn't need this right now. 'Yes Mum, Lily is divorced. I don't need reminding.'

'Well I should hope not, since you'll be taking the boy on.' Fran's eyes twinkled. 'I am proud of you, darling. There aren't many men who would take on another man's child.'

Sebastian almost shook his head in bemusement. Stepfamilies were not unusual in this day and age, but his mother appeared to have been frozen somewhere in the early eighties. He knew she meant nothing by it, though; it was just her way.

'He's a good lad.' Sebastian puffed up his chest, as if responsible for Denny already.

Fran grinned indulgently, then lowered her voice. 'I saw the … ex. In the car park. Do you think he might … try anything?'

'He'd better not.' Sebastian's words sounded tougher than he felt.

Fran nodded. 'It's not too late, you know.'

'Too late for what?' Sebastian said, frowning.

Fran raised her hands. A bemused smile shimmered across her face. 'Goodness me, aren't we a little defensive? I'm just saying, you wouldn't be the first groom to get cold feet.'

Sebastian sighed. He was being unreasonable. His mother had not been unsupportive of his marriage to Lily. And any misgivings she had were to be expected; after all, his and Lily's relationship had been the textbook whirlwind romance. He'd had many girlfriends over the years and loved every single one of them … for a short while, at least. So why wouldn't his mother wonder what was different about this one? It was probably his own stupid fault – he should have brought the two women together more in the nine months he'd been seeing Lily.

'I saw that young woman Lily's so close to – Triss, is it? – sitting outside in her car, too,' said Fran. 'Cutting it a bit fine, isn't she? I thought she was supposed to be the maid of honour.'

'She's with Lily now, Mum, no need to worry,' said Sebastian.

'Anyhow, darling, shall we go in?' Fran offered him the crook of her arm.

But Sebastian's gaze had wandered back towards the window. He'd caught sight of Maxwell's car again. Had he moved the vehicle closer still?

Sebastian thought he had. A Lexus with all the finishing touches, it looked grossly out of place among the saloon cars and people carriers. Even Fran's one-year-old BMW, almost fresh off the forecourt, looked shabby in comparison.

'Sebastian?' Fran prompted.

Through the window, he could see Maxwell sitting in the driver's seat, one hand on the steering wheel. He was as impeccably turned out as his Lexus. Shiny teeth, high cheekbones, close-cropped hair. The cuffs of his expensive-looking shirt were undone and flapping around his wrists in clearly contrived rebelliousness. Even dressed to the nines for his own wedding, Sebastian felt inferior.

Maxwell looked from the windscreen back towards the hotel, and the two men's eyes locked.

'You go in ahead, Mum…'

Sebastian didn't look back as he rushed towards the revolving doors. But before he'd even made it outside, he heard Maxwell gun the Lexus's engine. He arrived on the steps just in time to see Maxwell's penis extension roar out of the car park.

A smile passed over Sebastian's features. That was more like it. He knew it was ludicrous, but he felt the bigger man; he'd seen his rival off, even though he had not technically done anything.

Relieved, he allowed the tension of the morning to dissipate through his limbs, and strode back into the hotel.

He was getting married.

Three

I stopped on the landing as the wave of sound hit me: a scraping of chairs and babble of voices. My nerves prickled – it sounded like there were hundreds of guests. But I knew it was my mind playing tricks. Both Sebastian and I were only children, and we'd stuck to family and close friends. Even so, the guest list had hit nearly seventy, my extended family being large.

'It'll be all right, you know.' Triss adjusted her dress, so just the right amount of cleavage was showing.

I gave her a watery smile. As my oldest friend, she was not only my maid of honour, but was giving me away as well. My cousin Maya was a bridesmaid, following us up the aisle. Denny was the ringbearer.

'Can't see Maxwell's car.' Triss craned her neck to look out of the landing window. She grabbed her boobs and jiggled them, making sure they wouldn't fall out. Perpetually single, Triss would be looking for some action at the reception. I felt sure she would be disappointed; most of the male guests were either married or in their sixties.

'Good.' I handed her my bouquet and patted my hair, checking none of it was caught in any of the beading on my dress.

Triss sighed. 'It's a shame he's such a dick. Wouldn't mind a crack at that myself.'

I wasn't sure whether to be outraged or amused. 'That's the father of my kid you're lusting after and insulting.'

Triss shrugged. She handed me back my bouquet. 'Okay, missus … showtime!'

I raised an eyebrow. 'Seriously?'

Triss grinned.

One step at a time, we picked our way down the rest of the stairs. Hotel workers looked up and smiled at us. I knew they were not really seeing me: they were seeing the dress, the traditions and ceremony. Even so, I enjoyed basking in it all. There had been none of this laid-back attitude at my first wedding. Instead, I'd been drilled military-style by a wedding planner with a beehive hairdo and a clipboard. I'd felt less like a bride and more like a parcel, delivered to my new husband with a big white bow on top.

Sebastian and I were to be married in the Evesham Room. It was the biggest and the lightest in the hotel, with a view onto a large ornamental pond and trees. Of course, if you opened the triple-glazed windows you'd hear the zoom of traffic and realise it was just a narrow strip of green before the motorway. But the price had been right. Sebastian had wanted to spend more, but I'd told him not to. What was the point? I knew men didn't really care about this stuff and in truth, it was just one day.

Sebastian and I had the rest of our lives.

Denny joined us outside the big double doors, accompanied by Maya, who was from Dad's side of the family. I didn't see as much of her as I would've liked, but I could always count on her to attend big family occasions like this. She was wearing the same faded trouser suit she always did to formal events, yet somehow looked chic and effortless. With three kids under five and a full-time job she had no time for shopping – she'd sooner use the time for sleeping, she said. Me, too, and I only had one.

Maya's usually blank, exhausted visage lit up at the sight of me. 'You look gorgeous, Lil!'

I smiled. Next to Maya, Denny carried a small cushion, the rings in a little pouch on top. He stared at it with concentration, his little arms high, like it was a tea tray. His gaze did not leave it, even when we drew up beside him.

Maya dropped her voice to a murmur. 'So, *himself* turned up, I heard?'

Triss cut in before I could answer: 'Gone now.'

'I should bloody think so,' Maya muttered.

'Dad's coming back later though!' Denny declared in a sing-song voice, aware of whom we were discussing despite our best efforts. 'He's picking me up.'

I ruffled his hair. 'That's right, sport. Now, you got the rings? You haven't forgotten them, have you?'

Denny shoved the little cushion towards me. 'They're right here!'

'Silly me.' I winked at him. 'Now remember, even though I'm marrying Sebastian today, you're still my top man, okay?'

Denny shrugged, content and untroubled in the way only small children could be. 'I know. Obviously.'

'Well, that told you, Lil.' Maya grabbed the double doors with both hands, in readiness to push them inwards. 'Ready?'

I took a deep breath and exhaled slowly. Forget butterflies, I felt like I had a bellyful of eels. What if we opened these doors and Sebastian was not there? Or what if he changed his mind mid-ceremony? Which would be worse? I couldn't decide.

But I arrested these thoughts then banished them. Sebastian wouldn't do that to me. He was my soulmate. He would never let me down. He wasn't Maxwell.

Denny, Maya and Triss all looked at me, expectant.

'Ready,' I said.

Four

The ceremony seemed to be over in the blink of an eye. Suddenly Sebastian was writing his name in the registrar's book and there was Lily's new name, next to his: *Lily Adair*. Sebastian felt a rush of pride. No more Lily Stevens. He felt ridiculous for being so pleased that she'd rejected her ex-husband's name and taken his. Sebastian had tentatively floated the idea of changing Denny's to Adair too, but Maxwell wouldn't hear of it. They lived with Sebastian now though, not Maxwell. He could afford to throw Lily's ex a bone or two, he supposed.

The posed pictures on the lawn done, Sebastian shook the photographer's hand and sent him on his way. Taking a moment for himself, Sebastian surveyed everything around him, hands in his pockets. In the skies overhead, dark clouds threatened and there was a nip in the air – typical May bank-holiday weather. Next to the white marquee an old bouncy castle shuddered and lurched from side to side as children jumped and shrieked on it. A couple of adults jumped with them, shoes off. On the marquee's dance floor, Lily, still in her wedding dress, danced with Triss, Denny and some other children. He could hear the chords of an old rock number start up from the band behind them.

It had been a perfect day.

'Well, thank goodness that's over with!'

Irritation prickled through Sebastian as his mother appeared on the lawn next to him. He scowled at her.

Fran lifted her vape to her painted lips, then expelled a cloud of blackberry-scented steam. 'What?' she said, laughing. 'Oh, come on now, darling. You know that you and formal occasions don't mix.'

It was true, he'd always found formal occasions stressful, and as a result his inner jester always made an appearance. He could barely resist acting up. At school, he'd more often than not been excluded from prize-givings, meetings and even sports days. He'd spent many an hour as a child waiting outside the headmaster's office for shouting rude words, singing and generally causing a ruckus whenever heads were bowed and traditions were supposed to be observed. He'd been immensely relieved that Lily had chosen a civil ceremony. If he'd had to stand in a church and observe the wedding rituals, Sebastian had worried he'd have re-enacted yanking another boy's trousers down, exposing his friend's buttocks to the choir.

Any such thoughts had flown from his head on seeing his bride arrive in the Evesham Room.

Lily had flashed him an uncertain smile as she came towards him and Sebastian had been surprised to find tears pricking his eyelids. Denny had wandered behind, his focus very much on the little cushion in his hands; so much so, he nearly fell flat on his face. Triss was wearing a pale-lime silk shift dress and wrap. Sebastian had to do a double-take when Triss appeared: she looked completely different, her hair down, make-up on and in formal attire. At work, she'd often turn up in jeans and he'd have to remind her about the dress code.

'Yes sir!' she'd say, giving him an insolent salute. The day after one of these tellings-off, she'd turned up in bright-orange harem pants, green sandals and a white T-shirt with a yellow smiley face. Sebastian had given up after that.

At twenty-nine, Sebastian was one of the youngest primary-school head teachers in the country, with both Lily and Triss class teachers in the same school. Ever since he and Lily had announced they were engaged he'd had to suffer male colleagues complaining endlessly about the various excesses their wives had indulged in when organising their big day.

Lily had been completely different though. In fact, it had been Sebastian who had wanted to spend more. Lily had barely looked at the luxury hotel and service brochures Sebastian brought home for her. 'I just want to have a good party, with family and friends,' she'd said.

Sebastian was dubious at first. He was used to the women in his life claiming not to want a fuss, then condemning him when no fuss was made. His mother in particular was terrible for this. She'd always say she didn't want anything for Mother's Day or her birthday, then act offended when he took her at her word. 'It's a woman's prerogative to change her mind,' Fran would always say.

'I would have paid, you know,' Fran said now, interrupting his thoughts. 'For the wedding, I mean. Or your honeymoon. Just…'

Her words trailed off. Fran was staring into the marquee, an odd look on her face; a faraway, thousand-yard stare. Sebastian had seen that look many times in his life; in appeared at all major events: birthdays, Christmases, graduations. His mother was thinking about his father and how he should have lived to see his only son thrive in adulthood. A widow since Sebastian was a baby, every one of his milestones was bittersweet for her.

'I know you would have.' He put his arm around her, squeezed her to him.

Fran tapped her vape on her teeth. 'Well, never mind. You'll get it all soon enough – when I'm gone.'

Sebastian arrested a laugh in his throat. 'Mum, you're so morbid. You're barely into your fifties.'

Fran breathed out another vape plume. 'Right, I need a drink of the hard stuff! How about it?'

Fran slipped her arm through Sebastian's, keen on moving towards one of the waiters taking trays of Champagne around the lawn. Sebastian was pleased by her good humour and allowed her to sweep him along.

'Thank you, Mum,' he said quietly.

Fran grasped a Champagne flute from a tray. 'Whatever for, darling?'

'For … everything.' He felt his emotions welling up, and had to take a breath. His mother was old school; he didn't want to embarrass her. But it was his wedding day – the occasion called for an expression of gratitude to his only parent for delivering him thus far in his life.

Fran smiled adoringly. 'Thank *you*, darling. I think this calls for a toast, don't you? To whatever the future holds!'

She raised her glass and Sebastian clinked his own against hers. As they drank, Sebastian could see through the marquee's open flaps, onto the dance floor. Guests milled about beside a pop-up bar and more sat at tables decorated with chintzy fabrics, a heart-shaped balloon rising from the centrepiece on each.

From the makeshift stage, the singer of the band spotted him and pointed. 'Yo, Seb, time for a dance, innit!' A friend of Sebastian's from their fifty-grand-a-year school, he spoke as if he grew up on a sinkhole estate.

Caught in everyone's gaze, Sebastian froze. He looked to his mother; she gave him a wide grin and nodded her head vigorously as if to say, *Go on then!*

Sheepishly Sebastian joined Lily in the middle of the dance floor and the children fanned out around them, staring. Their mothers beckoned them to the sidelines as the first bars of Lily and Sebastian's first dance started up: 'Hero' by Enrique Iglesias – a somewhat uninspired choice, but one of Lily's favourites.

And as Sebastian held his new wife close and she mouthed the words of the song to him, he knew there was nowhere he would rather be.

Five

It had been a beautiful day, exactly how I'd imagined and wanted it to be, everyone kicking back and enjoying themselves. There had been none of this at my first wedding to Maxwell, who had micromanaged every aspect of the proceedings. Control freak that he was, he'd thrown toddler-style tantrums about the flowers, the cars, even the chocolate fountain. That would have been bad enough, but he had also tried to ensure there were certain places my relatives could and couldn't sit, plus he'd tried to leave them out of the photos. When I'd questioned him later, he'd suggested I was imagining it all.

In comparison, Sebastian had been the perfect host, meeting my extended family for the first time with a smile and handshake. He hadn't acted like he was better than them, or turned his nose up at their outfits. Everyone had been on their best behaviour. It had been perfect.

I should have known it wouldn't last.

Sebastian and I had just finished our first dance when I became aware of my ex-husband in my peripheral vision. I let go of Sebastian and gawked stupidly at Maxwell. In contrast to the rest of the guests, he was dressed casually, but had chosen his outfit with obvious care: a white shirt, freshly pressed jeans, aviator sunglasses despite the looming grey clouds overhead. He was standing by the marquee opening, Denny on his hip, watching the ongoing celebrations.

I wondered what line Maxwell had spun to get past reception and in here. I knew how amiable he could appear. But also knew, only too well, the mind games he played. I remembered waiting up for him night after night as he committed infidelity after infidelity, right under my nose. I remembered the drinking, the sneering contempt for my wellbeing, the control freakery.

Before I could make any move I saw Triss making her way towards him, sensing confrontation like a heat-seeking missile. I needed to intervene before this got ugly. I could hear their heated voices as I approached, even over the sound of the band behind me.

'I just wanted to say congratulations.' Maxwell's tone was stiff and defensive.

Triss's voice cut through the air. 'Pull the other one, it's got bells on. You don't "just" do anything.'

But Maxwell didn't seem to be paying Triss any attention at all. Instead, he was watching me approach, that infuriating smirk of his playing on his lips. I wished in that moment I had changed for the reception. For some reason, I just didn't want my ex-husband to see me in my wedding dress. This was *my* day, mine and Sebastian's. Maxwell had no place here.

I drew level with them. 'Thanks, Triss, I'll take it from here,' I said, my tone breezy, but carrying a warning. My best friend looked uncertain but moved away. Then, before I could speak again, Maxwell swooped towards me. I smelled his aftershave and the strong, sour tang of alcohol as he kissed my cheek.

'Lily, you look gorgeous. Doesn't your mum look gorgeous, Denny?' Thumb in his mouth and already sleepy-eyed after such a long and busy day, Denny nodded.

I swallowed down my fury. 'You've been drinking? It's barely five o'clock!' I hissed through gritted teeth.

Maxwell dropped his voice as he lifted his aviators. 'Just the one. Chill out, Lil.'

Another stab of irritation lanced through me as he used his old pet name for me. I would bet real money he'd done that on purpose. He was playing down his addiction as always, too. I'd never known Maxwell to drink a lot when he knew he was taking Denny in the car, but could today be the first time? I dithered a moment, wondering if I should tell Sebastian, cancel the honeymoon. Or maybe we should take Denny with us? No, that was ridiculous. We were staying in a hotel that was for adults only. For God's sake! This was typical Maxwell.

'You promise it was just the one?' I demanded quietly.

Maxwell fixed me with a stare from those endless blue-pool eyes of his. 'I give you my word.'

'Lily—' Fran appeared on the fringes of the group now, her concern evident as her gaze jumped from me, to Maxwell. 'Is everything all right? Shall I take Denny for a drink or something?'

I didn't know my new mother-in-law well, but in that moment I loved her – for playing granny and wanting to shield my boy. I turned towards her and patted her arm. 'It's fine, Fran. No harm done.' I gave her a gentle smile.

Fran moved her gaze over to Sebastian, who had now appeared beside her.

He gave her a supportive nod. 'It's fine, Mum. I'll catch you up in a sec.'

Reassured, Fran smiled and moved back into the throng.

Maxwell offered Sebastian his hand. A sudden flash of a memory pierced its way through my mind: I was emptying a bottle of his most expensive whisky down the sink as I waited for him to return from yet another jaunt. Maybe I hadn't always behaved with aplomb, either. But then my ex-husband could try the patience of even the most committed saint. Bloody Maxwell! I didn't want to have to deal with him today, of all days. I willed my new husband not to take my ex's hand.

He did, of course.

'You take good care of her,' Maxwell said, voice soft with what – regret?

My eyes bulged outwards at the hypocrisy, but I saw only a polite smile on Sebastian's face. Counting to ten, I reminded myself that Sebastian was a peacemaker; that's what I liked most about him. No, scrub that – what I liked most about Sebastian was not just that, but the fact he was the opposite of Maxwell in almost every way.

His point made – whatever it was – Maxwell's attention snapped back to me. 'So, I guess we'd better get going. You got Denny's things?'

Obviously, I wanted to say. When Maxwell and I were married,

Denny had always been *my* child. I was the one who did the breakfasts, bathtimes and bedtimes. It was only now I'd left him that Maxwell showed his child any interest.

'...Right here!'

Triss appeared, Denny's rucksack in hand. I hadn't noticed her slip away to collect it for me. I was surprised. How had she thought to get it? Triss was not exactly known for her own organisational skills, even if she was a teacher. The few times I'd asked Triss to babysit Denny for me, he'd be returned to me on a sugar high, hair unbrushed and shoes on the wrong feet. Even so, I nodded my thanks. Maxwell looked almost disappointed as he took it from Triss's outstretched hand. What was he expecting? To go up to the bridal suite with me to get it?

'We don't want to keep you.' Sebastian indicated Denny, whose eyelids were getting increasingly droopy.

Maxwell took Sebastian's pointed gesture in his stride. 'Well, we'll see you in a week, then. Say "Bye Mum".'

Denny gave me a halfhearted wave. Maxwell shot us that smirk of his again, but I was glad to see it accompanied by a slight awkwardness now. He turned and stalked off, back towards the hotel.

On an ordinary day I hated having to hand my boy over to Maxwell, but today it somehow felt a hundred times worse. It was like Maxwell had managed to tramp all over the occasion; everything that had felt so good was now spoiled. All of sudden I was done with the wedding; I just wanted to leave.

'What time are our flights?' I murmured to Sebastian.

He looked at his watch. 'Oh, not for five or six hours yet, we've got ages...'

He spotted the expression on my face and realisation set in. Even less than a year into our relationship, he knew me well.

He draped his arm around my bare shoulders. 'Why don't we say our goodbyes, now? It'll take a while, then we can go get our stuff. Maybe have a drink at the airport, get the honeymoon off to a *flying* start?'

I rolled my eyes at his horrendous pun, smiling despite myself. I hated that Maxwell could still do this to me, even on my wedding day. At least Sebastian didn't hold it against me.

It took nearly an hour to extricate ourselves from the throng as family members and well-wishers all wanted to bid us goodbye. I made sure to tell everyone not to follow us out: that they should make sure they leave when *they* wanted. It made no sense for them not to finish the buffet, or fail to drink the free bar dry, I said, over and over.

It was only later, as we were waiting to board our flight, that I realised.

We hadn't seen or said goodbye to Fran.

Six

Sebastian yawned, irritated as he watched the departures board flash yellow with yet more updates and delays. He shifted his body in the hard, plastic seat near the desk. Directly in front of him, a businessman in a rumpled suit argued with a pained-looking young woman whose gaze kept flitting back to her computer screen. Beside Sebastian, a family slumped, morose. The parents muttered to each other in a language Sebastian didn't recognise. Two small children lay either side of the father, asleep across his lap, on top of each other and unconcerned, like puppies.

At the desk, the anxious young woman tried to contain the annoyed customer. Behind him, a queue was growing, with yet more resentful faces.

'I can only apologise for the delay, sir…'

The annoyed customer was a tall man whose jacket stretched across his sizeable beer belly. At his feet was a small case on wheels that seemed dwarfed by his stature. The man's complexion was flushed, the legacy of a combination of high blood pressure and too many liquid lunches, perhaps.

The man kept emphasising the young woman's name, displayed on her badge, pronouncing each syllable slowly, as if it were an insult. 'Yes, you keep saying that *Ka-tie*, but funnily enough, that doesn't appear to be making the slightest bit of difference, does it, *Ka-tie*?'

'With all due respect, all this isn't making any difference either, is it?'

The words were out before Sebastian had thought them through. As the annoyed customer turned, Sebastian groaned at himself. Peace-making was so ingrained in him, he couldn't stop himself doing it. If he admitted it to himself, it wasn't always strictly for others' benefit, either. Sebastian abhorred chaos and conflict; it was why his years at boarding school, regimented and predictable, had been some of the happiest of his life. He wanted the quiet life; for everyone to get along.

Already regretting intervening, Sebastian stood up to meet the other man's antagonistic gaze, palms out in a conciliatory gesture. 'Look, it's late. Why not go have a drink?'

The tall man's eyes narrowed, as if making a decision. Though the airport floor was solid under his feet, Sebastian felt as if he was walking a tightrope. He'd always been afraid some rowdy man would get physical with him. He hadn't been in a fight since school, where they were never more than a tussle, anyway: the grabbing of shirt collars, the yanking of boxer-short elastic. He was not a big man, nor particularly strong. Against this powerhouse in front of him, he knew he would lose.

And it would hurt. A lot.

'Katie will put a message out on the tannoy when your flight's ready to board … won't you?' Sebastian looked to the young woman.

She nodded, eyes wide. The man blinked. Then his shoulders appeared to sag, his fury dissipating. He took in the people standing behind him, their hostile stares.

'Good idea,' the man mumbled.

He grabbed the extended handle of his little carry-on case and stalked off in the direction of a Starbucks, pretending not to notice or hear the clap of the people in the queue.

'Thank you.' The girl gave Sebastian a grateful smile.

He found himself grinning back, pleased with himself.

Sebastian returned to his seat, just as his pocket started vibrating. It took him a moment to realise it was a call; he'd forgotten to switch the ringer back on after the ceremony. What now?

The word 'MUM' flashed on screen. Her photo accompanied it: a picture of her one Christmas, wearing a purple paper hat, throwing her head back laughing. Sebastian liked this photo because it was one of the few of her without that self-conscious smile she so often adopted that made her look like a James Bond villain.

Sebastian's thumb hesitated over the screen. He was aware that he'd told her he would come and find her after the Maxwell incident at the wedding, but he hadn't. Fran, in comparison to him, could be more mercurial and prone to fits of pique. Sebastian had spent his life trying to guess her moods, appease her; then he could get what he wanted while making it look like her idea.

Knowing Fran as he did, Sebastian knew she would be disappointed. She would have wanted to have a final word with him. She'd probably had some kind of speech or life advice to give him; she collected motivational and inspirational quotes and memes on her Pinterest boards like a million other women online. He feared an argument.

No, that was not right. Sebastian never *argued* with his mother. She would simply scold him for not saying goodbye. And, of course, he would take it. Then he'd hang up and wish he'd said something … He was supposed to be jetting off to paradise with his new bride. For God's sake, the last thing a man should be thinking about on his honeymoon was his mother!

All the same, he dithered. Then a burst of static emitted from the tannoy, along with the flashing yellow words on the LED screen in front of him. They were calling their flight. His mind finally made up, Sebastian swept a finger across the touchscreen and pressed the red phone icon.

The call rejected, his mother's face disappeared from Sebastian's mind as quickly as her photo left the screen.

◉

29th May

Up all night. Adrenaline, I suppose. Maybe a touch of frustration, too. I'd put everything into the wedding plan and I guess I hoped there would be more of a scene? But I don't want to peak early. Every piece of this puzzle has been planned to perfection: I can't have anything fall out of place. Not now, when so much is at stake.

I just hate the idea of you on your honeymoon: the thought of you enjoying yourself with someone else, seeing only them, makes me feel sick. I should be the one with you. I should be the one you turn to, wonderment in your eyes. It should be me you shower with gratitude. It's going to be such a long way back for us.

This torture will be worth it.

30th May

Fuck. FUCK. FUCK!

1st June

How can you be gone only three days and I feel so nauseous? It's like I am a lovesick teenager all over again. I'm pacing the floor, unable to eat, restless. All I can see in my head are sandy beaches, blue skies, cocktails on the beach. You, smiling in the sunshine. This isn't fair. I thought it was bad before, but it was nothing compared to this. Back then, I knew you would return; there was no rush. You would see the error of your ways and come crawling back to me. I was such a fool, so complacent. Now your marriage threatens to sever the ties between us forever. Some would say they've already gone, but those people are just quitters. Not me. One thing I've realised over the years: it doesn't matter how much time it takes, if you're willing to put the hours in, you can reap the rewards. It's never 'if' but when.

You will be back.

2nd June

So, I went out to the airport and moved the car further away from where it was parked. Childish, I know, plus it wasn't even on my schedule … But I had to feel like I was doing something. Sitting here, left behind and twiddling my thumbs was driving me crazy. Now I'm struck by the worry you might notice, or worse – that I was caught on CCTV. But I have to calm down. It's not like I stole it. No one is going to sit through hours of tapes just for that. But I can't be so reckless again. I must stick with the plan; I mustn't deviate again. No matter what.

3rd June

Feeling calmer now. Yesterday was the worst, but I have managed to get my thoughts back under control … though I am still restless. I soothe myself by going through my plans. I have a folder on my desktop dedicated to this project, complete with schedules, spreadsheets, even saved emails and phone recordings. I like to keep meticulous records anyway, but given the sensitive nature of this task, I must be extra careful. I have been deleting everything from the rest of my computer just in case. I found some nerd on an internet forum. He was only too happy to meet me in a backstreet pub and discuss the finer points of black-hat cyber security for fifty quid. He looked like he hadn't gone outside in about a year, lank-haired, pale and blinking. He told me about the cache – a digital shadow of everything you do online, basically – and how to get rid of stuff from it. He taught me how to hide the location of my computer and even how to make it look like someone else's. Yes, very useful indeed.

You'll be back in a few days and then I can begin in earnest.

You're not going to know what's hit you.

Seven

'Cheers!'

Sebastian clinked his glass with Lily's, enjoying the rapturous look on her face. It was one of the things he loved about his new wife: her ability to enjoy the moment. It was why he'd wanted no expense spared on their honeymoon.

'This place is gorgeous!' Lily had exclaimed at the end of their first twenty-four hours, and let out a gratifying squeal as they had strolled, hand in hand, down a fantastically long stretch of a white sandy beach.

Sebastian had spent an age arranging the honeymoon. The fact they wanted to marry soon had proved difficult, since so many resorts were already fully booked. But Sebastian had never shied away from a challenge. Besides, he wanted to outdo Maxwell, who had only taken Lily to Paris for a long weekend. Sebastian knew that would have been impressive enough for her, as she'd grown up in a house where money was always tight. He really wanted to blow her socks off though.

They'd gone on a small tour that first day. Sebastian had hired a rotund guide, who had regaled them with a full spiel they later joked sounded like he'd lifted wholesale from a website. He'd pointed out the French colonial mansions and told them about the various exotic plants that could be found in the islands' old botanic gardens.

After, they'd wandered through an old Indian marketplace. Sebastian had told Lily about the nature walks he'd arranged for them to take through the biodiverse climate, and how they'd be visiting the pristine offshore islands, reachable only via catamaran. Lily was as delighted as he'd hoped she would be.

Later in the holiday, they'd also viewed imported African animals at Casela, the island's eco-adventure park. There was time for horse riding, rum tasting and even quad biking.

But it was Sebastian's *piece de resistance* he'd most savoured: swimming with dolphins. To do this had been Lily's childhood wish. He'd delighted at the childlike wonder in her face when he'd broken to her that this was his plan for that day. Sebastian had thought he'd seen her eyes momentarily go glassy with tears, so like a little girl's, rather than the thirty-six-year-old woman she was. It made his chest puff up like a pigeon's.

Now on their final night in Mauritius, Sebastian could feel his typically British, pale skin glower, as if it retained heat. He felt hot, sweaty and uncomfortable, in comparison to Lily who looked cool and at ease. She was wearing a red skirt and a white peasant blouse that tied together at the bust, accentuating her cleavage in a way that drove him wild.

'Back to reality tomorrow,' Lily said.

Her expression was wistful. Sebastian could not help but notice her gaze wander towards her phone, which was sitting on the table next to her hand. A picture of Denny filled the screen – a huge, gap-toothed grin on his little face.

'He's been fine with his dad.' Sebastian placed a hand over Lily's. 'You've spoken to him every day.'

Lily nodded. 'Just miss my boy, that's all.'

'We'll be back soon,' he soothed.

Lily pretend-grimaced. 'Yup. Back to the grindstone!'

They would be flying back in fewer than fifteen hours. Half-term holiday over, it was school again on Monday. They'd barely have time to reacclimatise before going back to work and sending Denny back to school. It had seemed like such a good idea when he'd booked the honeymoon, but now, faced with the mammoth journey, Sebastian's stomach lurched.

'It'll be fine,' Sebastian said, for himself as much as for Lily.

'It's the summer soon,' Lily smiled beatifically, her head clearly still filled with vacation.

Sebastian picked at the tablecloth, zoning out a little as his new wife talked about all the things they could do together as a family when the school holidays started. The idea of parks and pets' corners and laser tag all seemed a little boring to Sebastian, but then he guessed small boys normally liked that kind of thing. Lacking his own father figure, he'd done none of those things as a child. When he was a boy, and was back home from boarding school, he'd been used to accompanying Fran to museums, plays and stately homes. But despite her efforts to give him a grounding in culture, all she had done was instil in Sebastian a love of staying at home, playing music and reading comic books. He made a mental note: he would buy Denny some comic books at the airport – a little present for his new stepchild. He'd be sure to like them. No little boy could resist superheroes.

'Just can't believe we have to deal with the inspection,' Lily was saying as he tuned back in.

He made sympathetic noises. He wasn't looking forward to that, either. The spectre of the upcoming school inspection was now on the horizon. They'd been due one for a while and he had hoped to get it over with before the wedding. But those government types loved to keep schools and their head teachers guessing. But perhaps it was better that way. It would only be another eight weeks before the summer; then they could have a nice, relaxed time, their first long break living together.

Sebastian did not bother putting the empty bottle back in the ice bucket. A short, conscientious waiter swept by almost instantly to pick it up, an unspoken question on his tanned face. Sebastian shook his head: no more wine. He indicated for more water, instead. The young waiter smiled and was back again quickly, bringing a big, cool jug of water, with slices of fresh lemon floating in it.

Lily poured herself a large glass. 'Maybe we should go on a detox. No booze until the end of term?'

'Is that code for we *are* going on a detox, Mrs Adair?' he grinned.

Lily laughed, then pulled a mock-serious face. 'Well, I have to look after you now, don't I? It's my job.'

'Yes, it is,' replied Sebastian, playing along. 'And I have to do what you say. Like they say, "Happy wife, happy life"!'

Lily's eyes sparkled. 'Can I have that in writing?'

'I think you already did, Mrs Adair. Remember the wedding, barely a week ago?' Sebastian laughed.

Lily grinned and raised her water glass in a toast. 'Okay, then … To a happy wife and a happy life.'

'Forever.' Sebastian clinked his glass against hers.

Eight

We arrived back in the UK to find June had arrived, but had failed to clear away the ominous clouds we thought we'd left behind on May bank holiday. There was a metallic taste to the air: a storm coming.

I rolled my neck and shoulders as I waited for Sebastian to bring the car round to the pickup point. Similarly tired and jet-lagged people trudged past me out of the white halls of the terminal, dragging trolleys of luggage. A couple of kids were piled on top of one, sucking their thumbs, eyelids heavy. The older one, a girl, had her arm across her little brother, protective.

Not for the first time, I let thoughts of a brother or sister for Denny wash over me. Though I'd never felt neglected when my parents were still alive, I felt the absence of a sibling keenly now. Triss was the nearest thing I had to a sister, but we didn't have the shared genes and experiences that people growing up in the same family unit do. What I wouldn't have given to have a sister in my bridal suite, too. Or a brother, so a man could have taken me down the aisle as tradition demanded.

But perhaps that was my baggage. Maybe thoughts of siblings would never enter Denny's head. Besides, I'd had a difficult pregnancy – and an awful labour. And thanks to Maxwell, it had been hard to juggle a career and parenting even with only the one kid. I couldn't fathom how other working mums managed with two or more.

I'd seen my way through it all, though. I remembered how proud Dad had been when I got into university – one of the first in my family. Because he was so well off, everyone assumed Maxwell had paid my fees; but no, I'd shouldered the debt myself and managed a part-time job at the same time as my studies. I'd wanted to do it all on my own. Maybe even before Denny, I'd somehow realised my days with Maxwell were numbered. This may have been why I'd gone on to complete an MA in education through the Open University when I was pregnant. I'd felt a need for my own career, but perhaps what I was unconciously looking for was an escape route.

It had worked – not just for me, but for Triss too. Triss had been one of those lost kids, the type who couldn't see her way through without a trusted ally to run every decision past. Her own parents had been useless drunks, so she'd been at my house every night after school when Dad was at work; and most weekends. She'd stuck to me like glue all the way through school, and worked at the hospital canteen with me too – which was where I met Maxwell.

When I applied to study education at university and then to do my teacher training, Triss announced she was doing the same. We both graduated together. Our only time apart was our first year as newly qualified teachers, when Triss had had to move to Reading for a job. She'd been as homesick as hell, so the moment a position opened up at my school – Avonwood – she applied for it. Of course she got it. As scatty as she was, Triss was a great teacher and had a brilliant rapport with the kids, even though she always insisted she hated them. The end result was that we were back in each other's pockets again – just like we always had been. The only difference now was that I had a new husband. But Triss seemed to accept Sebastian. And he her. Anything else would have made my life very difficult. I wouldn't have been without Triss. And I was certain she couldn't do without me.

Sebastian drew up in the car at last. Grabbing the suitcases from me as I rolled the trolley back, he frowned. 'I swear the car wasn't that far away last week. I reckon someone moved it to the furthest car park!'

Exhausted, I smiled anyway. 'As if! It's just cos you're more tired now than last week.'

Sebastian affected a mock strong-man pose. 'Well I better limber up if I'm carrying you across the threshold.'

Nine

Outside Maxwell's home, Sebastian let the car coast to a halt then opened his door before Lily could even get her seatbelt off.

'I'll go and get him,' he said.

He saw Lily sigh with relief. 'Thanks.'

She was tired, and he didn't want her upset by the likes of Maxwell on their first night as a family. He knew that try as she might, Lily could never quite keep from being irritated by her ex's barbed comments.

Sebastian gave his new bride a reassuring smile, got out and walked towards the pathway.

Maxwell's home was a well-laid out town house in a west suburb of Epsom. Surrounded by tall leylandii, it was private, with large front and back gardens. It was the perfect family home, but then Maxwell prided himself on keeping up with the Joneses, even if his private behaviour left a lot to be desired.

Sebastian undid the latch on the garden gate, leaving it open behind him as he trudged towards the porch. He opened the outer door – there was no need for him to ring the bell, as inside, there was a scrabble of claws as a large animal bounded at the glass inner door: Ginny, Maxwell's mad collie, had erupted in a flurry of barks, alerting her owner to Sebastian's presence.

The door opened, letting out a waft of dog. Without a greeting, Maxwell launched straight into conflict, his voice appearing almost before the rest of him: 'Bit late, aren't you? I was expecting you nearly an hour ago.'

Maxwell's hands were gripping Denny's little shoulders as the boy stood in front of him. The significance of the gesture was not lost on Sebastian: *This is mine.* Denny stood between the two men, staring up at them with wide eyes.

Sebastian swallowed down a sarcastic retort. 'We did say between midday and one.'

'Really? Midday, Lily said.' Maxwell smiled, but there was a steely glint in his eye. Before he released Denny's shoulders, he gestured to his cheek. 'Give Daddy a kiss, son.'

Daddy. Son. Words chosen for Sebastian's benefit. Sebastian averted his eyes from the display of affection, then stepped back, allowing Denny to pass.

'Well, thanks for having him,' Sebastian said, careful to keep his tone neutral.

But Maxwell was not having that. 'You don't have to thank me. I'm his father. I'm supposed to look after him.'

You said it, Sebastian wanted to fire back, but resisted.

He turned on his heel and extended a hand towards Denny. But the little boy jerked away, giving him a wide berth. Sebastian sighed, careful not to look back; he knew he'd see satisfaction on Maxwell's face if he did.

Denny's face, on the other hand, was drawn into a scowl. The child seemed different from the week before, more closed off. He often came back from Maxwell's in this mood, almost like he needed to re-establish his connection to Lily. Sebastian supposed most kids from broken families had the same problem. How would he know? Sebastian had never had one dad, never mind two.

'Hi Denny, I missed you!' Lily said. Sebastian could hear the warmth in his new wife's voice at seeing her son.

But Denny barely acknowledged his mother as he got in the car.

'Did you miss me?' she asked, her pleasure clearly dented.

The little boy shrugged, staring out the window as Sebastian started the car.

He could see Lily trying hard not let the hurt show on her face. He smiled at her, tight-lipped, as if to say, *Kids, eh?*

Sebastian pulled the handbrake on. 'Home sweet home!'

Lily flashed him a weary, jet-lagged smile. Sebastian's – and now Lily's – snug little maisonette was near Epsom Playhouse, in a converted Magdalene house. Like so many listed buildings, the only direct access was on foot; they had to park in the car park behind the building, at the rear of a couple of exclusive boutiques and an American-style ice-cream parlour. On bright days, the sun shining through the parlour made the silhouette of the cartoon polar bear on its back window tread its way across the courtyard, until three o' clock, when it retreated again, back into the shadows.

'Hurry up!' Denny opened the car door and practically fell out onto the tarmac.

'Hang on!' Lily chastised as he raced off towards the alleyway that led to the maisonette's front door, halfway down. Dark with half-timbered walls, the alleyway was paved with slate. The little boy waved, a silhouette, the light behind him. Just a few feet from the neon signs of the high street, it was like stepping into another time.

The luggage retrieved from the car, moments later, Sebastian grappled with the keys to the front door. Lily hovered on the doorstep of the maisonette, a bag on one elbow, another between her feet. The long flight and the thought of sorting school stuff out for the next day felt like a giant invisible hand pressing them both down from above. Finally, the key turned and the door opened. Lily began to walk inside.

'…Wait!' Grinning, Sebastian opened his arms up for her. Lily laughed, put one hand on his shoulder and hopped up into his arms, throwing hers around his neck.

'I love you,' she said.

Sebastian rested his forehead against hers. 'And I love you.'

Lily was no waif, but she was trim and light, so it was not difficult to carry her across the threshold into the tiny, dark hallway. He'd been expecting the stale air you always met when a home had been locked up for days, but now an oddly sweet smell came with it. Like rotting fruit. His stomach plummeted. Could a pipe have burst while they were away? They had no downstairs neighbour in the bottom flat, so no one would have known.

'So. Home sweet home!' Sebastian tried to keep his voice bright.

'Come on, then!' Denny pushed past Sebastian, his trainers clumping on the wooden staircase. Before the little boy could ascend, Sebastian blocked his way with one arm. Lily slid from his arms, back onto her feet.

'What's wrong?' Lily said, then followed his pointing finger. 'Where's the stairgate?'

Sebastian didn't answer. 'Just wait here.'

He thumped his way up the stairs, purposely making his steps loud. If there was still someone inside, he wanted to make sure they took their chances and escaped out of a window, hopefully across the kitchen extension roof on the second storey. Jet-lagged, he didn't fancy his chances against a burglar.

When he made it to the top of the stairs, he let out a groan. 'Oh my God…'

At first, his brain could not process what his eyes were seeing. Then, bit by bit, he picked through the chaos: the broken glass bottles and jars that had been thrown across the floor tiles, jams and condiments mixing in gelatinous puddles. The bin had been overturned, onto the floor and the sofa. Bottles of cordial had been emptied over the surfaces. Books and papers were everywhere, scattered like giant confetti.

The maisonette was well and truly trashed.

'What is it?' Lily came thundering up behind him. As she took in the destruction, a hand flew to her mouth. 'No! Who would do such a thing?'

Sebastian picked his way through the the devastation as best as he could and rushed up the stairs to the second storey, taking a glimpse at his and Lily's bedroom as he passed. It was a sorry state in there too, all their clothes pulled from drawers and the wardrobe, plus a can of red emulsion had been poured over the double bed.

More paint had been splashed around the bathroom, their toiletries squeezed from bottles and tubes into the sink and bath.

Sebastian opened Denny's door, expecting the window to be open. There was a flat roof beneath the little boy's window, which was why he had chosen to move the child in there. It lacked the perilous drop should Denny get ideas about climbing on the window ledge.

A major disadvantage though, was the fact that it was also a security issue. A determined burglar could shimmy up onto the roof, making breaking in to the maisonette relatively easy from this side. Had he remembered to shut the window properly before they went away? Perhaps not. A horrible thought occurred to him: had someone been watching the maisonette, and taken the opportunity while they were away to do all this.

But why?

Yet the window didn't look like it was open. He strode over and pulled at it, expecting it to yield immediately. It didn't.

As Sebastian turned from the window, he took in Denny's room. He was taken aback. Unlike the rest of the maisonette, it was pristine. The little boy's bed was made; his books and DVDs were lined up next to the television. His toys were all in the toy box, exactly where Lily had thrown them in a hurry before the wedding and their honeymoon. She hadn't wanted to come home to a mess.

Then the realisation dawned on Sebastian. Maxwell. Denny was *his* child, so why would *he* trash his own son's room? Anger now wound tightly around Sebastian's stomach. A flash of Maxwell's hands on Denny's shoulders again: *This is mine.*

Maxwell had done this.

Ten

I hurried Denny to his room, the only safe place in the whole of the maisonette. I told him he could play on his Xbox as long as he wanted. He looked confused as he juggled the pleasure of more games time with the chaos he'd seen downstairs. I kissed him and shut his door; there wasn't much else I could do short of ringing Maxwell to take him – and I wasn't going to do that. I was just grateful to be able to distract Denny and keep him occupied. He'd started bawling at the sight of his home in such disarray and I didn't blame him. I wanted to cry myself.

Denny settled, I went downstairs to find Sebastian on the phone to the police. Two uniformed officers turned up about forty minutes later, their radios buzzing with static as they took in the destruction we'd had to stand about in as we waited.

'And nothing was taken?' The first one was much older than his colleague, and tall and thin with it.

'Nothing.' After we'd got over the shock, we'd checked for everything of value. Both our laptops, Denny's Xbox, the television, all Sebastian's gadgets and everything else remained where they were supposed to be.

The police made notes, took a look around, asked a few questions, then told us it was probably kids. They asked if we were sure we'd shut the front door properly when we'd left the morning of the wedding. Apparently that was the most likely way they'd gained entrance.

'Of course I closed the front door properly!'

Sebastian had been the one here last. I had stayed at Triss's the night before the ceremony. But he couldn't consciously remember locking the door. That was enough for the police. I had the feeling they were looking for the easiest explanation.

The police then asked if we had any enemies; Sebastian dutifully shook his head … no. He glanced at me and I knew what he was thinking. When he'd come downstairs earlier, bursting with his theory that Maxwell had trashed the maisonette, I'd refused to believe it. Why would Maxwell ruin his child's home? It didn't make any sense.

Once the police had left, I called Triss – to tell her we were back, and to tell her what we'd come back to. She agreed with me. 'That doesn't sound like something Maxwell would do,' she said when I mentioned Sebastian's suspicions.

Triss had known Maxwell as long as I had; she'd even been serving at the till in the hospital canteen when he'd appeared to pay for his latte.

'This and … your friend.' Maxwell had told her, smirking playfully and pointing to me.

I'd been presiding over the fried eggs, sausages and bacon under the white-hot heating lamps, moving the older ones to the front with a spatula. I'd even looked behind me, sure he must have meant someone else.

Triss had snorted with laughter. 'She's available tonight,' she said.

I abandoned my spatula and stood up, hands on hips. 'Oh, am I?'

'Yup. You can pick her up at eight.' Triss didn't even look at me, just accepted Maxwell's business card, as well as the pocketful of change he dumped in her palm.

Maxwell looked though. Intently, as if drinking me in. Those blue eyes had captivated me back then. 'See you at eight then, beautiful.'

Despite myself, a tingle worked its way through my body. Even wearing a hairnet and a tabard covered in grease stains, I *did* feel beautiful in that second. That's what Maxwell could do.

Triss had appeared by my side. 'Oh. My. God. Dr Dish luuuurves you!'

'Pretty sure he's a consultant.' I said, my tone lofty.

Triss waved the card in my face. 'So, you don't want his number, then?'

I'd snatched it from her fingtertips.

'I know, right?' I said now, as I picked my way through the detritus and sticky substances in the kitchen. This clean-up was going to take hours. We needed all hands on deck if we were going to get the place straight before school the next day. 'Would you mind coming over and giving us a hand?'

'Oh babe, I can't.' Triss lamented. 'Much as I'd love to play *Stig of the Dump* with you, guess who left her marking to the last minute this half-term? I'll be up till midnight as it is!'

I sighed, good-natured with it. It *was* typical of Triss. She wished me goodbye and good luck. I said the same to her, before rejoining Sebastian in our trashed bedroom. I felt my stomach plummet. New brides were meant to come back to maybe a few rose petals on their bed, not red emulsion splattered everywhere. Sebastian saw my face and put a consoling arm around me.

'It's not as bad as it looks.' Sebastian tried to force authority into his voice. He obviously wanted to believe it as much as me.

I gritted my teeth for the task ahead. 'Let's just get it done.'

Resolving to be positive, we attacked the mess with gusto. As I threw empty bottles and other rubbish into black bin liners, Sebastian vaccumed behind me. I stripped the bed of ruined linen and Sebastian aired out the room, then scrubbed at a suspicious stain on the carpet.

'You know, I still think it was Maxwell,' Sebastian said, still crouched on his hands and knees. 'Because Denny's room was the only one that wasn't trashed…'

I just couldn't reconcile this with the Maxwell I knew. 'Maxwell is super-clean and finicky – he's a surgeon! The idea of him wrecking the place – spreading filth everywhere? No. I don't think so. It was kids or someone, and they were interrupted before they got to Denny's room.'

'I know I locked that front door. I always do,' Sebastian insisted. 'Whoever did this had a key.' Sebastian tried his best to keep his tone from sounding accusatory. 'Did you give him a key, maybe? For emergencies, with Denny? I won't be angry, I promise.'

Irritation lanced through me. '*Of course* I haven't given Maxwell a key. What do you take me for?'

The doorbell rang. We looked at each other in surprise. *Who the hell could that be?*

'I'll get it.' I said, clumping down the stairs to the first floor, then down to the front door. I wrenched it open, expecting to see the police there again; maybe they'd forgotten something.

But it was Fran, her arms wrapped around a gorgeous bouquet of white roses.

'Oh, hello my dear! I won't stop, I know you're bound to be busy, with school and whatnot starting again tomorrow. I just thought I'd drop these off – a little welcome-home gift for you both.'

I stared from her to the flowers, and started to cry.

Ten minutes later, Fran had rolled up her sleeves to enter the fray and help us put the maisonette to rights.

She talked about her parents and 'Blitz spirit', and set about clearing up and fixing. It turned out she was armed with a variety of home remedies and little-known cures for the problems we were facing – such as getting rid of the paint in the bathroom.

'A little surgical spirit should do the trick,' she said, bending over the bath and scrubbing with a tough sponge. She sat back on her heels and admired her handiwork: the paint spatters really were disappearing. 'Any remaining stains, we can use wire wool dipped in wax, as long as we scrub lightly…'

As Fran stood, she staggered backwards. Alarmed, I rushed forwards, catching her elbows with my hands to steady her.

'*I'll* scrub lightly,' I said, taking the white spirit from her.

'I'm fine! The blood rushed to my head, that's all.' Fran's manner was abrupt. But I recognised why instantly: she was embarrassed.

'Are you sure you're okay?'

Fran smiled, though I noted her sunken cheeks, how pale her skin was. She patted my arm. 'I should be asking you that, dear. What a dreadful welcome home.'

With Fran's help – and Denny distracted – by the time it was dark we'd managed to get the place back into a liveable state. As Sebastian had thought, most of it was cosmetic: once we'd got rid of the broken glass, empty bottles and rotting rubbish from the emptied bin, it wasn't so bad. We could replace the ruined sheets and wash or scrub everything else. I tried not to dwell on our bad luck, or the fact Sebastian must have left the maisonette unsecured. He'd been excited, going to our wedding. But we hadn't lost anything, except time. It didn't matter. We had each other and Denny would soon forget this had ever happened. Everything was fine.

But we couldn't just accept Fran's help and then chuck her out, so once everything was straight, Sebastian called for a Chinese takeaway and grabbed a bottle of wine from the corner shop. As we tucked in, I noticed Fran was only toying with her food, twirling noodles around and around her fork. She didn't lift it to her mouth.

'Not hungry, Fran?'

She gave me a vague smile, pressing a hand to her perfectly flat stomach. 'Not really, dear. Dicky tummy. I feel rather bloated, truth be told.'

'Well, you don't look it.' Sebastian declared, shovelling egg-fried rice into his mouth. I had to smile at his big appetite. 'How's the cough?'

I raised an eyebrow. Sebastian hadn't mentioned this to me. Fran kept talking, probably assuming he had.

'Oh you know, darling. If it gets any worse, I'll be sure to see a doctor, don't you worry.' As Sebastian nodded, Fran turned to me. 'I hear you went swimming with dolphins?'

I was surprised she knew already. But maybe Sebastian had texted her, or had told her the plan before we'd gone? I grinned at the memory. Before I could reply, Denny interjected.

'I want to swim with sharks.' Denny speared a prawn ball with his fork.

'Oh goodness, that would be rather dangerous,' Fran replied, putting her full plate aside on the coffee table.

'Nope.' Denny said. 'Sharks only kill five people a year. Did you know? Dogs kill thirty people a year. Hippos kill nearly three thousand people a year. Volcanoes kill over eight hundred. Aeroplanes … twelve hundred!'

'Okay, okay thank you!' I interrupted. Denny loved facts; we could be here all night. I wondered where his sudden interest in death had come from. I made a mental note to find out what he'd been looking at on YouTube.

I distracted Denny with more noodles as Sebastian described our wonderful week away. The sunshine, the culture, the food, all the fabulous tours and activities we'd done.

'I'm sure it was heavenly, darling.' With a pang, I saw that Sebastian's mother's eyes were glassy with tears and the expression on her face was pained. But then a wan smile appeared on her lips.

I guessed she was thinking about his father. Sebastian had told me what had happened to his dad. They'd had barely two years together. They'd married after a year, his father's unexpected death coming when Sebastian was just three months old. It must have been horrific for her, I thought, having the love of her life ripped from her after so short a time together. Unable to help myself, I leaned forwards and placed a hand on hers. She patted it with the palm of her other hand and dabbed her eyes with a tissue. The moment quickly passed.

She left soon afterwards, with us still thanking her profusely as we followed her to the door.

'Really, Mum, thanks again for all your help.'

I nodded. If it hadn't been for Fran, especially with her cleaning tips and tricks, we'd still have been hard at it. I shuddered at the thought.

'Really, that's what I'm here for!' Fran gave a little laugh. 'I will always move heaven and earth, you know that.'

Sebastian hugged his mother and Fran made her way down the alleyway, towards her car. We waved until she disappeared from sight.

Eleven

Sebastian's first day back at work was a nightmare: a constant stream of paperwork, phone calls and various appointments. Two sets of parents from the PTA turned up out of the blue, demanding to be seen, both saying it was urgent. One was about the upcoming school fête; the other about getting new sponsors for the football kits. Both could have waited. He rebuked his secretary, Rosanna, who stared him out over the top of her smartphone. She really was useless. But Sebastian knew he wouldn't fire her. He had too much to do and could not add interviewing new help to his burden.

Shaking his head, Sebastian walked into the small closet-like en suite next to his office, flicking the light on as he went. He peed quickly, shook himself off and turned to wash his hands. As he did so, he caught sight of his reflection in the mirror. Under the white glare of the overhead strip-light his cheeks were as sunken as the dark circles under his eyes. He looked haggard, older than his twenty-nine years. Not for the first time he wondered if he really was too young for this job.

As Sebastian returned to his desk, the bell went for lunch. He didn't have time for anything other than a sandwich at his desk today. He rolled his head around his shoulders, feeling the tense *crack* of his neck. After a horrible afternoon the day before, he'd had a terrible night. The jet lag had bitten deep and he'd found himself awake at three-thirty in the morning, sweating, his heart racing. He'd sat up in bed, taking deep breaths to calm himself. An envious sigh had escaped him at the sight of Lily, asleep and unruffled, next to him. Denny had joined them too: clad in his Batman pyjamas, the little boy was lying across the foot of the bed, a toy car still in one hand, a bubble of saliva in the corner of his mouth.

Sebastian had grabbed Denny up in his arms with difficulty. A small child, he still felt as heavy as a brick when he was sleeping. As he staggered through to the child's bedroom, Denny's weight felt symbolic to Sebastian: he hadn't just married Lily, he had taken on the responsibility of stepfatherhood. Was it too soon? It didn't matter now; it was done. Even so, Maxwell's jealousy and possessiveness burned in his brain. Was he going to back off? He had to. Even Maxwell would realise that ship had sailed, surely. And perhaps Lily was right. Maybe it was just a coincidence; maybe Sebastian had left the door ajar and kids had got in and trashed the place.

Yet something in Sebastian's gut told him he was right and Lily was wrong.

A deep sleeper, Denny hadn't stirred. Sebastian placed the child into his half-sized bed, tucking him in with a selection of soft toys. He envied him. Life must seem so straightforward. Lily really was an exemplary mother, even if her methods were at times a little unorthodox. Denny was allowed to be a child, carefree and able to find his own limits – two things always denied Sebastian when he was growing up: first by the rigid structures and expectations of his mother, then by boarding school, university and the world of work.

Now, as Sebastian consulted some spreadsheets, he heard the *ting* of the reception bell. He ignored it; that was Rosanna's job. But when the sound came again, he looked up, exasperated. Through the internal window from his office, Sebastian could see that Rosanna's chair was empty. Her bag was missing from the pegs near the main reception desk. Momentary rage engulfed him before he realised it was perfectly reasonable for even the worst secretary on earth to take a break for lunch.

He sighed, kneading his forehead with one hand, then opened his door and appeared in the reception area. On the other side of the glass that surrounded the desk stood a small woman, only her head and shoulders visible, like one of the children.

Sebastian opened the reception door and appeared outside. 'How may I help?' he asked, painting on a smile that might well have looked like a grimace.

'I need to speak to Jim Masterson.' The woman's words were clipped. Barely five feet tall, she had an oddly cramped posture.

Sebastian didn't let his tense smile drop. 'Regarding?'

'I'm his wife.' Her expression was grim: deep-set eyes, pursed lips.

Sensing he wasn't going to get much more from her, Sebastian nodded. He went back behind reception and rang down to the gym, then offered her a seat on one of the threadbare reception chairs, near the giant papier-mâché sculpture of two cupped hands around a globe. Returning to his desk to sort more paperwork, Sebastian watched through the reception window as she picked at her black sleeves, smoothed down her skirt, her drawn features impassive.

About five minutes into her vigil, Jim arrived – almost at a run and with a strange expression on his face, which Sebastian couldn't place for a moment. Then he realised what it was: anxiety. He'd never seen anything but laughter lines on the big man's visage before. To him Jim was a big, jolly bald man with a thick white beard like Santa. The kids loved him, not to mention his imaginative games in gym, such as 'lavaball', a hybrid of dodgeball and the classic kids' favourite, 'The floor is lava'. Jim had proved himself able to get even the least enthusiastic child moving.

Yet he did not appear to have any such effect on his wife. As soon as she saw her husband the tiny woman's blank expression twisted with rage. Jim stooped towards her, his look earnest, and attempted to usher her towards a side room, but she jerked her arm away from his, as if she didn't want him touching her. Sebastian couldn't hear what they were saying through the glass, but from Jim's body language, it was clear: he was trying, desperately it seemed, to placate her.

But she wasn't having it. She stood, one hand on her bony hip, wagging a finger at him like a parent. Even the bell going off again failed to stop her. A line of kids coming back in from the playground eyeballed the confrontation, parting around Jim and his wife as they made their way past reception, then reconvening like ants. The wife was so intent on telling off her husband she did not seem to notice this. Jim hung his head, mortified.

You never can tell what goes on behind closed doors, Sebastian's mother always said. Sebastian had always thought it rather a stupid saying; he'd been sure most people were poor liars, their troubles easy to see, if only people would look. But now … He'd never had an inkling Jim had any trouble at home.

Mrs Masterson finally left, and as Jim slunk back towards the PE department, Sebastian found himself reconsidering Maxwell. Up until that point, Lily's ex had seemed more pathetic than anything. But could he be worse than they feared? Sebastian made a mental note to be extra wary. He wasn't going to give Maxwell any chance to come between him and Lily.

When the bell rang for the end of the day, Sebastian found himself suddenly sick of all the paperwork and admin. He decided to take his laptop home with him and go through the remainder of his emails after dinner. Juggling box files, his laptop bag, empty lunchbox and coffee cup, he bid Rosanna goodnight, taking delight at her bulging eyes – he was leaving before her for once.

Back to *his* family.

Twelve

The first week of school zipped by. I sleepwalked my way through it and suddenly it was Friday morning. I kissed Sebastian goodbye before he left, bleary-eyed, his travel mug of black coffee in hand. Being the boss, he always went in to school before me.

Denny sat at the table, hunched over his cereal, his bad mood etched into his little face. One by one, he took Cheerios out of the bowl and crushed them under his spoon.

'Stop that,' I chided gently.

Denny pouted. 'Don't wanna go to school.'

I took a bite of toast, thinking, *You and me both, kiddo*.

Sebastian had taken the car, but the school was only a ten-minute walk away. With Denny in a mood, it took twenty-five and I practically had to drag him to the door of his year-one classroom.

'Oh dear, Denny, like that, is it?' Kelly, the before- and after-school club leader, was waiting at the door. She attempted to ruffle Denny's hair, but he jerked his head away as he stalked into the classroom, hands in his pockets. Kelly shrugged, the amusement of someone used to kids written all over her face.

I raced to the staffroom for the daily morning meeting, arriving ten minutes late. I heard a couple of the other teachers mutter as I searched for a seat. They all thought Sebastian gave me special treatment, but in reality I was like this before I was even seeing him. The plight of the working mother – never enough time.

I cast a look around my colleagues, and realised with surprise that Triss hadn't arrived yet. Even though she was the flighty type, she was always at work super-early. I knew it was the legacy of growing up in a household where her parents prized booze over punctuality. She'd always hated arriving late to school, having to skulk in after the bell as everyone looked at her from their desks.

At the front, perched on a desk, one foot behind him, Sebastian looked drawn and tired. Behind him, a digital clock read 08:23. Jim, the PE teacher, sat on a chair at the front, arms folded, legs spread wide.

'Marriage obviously suits you, boss.' He laughed at his own good-natured heckle. The others joined in as Sebastian tipped an imaginary hat to me. Polite applause followed, which I acknowledged with a smile. Fortunately, everyone was then distracted: Triss had finally arrived. She faltered on the threshold for a moment, then covered up her embarrassment by giving Sebastian a salute.

'Sir!' She always called him this, like she was still a pupil herself.

Sebastian nodded as Triss scuttled through and took the seat next to me, then it was down to business. He took us through the various points: this year's end-of-year tests; the upcoming school inspection; the child-protection hoo-ha. Avonwood was not a rough school, but we did have some challenges the more privileged Epsom schools didn't face. Most of our pupils were from low socio-economic backgrounds, and there was some tension between those who had deigned themselves more middle class and the poorer parents. English was also not a first language for a larger-than-average percentage of our students. Resources were stretched and finances limited, but our pastoral care was excellent and as far as most of us were concerned, we were a big family, ready to take the knocks.

I wouldn't have taught anywhere else.

The bell went and we all stood up, rushing off in various directions for registration. I found myself in my classroom about one minute before the first children filed in. It smelled of paint and PVA glue. The children's artwork lined the back wall, and on the side there were a number of half-finished clay pots. My kids ambled in with lunch-boxes and sports kits, their faces expectant and open. My class were between eight and nine, my favourite age: not yet old enough for the kind of guarded cynicism that hit tweens and early teens. This year the boys in my class outnumbered the girls three to one. It sometimes happened with one gender, especially in baby-boom years.

'Good morning, Mrs Stevens!' They chorused in unison, even though I'd written *Mrs Adair* surrounded by arrows in big blue letters on the whiteboard. I shrugged. Not to worry. They'd get it by the end of the term.

And then it was as if I'd blinked and the school day was over. I usually picked Denny up from after-school club just before five, after I've done my marking. But there was none to do today, because it was Friday. I took the opportunity to catch my breath and tidy up, placing escaped pencils and pens into their tubs, returning glue sticks and scissors to the trays of the brightly coloured drawers.

My thoughts returned to the scene of destruction we'd come back to. Could Sebastian have been right? Could Maxwell have been responsible? No, Maxwell was a neat freak. He liked everything just so, lining books and CDs up in alphabetical order. He let one of his poor cleaners go when he discovered she hadn't been vacuuming underneath the sofa. Anyway, he'd have had to swipe a key from our rack when he'd picked up Denny, and then replaced it. That was too creepy for him. Maxwell was a prick who loved himself, but he wasn't someone who'd do something like that.

Was he?

Denny seemed to have recovered from his morning grumpiness. He chatted all the way back to the maisonette. I struggled to call it home just yet; secretly, I still hoped we would move to one of the new estates – preferably on the opposite side of town to Maxwell, and nowhere near Fran, either. I liked my mother-in-law – especially after her help cleaning the maisonette – but I wanted somewhere just for us. I would have to be careful about suggesting this to Sebastian, though; he was attached to his characterful pad in the town centre.

As ever, as soon as I opened the door, Denny bounded up the stairs two at a time.

'No Xbox till after tea,' I called. 'You know the rules!'

There was pause, then he yelled, 'Muuuuuuuum!'

I sighed at the angst in Denny's voice and shut the front door, plunging myself momentarily into the darkness of the windowless hallway.

'What?' I called back as I walked up the stairs through the dim light from the kitchen-diner. I had long ago ceased bothering to tell Denny to stop hollering at me from afar. Kids never learned that lesson.

'The light's not working!' Denny bellowed, unaware I had appeared behind him. I winced.

'All right, foghorn.' I made a show of putting my hands over my ears, making Denny cackle.

I pressed the light switch in the gloomy living area. Nothing happened. Denny was right. I picked up the remote control and tried to turn the telly on. No sign of life. I pressed various buttons, but nothing at all.

Brilliant, a power cut.

'Can Seb fix it?' Denny said, eyes wide, a tremor in his voice. 'What about my Xbox time later?'

Panic was not far away: he loved his Xbox that much. I made a mental note for myself: I should probably have a think about machine detoxes, or limiting screen time.

'*I'll* fix it.' I took a deep breath. For a child who'd been raised practically single-handedly by me – even when I was married to his dad – Denny was surprisingly reliant on male intervention for mending things.

I traipsed down the long corridor to the bathroom, where the fuse box was located. It was high, out of reach, so I had to clamber onto the closed toilet seat to pull the cover off. I had already bet myself it was our bedroom that was the problem; I'd detected a slight burning smell that morning when I was blowing out my curls. I'd thought I'd caught the end of one of them, but perhaps it was the hairdryer itself. I hoped not, because that meant we'd have a freezer full of defrosted food.

But the bedroom fuse was not blown. None of them was. All the switches were aligned perfectly. I furrowed my brow in confusion. *Weird.*

'Mum?' Denny called down the corridor. 'You still there?'

'Yes. Hang on, mate…'

I wandered into the kitchen. With a stab of guilt, I realised I had no clue which electricity company Sebastian was with. This still wasn't my home, really. I sighed and pulled my mobile from my cardigan pocket, intent on calling him, but as I did, my gaze alighted on the fridge door, on which was emblazoned a red electricity bill.

I grabbed it from under the Dennis the Menace fridge magnet and quickly scanned the top sheet, taking note of the recent date and realising what must have happened. With the wedding and everything else that had been going on, Sebastian had simply forgotten to pay it. Well, that was soon rectified. Bill in hand, I pressed my phone to my ear again as I went in search of my purse.

Denny appeared in the kitchen, clearly wanting to find out what was going on.

'Okay. Just hang on…' I said, indicating the phone, the tone ringing in my ear, debit card at the ready. Denny pulled a comical face, full of six-year-old angst, and mimed *Hurry up*. I ignored him, keying in all the account numbers from the bill, so I could pay via the automated system.

'One moment, please,' said a robotic female voice.

I waited.

Then, that tell-tale click as the computer caught up with itself.

'Sorry, we have no record of that account,' said the robotic voice at last.

'What the hell?' The words burst out of me. At my feet, Denny regarded me, open-mouthed with both joy and mischief. I never said rude words – around him, anyway. I sighed. The automated system must have a fault. At least now I'd speak to a real person.

'Putting you through to a customer-service advisor,' the robotic voice continued. 'You will be answered as soon as possible. Please stay on the line, your call is important to us.'

Three muzak versions of Taylor Swift songs later, a bored-sounding Scottish man came on the line. 'Hello, how can I help you today?'

'Your computer thing's not working, I need to pay our bill.' I hardened my voice, just in case he tried to sell me something.

But the man on the line seemed as uninterested in conflict as me – he didn't ask for details, or argue. 'Name and account number, please,' he said.

I gave them. There was some tapping, then nothing. I thought I'd been cut off. But then the man spoke: 'Aye, your bill's been paid already.'

'When?'

The man made no attempt to stifle a yawn. 'Today.'

Now I was really irritated. 'Then you guys have made an error. I've just come home and we have no power.'

No reply, but instead, more tapping. 'That's right. Disconnection. A Mr Sebastian Adair requested it this morning.' Then he quoted the maisonette's address and account number.

This made no sense. Why would Sebastian disconnect the power? 'That's my husband, but I don't understand why he's cut our power off…' An odd, sick feeling had formed in my belly.

There was another pause. 'There's a note on the system. You've moved out, it says.'

'No we haven't – we still live here!' I gestured angrily at Denny and myself, even though the guy on the other end of the line could not see us.

And then a connection formed in my brain. My stomach lurched now and I emitted a low groan. I knew exactly who'd done this.

'All your calls are recorded, right?' I said. 'Can you tell me what time you received this disconnection request?'

Utterly unflustered, the guy on the end of the phone tapped away again, and then said, 'Eight twenty-eight this morning.'

A flash of the big, red digital clock in the staffroom appeared in my mind's eye. Sebastian could not have possibly have made the disconnection request – he'd been leading the back-to-school staff meeting at that time. So, if a man had called the electricity company, paid our bill and had us disconnected, that left only one other option.

- From: Mr.M.Stevens@cromwellhealthtrust.com
- To: receptionist@avonwoodschool.edu.com

7 June 2018

Hi there, my son Dennis Stevens is in Year 2 and tells me there is a school fête soon. He brought me a letter, but I'm afraid I threw it in the recycling by accident. If you could let me know the date and times, I would be most grateful. Best wishes, Maxwell

- From: receptionist@avonwoodschool.edu.com
- To: Mr.M.Stevens@cromwellhealthtrust.com

28 June 2018

Dear Mr Stevens, please don't worry. I can confirm our school fête is later than usual this year – Saturday, 14 July, 10 a.m.–3 p.m. This is to accommodate the upcoming school inspection we are expecting before the summer holidays. Should you require any more information about the fête (including bad weather contingencies, parking details and a PDF school map you can download), please check the school blog and/or our Facebook page and Twitter feed. Many thanks, Rosanna Taylor

- From: Mr.M.Stevens@cromwellhealthtrust.com
- To: receptionist@avonwoodschool.edu.com

28 June 2018

Thank you Rosanna, this is most helpful. M

Thirteen

With the electricity reconnected, the gravity of the situation hit me. Maxwell had somehow got hold of a key, been in our house … That was bad enough, but his actions once he'd got inside seemed to hint at some even darker intention. Like Sebastian had said, he hadn't trashed Denny's room, but he'd wrecked all our stuff. For a neat freak, that was deeply out of character. Then he'd cut off the power. Knowing Maxwell as I did, I knew his game: he wanted to show us who was in charge. Were we in danger? I pushed this thought out of my mind. No. Maxwell might be many things, but he was not a psychopath. These were just mind games, to freak us out. And they were working.

I wanted Sebastian. When I'd discovered the issue with the electricity and Maxwell, I'd left a voicemail and several texts on his phone. All to no avail. Sebastian rarely checked his phone – one of his few annoying habits. I opened a bottle of wine to calm my nerves.

Two glasses later, he finally appeared.

'Where have you been?' I took his briefcase from him automatically, like the good little wife. I stared at it in my hands. Now what? I dithered, then shoved it next to the boots and shoes by the coatrack.

'At work. Where else?' Sebastian undid his tie, sinking onto one of the stools by the breakfast bar. He grabbed his phone from his pocket and started scrolling through.

'Something happened…' I turned to the sink, not able to look him in the eye. 'You might have been right about the break-in.'

I waited for him to catch up on his texts. 'Oh, it was you messaging me…' Then: 'Wait – Maxwell did *what*?'

I turned back towards him and, leaning against the countertop, I quickly filled him in on all the details. I said that I guessed Maxwell must have taken one of our bills off the fridge then pretended to be him and disconnected us.

Sebastian's expression grew more puzzled. 'But Denny lives here, too. What's the point?'

I shrugged. 'He loves mind games. I guess he knew we'd put it back on again, straight away. He's just messing with us. Reminding us he can do whatever he wants.'

Sebastian massaged his forehead, as if he was warding off a headache. 'Maxwell has a key?'

'Presumably,' I replied, discomfort crawling across my skin like a million spiders.

I hated the idea of Maxwell being in our space without our knowledge, going through our things. The congratulations cards were still on the mantelpiece from our engagement, waiting to be replaced with our wedding cards. Maybe Maxwell had looked through our gifts, too, made comparisons with the ones he and I had received for our wedding. What else had my ex seen? An image of the medicine cabinet flashed across my mind's eye: my contraceptive pills; sexual lubricants; a jar of massage oil. I shuddered. Then hot fury replaced my uneasiness. *How dare he?*

'How the hell did he get a key?'

I could hear the hot anger in Sebastian's voice and I winced.

He saw me do so and raised both hands. 'I'm not blaming you. I know you wouldn't have given him one.'

Relief filled my chest. I didn't want to argue. 'I suppose he must have taken one from the key rack last time he was here to collect Denny. Copied it. Easy enough to do. Then replaced it without us realising.'

'Right.' Sebastian stood up, shoulders back, arms bent at his sides, hands curled into his fists.

I knew instantly what he was planning. Before he could move towards the stairs to storm back out, I blocked the way.

'Don't go over there all guns blazing,' I said. 'That's exactly what he wants. You'd be playing right into his hands.'

Sebastian seemed to wilt. 'You're right.' He sat down again, swiping the screen of his phone. He put it to his ear.

'You're not ringing him?' I said.

'No…' He waved me away, turning as whoever he was calling answered. 'Ah, hi – your website says you do twenty-four-hour lock replacements?'

The tension in my body seemed to unfurl as I heard him book the locksmith.

A young, red-headed man with tattoos and an eye-watering fee appeared on the doorstep half an hour later. As I bathed Denny, I listened to Sebastian lay out exactly what we'd agreed upon.

'So, a new front-door lock, plus a chain, plus a deadbolt and locks on all the windows. Gotcha,' the locksmith said, dragging his heavy tool kit towards him. I heard him test his drill. 'This place'll be like Fort Knox when I'm done. No one will be getting in.'

He was surprisingly speedy. By the time I had Denny in his pyjamas and had read him a story, the locksmith was putting the finishing touches to the new bedroom window locks. Denny wanted to investigate what was going on, but I told him to stay in bed and look through his comic books. With the drill finished, he'd drift off soon enough.

The young locksmith bid us a hearty cheerio, and Sebastian saw him out before joining me on the sofa in the living area. He had a bottle of white wine on the coffee table, a large glass already poured for me. Grateful, I took it and knocked back a large swig.

'Safe now,' Sebastian said. 'He can't get in again.'

I nodded, resting my head on his shoulder.

I could not, however, get the thought of Maxwell being in the maisonette out of my head. Brushing my teeth the next morning, I opened the medicine cabinet and regarded its contents, fury building inside me with the force of a volcano. When we were officially his family, Maxwell had given every sign that he didn't want us – me, or even Denny, for that matter. Now he was trying to lay claim to us, get in the way of our new lives, playing stupid mind games with me and Sebastian. Who the hell did he think he was?

I brooded throughout the long school day. I barely acknowledged the pages of sums and sentences presented to me as I worked through my classes on autopilot. But, as I ate a sandwich in the staffroom and listened to Triss prattle on about some movie she'd watched, I made a decision. That afternoon, as soon as school finished, I would ignore my advice to Sebastian and pay Maxwell a visit myself. I dumped down my ham and cheese and fired off a quick text to my ex-husband:

You in about 4 p.m. today?

The reply was almost instant:

Yep

I have to see you, I started to type … then realised how Maxwell was likely to view it as some kind of declaration of need, or even love. I shilly-shallied over how to reply, before deciding I didn't actually need to, then I put the phone back in my pocket.

As soon as the school bell rang for the end of the day, I gathered up my things and hurried out to the taxi I'd ordered; it was already waiting in the car park. I didn't really have time for all this – I had marking to do and Denny to pick up at five. And I also worried that Sebastian might look out of his office window and see me furtively sneaking off to see my ex. But he didn't know Maxwell like I did. I needed to show him I was onto his game; I had to demonstrate I was unimpressed and he was wasting his time.

Arriving in Maxwell's road, I told the taxi driver to wait, then, shielded by the leylandii surrounding Maxwell's ridiculously osten-tatious house, I traipsed up the path and wrenched open the porch door. Maxwell must have been watching for me because he was opening the inner door before I could press the doorbell.

'Lily, hi.' He was dressed in sweatpants, his tone purposefully nonchalant, though his blue eyes roved up and down me like I was a particularly tasty morsel. I noted he was wearing a tight white T-shirt. Maxwell had a home gym. When he wasn't working, he could lift weights for hours at a time. I could see the outline of his well-defined torso and pecs, the vee of sweat starting at his throat. But his body, like the rest of him, was purely decorative.

He indicated the hallway. 'Come on in.'

I stayed where I was. 'I don't think so.'

Maxwell cocked his head. He leaned against the doorframe, folding his large arms. 'So, why are you here, Lily … is it about Denny?'

White-hot anger pooled in my chest, but I took a deep breath. I needed to keep it in check. 'You know what this is about.'

Maxwell's brow furrowed. 'I can assure you I don't. Have I forgotten it's my day to have him for tea? It's not my day … is it?'

'No. It's not your day,' I muttered through clenched teeth. 'I don't know what you were hoping to achieve, but this stops now…'

Maxwell stood up straight and held out both hands. 'Look. I really don't know what you're talking about—'

I continued, regardless. '…Or your access for Denny will get very complicated. Do you hear me?'

Maxwell's features slackened in shock at the threat, then twisted with exasperation. He was still trying to make me believe he had no clue what he was supposed to have done to us.

'You can't do that!'

'Watch me,' I hissed.

Maxwell's confidence returned as quickly as it had left. 'Sebastian put you up to this. He wants you both to himself. Well, that's not on. Denny is my son, not his.'

I shook my head at him. 'Sebastian is twice the father you were already and we've only been together five minutes.'

I saw pain shimmer across Maxwell's blue eyes and shame lanced me sharp in the chest. There'd been no need for me to say that. As much as I thought Maxwell's efforts with Denny were not good enough, I had said it to hurt him, to score points. That wasn't me. I needed to rise above all this crap. I couldn't let him drag me down to his level.

Suddenly sick of it all, I turned on my heel and strode down the pathway, grinding my teeth. I felt angry tears prick my eyes.

I opened the taxi door. The meter flashed as bright red as my mood. The driver regarded me to in the rear-view mirror.

'Where to, now?' he said.

I stared ahead, my thoughts still at my ex's doorstep. I took a deep breath and closed my eyes, swallowing down my loathing and resentment. I visualised a calm place: a stereotypical meadow, buttercups and birds, a bright-yellow sun on the horizon – a child's drawing. It worked.

'Back to Avonwood School,' I said. 'And then … home,' and I gave him the maisonette's address.

Fourteen

Sebastian locked the car and turned down the narrow alleyway, past the half-timbered buildings on either side, to the maisonette's front door, only to see a figure ahead of him. The afternoon sun behind her, she was just a black shape, one arm raised in front of her to press the doorbell. On her wrist a collection of bangles; one of them caught the light and flashed, making him raise a hand to his eyes.

'Hello…?' he called.

'Is that you, darling?' Fran's voice was light and airy as her perpetually neat form emerged from the shadows.

'The one and only.' Sebastian gave his mother a tight smile as she swooped in, air-kissing each of his cheeks. He dug in his pocket for his keys. 'Lily not let you in?'

Fran's eyes roved around the dark and enclosed alleyway, taking in the old beams threaded through the brickwork. 'Oh, I've been standing outside a while. I don't think she's home yet.'

Sebastian checked his watch. That was odd; she and Denny should have been home at least half an hour ago. Perhaps Lily had been held up. 'She should be here with Denny any minute. Why don't you come on up?'

His mother looked towards the maisonette's front door. 'Well, only if you're sure. I've got a little something for Denny.' She indicated her oversized handbag.

Sebastian smiled, imagining some sweets in there for her new stepgrandson.

'Lovely.' He replied, opening the door for them both.

◉

'Hi honey, I'm home!'

Lily's jokey tone filtered up the stairs ahead of her. The *thunk* of rubber-soled shoes heralded Denny's arrival: he bounded up the stairs, dragging his school bag behind him. Lily's head bobbed up above the bannister, into the kitchen-diner. She gave Sebastian a brilliant-white smile, then her expression froze, surprised, at the sight of Fran at the kitchen table.

'Look who I found on the doorstep.' Sebastian nodded a little pointedly at Fran, who gave Lily an awkward little sideways wave, like she was the Queen of England.

'Fran! Lovely to see you,' Lily enthused, homing in on Denny, who was shovelling three or four biscuits out of the barrel with his little hands. She grabbed two back, peeling his fingers off them. Left with one chocolate chip cookie, Denny bit into it and shrugged.

Lily stalked straight to the sink to fetch a glass of water. 'It's so humid out there.'

Across the table, Denny gave Fran a toothy grin. His middle two were missing. 'Hiya, Mrs Adair.'

Fran fixed the boy with her best child-friendly smile. 'Oh Dennis, no need to call me Mrs Adair. Why not call me Fran?'

Denny nodded. 'Okay. But only if you never call me Dennis again.'

Sebastian's stomach lurched. His mother would never have stood for such backchat from him as a child.

But Fran laughed, catching Lily's eye. 'That told me!'

Lily laughed too.

Fran put her large handbag on the table and unzipped it. 'I have something here for you, if Mum says it's okay…?'

Fran looked to Lily, who nodded readily. But her eyes narrowed as Fran pulled a box from her bag. Not sweets, then, Sebastian thought as he saw Lily's eyes widen and her brows contract in a frown.

'Is that a—?' she began.

'Phone!' Denny interrupted with a squeal as he took the box. 'Wow, thanks Mrs … Fran!'

He gave Fran a quick hug and then set to work opening the package. Fran watched him, grinning like a Cheshire cat.

'Can I speak to you a minute, Sebastian?' said Lily, her tone careful and measured.

She clambered off the kitchen stool and disappeared into the hallway that led to the bedrooms. Sebastian smiled at his mother apologetically and followed, Fran appearing not to notice him leaving, captivated as she was by Denny's enthusiasm for his new gadget.

'A phone? Seriously? He's only six!' Lily murmured. Sebastian saw that she was clenching her fists.

Sebastian kept his voice low. 'She's trying to do a nice thing. She wants to show she's taking this stepgrandmother thing seriously.'

Lily grimaced. 'I realise that and honestly, I do appreciate it. But a gift like this? It's too big – and he's too young!'

Sebastian sighed. 'It's not too big, it's—'

'Phones like that are about two hundred pounds!' Lily interrupted.

'That's what I mean,' Sebastian explained. 'Two hundred pounds is nothing to my mother. If she'd turned up and given him something that cost a tenner, would you think that was such a big deal?'

Lily opened her mouth as if to say 'No', then seemed to think better of it. 'I guess not.'

'Well, think of it like that.' Sebastian hugged Lily; she let him. 'I know it's weird, you growing up with so little. But Denny doesn't have to.'

'I just didn't want him to have a phone at six years old,' Lily muttered, into Sebastian's chest.

He released her. 'Well, then let's tell her that.'

Holding hands, they headed back into the kitchen. Lily smiled at Denny and sent him, clutching the phone, to his bedroom. The little boy was only too happy to acquiesce, still staring at the screen in his hand. Sebastian stood to one side to let his stepson past.

'We wish you hadn't given him that, Fran.' Lily looked to Sebastian, who nodded earnestly in agreement. They were a unified front.

His mother was still seated at the kitchen table, her hands in her lap. Her eyes widened, like she'd been caught in car headlights. Confusion registered on her face. 'But you said I could give it to him…'

Sebastian sighed, pinching the bridge of his nose between his thumb and forefinger. He could feel the tension in his brow, leading down to his jaw and neck.

'You said you had *something* to give to him,' said Lily. 'I thought it was just a bag of sweets.' She attempted, unsuccessfully, to hide an exasperated sigh.

Fran shot a beseeching look at Sebastian. He wanted to reassure her, to tell her he got what she was trying to do. But he had to toe the party line. 'Lily's right. It was up to us to decide when Denny has a phone.'

A pang sliced through his chest as he saw the suggestion of tears in his mother's eyes. They'd got on so well during the clean-up on the day they'd returned from holiday. Now the three of them were rubbing up against one another, clashing, all sharp edges. Was this normal? Maybe it was for stepfamilies. And the added stress of Maxwell wasn't helping. Sebastian had never done this before, but to be fair to Fran, she hadn't either. They'd grow accustomed to one another soon, surely? They had to.

'I see.' Fran gathered her bag's handles together and stood, her head hung in shame. 'I thought I was doing something nice for the boy.'

'Yes, we appreciate that, but—' Lily began, but Fran held up a hand to silence her.

'It's all right, Lily. I understand.' With an effort, Fran got up from her chair.

'You don't have to go,' Sebastian was dismayed.

'No, please stay,' Lily echoed, though it didn't sound like her heart was in it.

'It's fine, I have bridge club tonight anyway.' Fran flashed them a watery smile and leaned heavily on the bannister at the top of the stairs.

'If you're sure,' Lily said.

Fran disappeared down the stairs, slowly, one at a time, as if she was scared of falling.

As the front door slammed, Lily looked to Sebastian for reassurance, biting her lip.

But he didn't give it. 'Well, that went well.'

Lily stood her ground, one foot in front of the other, hands on her hips. 'Sarcasm is not helpful.'

'I know, I know, I'm sorry.' He encircled her in his arms again. 'She should have asked us first, you're right.'

Even so, Sebastian could not help feeling that if Lily hadn't been so irritated by Maxwell's recent behaviour, she would not have put her foot down like this over the phone. It felt as if they were punishing Fran for Maxwell's trespasses. But he could see Lily's point. There were only two of them in this marriage, after all. Denny was part of his family now, as was Fran – but he wasn't married to either of them. Lily was his wife. His honeymoon toast rolled back into his thoughts: *Happy wife … happy life.* That was the way he had to play it. He could make it up to his mother.

Somehow.

Fifteen

The rain promised all week rolled in just after school finished for the day. As I checked through my students' exercise books, I glanced up to see the water pouring off the school roof in steady streams. It hit the tarmac of the playground with a hiss; a smell of ozone wafting through the open window. As I closed it, I heard the distant rumble of thunder and was startled when a flash of sheet lightning illuminated the sky. The muggy June weather had broken at last. I was grateful the kids had already gone home. Bad weather and children was never a good mix: it got them antsy, jumping around in their seats like cats in spring.

I checked my watch and groaned. After five o'clock. I should have been at after-school club picking Denny up, right then.

I gathered up my papers and my laptop bag then almost tripped on a miniature chair left in the gangway near my desk. Leaving my classroom, I crossed the school atrium. No one was staffing reception, but that was nothing new. Sebastian's receptionist, Rosanna, was a nightmare. In fact, ranting about her transgressions, both real and perceived, was one of his favourite things to do at the end of the day. Unlike with Maxwell though, I didn't need to worry about Sebastian having an affair with his secretary.

Through an inner window decorated by kids' paintings, I could see Sebastian's desk was customarily neat – empty of papers, pens or cups. His jacket and bag were nowhere in sight. Sebastian usually worked until six, arriving home approximately an hour after Denny and I, in time for a 'shake-and-bake' dinner of something like potato waffles and fish fingers.

But I did not slow down. I was unconcerned that Sebastian was not at his desk. *I'm his wife, not his jailer.* The thought brought a smile to my lips. My dad would say that to my mother, whenever she asked where he'd been. It was a running joke between them: she'd send him to the shop for a loaf of bread and up to forty minutes later he'd trudge back, trailing the loaf from one hand, the other in his pocket.

'Where did you get to? Was about to send a search party out,' Mum would rebuke him in good-natured fashion.

'Eh woman, you're me wife, not me jailer,' Dad would grin.

Now Kelly, the after-school club group leader, appeared from a side room, surprising me. 'Late again, Lily,' she said. The club moved around the school and I could never remember which room it was in. Today it was in one of the larger communal classrooms and I'd rushed straight past. Kelly flashed me a confused smile.

My words tumbled from my lips as I tried to catch my breath. 'I know, I know. I'm so sorry. Completely mad, since I'm actually here, too.'

Kelly's tone was bright and breezy, but I could detect a steely undertone. 'I know it's hard being a working mum.'

Was that disapproval? I was stung, even a little outraged. Kelly was well known in Epsom as a good-time girl, propping up bars every Saturday night, doing the walk of shame down an empty Epsom High Street most Sunday mornings. I'd even seen her myself once, wandering past the Co-Op as I bought a pint of milk. Her unbrushed hair resembled a bird's nest. Shoeless, wearing a vest top and a barely-there skirt, she'd had a dreamy look in her panda eyes, her pasty skin still smeared with the previous night's make-up.

I laughed off any criticism Kelly might have of me; she could go and sort out her own life before she passed judgement on mine. 'Anyway, if I could just pick up Denny?'

Kelly's brow furrowed. 'His dad came and got him about half an hour ago.'

The sight of Sebastian's empty office and desk came back to me. I was puzzled though: he hadn't told me he was picking up Denny and taking him home by car. When he did that, he normally took me as well. Had I forgotten something? A football match, a dentist's appointment, a friend for tea? But those were all *my* department; Sebastian wouldn't just take over without telling me. And then a sharp pain hit me low in my abdomen as I realised what had happened. I felt compelled to check, even though I knew I was wrong:

'You mean Mr Adair, right?'

Nervous, Kelly licked her lips and hesitated before sighing heavily. 'No. Mr Stevens. His real dad.'

Sixteen

Sebastian watched the rain pour down from the gutters from one of the top classroom windows. He'd finished his admin for the day, first doing data input, then responding to emails, as well as sending various press releases to the local newspapers about student achievements. He'd decided to do his nightly patrol around the school early for once, hoping to intercept Lily and Denny on the way back and give them both a lift home.

He discovered a few forgotten coffee cups and balls of paper that had missed the bin in E6; he even cleaned the whiteboard that Ms McCarthy had forgotten. She was becoming increasingly scatty. Twice that week she'd come into school with two different shoes on. Sebastian had thought it was a myth that 'baby brain' took hold of pregnant women, but if she was anything to go by, it was very much a thing. Perhaps even loudly self-anointed feminists like Ms McCarthy couldn't help but play to type when it came to biology? It smelled like bullshit to him, but what did he know?

Weary, Sebastian climbed the winding staircase to check in at student resources, which was at the back of the library. Both of the female support staff there were stocktaking, unpacking new books and boxes of exercise books and pencils. They were flabbergasted to see him unannounced. He normally made his circuit of the school long after they had gone home.

'Everything okay up here?' Sebastian felt awkward, suddenly aware he always expected the librarians to get on with things by themselves, making the most of their ever-decreasing budget.

Head librarian, Mim, a small, round woman with an unfortunate penchant for orange, nodded with vigour, her double chin wobbling. 'Everything's okay with me … You?' She turned to Lena, a young, tall, willowy woman – Mim's opposite in every way.

'It is all okay, yes,' said Lena.

Lena was German but, apart from her blonde hair and blue eyes, she was as far removed from the gruff, ice-maiden national stereotype as you could get. Maternally minded, with a wickedly puerile sense of humour, Lena was a huge hit with the kids and often doubled as a teaching assistant when Avonwood was understaffed, which was always.

'Okay.' There was an awkward pause as Sebastian drank this in. Both women stayed where they were, smiles frozen on their faces. 'Well, keep up the good work.'

'Yes, sir!' Lena gave him a mock salute as he left.

As Sebastian made it back into his office on the ground floor, he heard the persistent vibrating buzz of his mobile. It stopped, but before he could cross the room to the desk, it started again. He snatched it up, seeing 'LILY' on the screen, along with '15 MISSED CALLS'. Trepidation jumped from his chest to his throat. Lily was not prone to panic. She tended to call once or twice, then give up. This must be serious. He pressed the green button to answer.

Before he could even ask what was up, Lily started to babble. Something about Maxwell taking Denny. Immediately, Sebastian's anxiety abated. Maxwell was the boy's father, after all. But confusion was not far behind: Maxwell had come into the school? How? That was not difficult to guess, he thought: Rosanna had probably let him in without a second's thought, she was that careless. But Sebastian had thought better of Kelly. Maxwell had never picked his son up before, not even when he and Lily were still married.

'What was Kelly playing at?' Sebastian wondered aloud.

'I don't know,' Lily said. 'Some crappy excuse about Maxwell still being on Denny's school registration form. That doesn't matter now!'

'I'm on my way.' Sebastian ended the call and grabbed his stuff.

Lily was waiting for him in the corridor that led from the big hall out into the school car park. They swept out of the school, into the rain, chucking their belongings into the back seat of his car and belting up.

'That bastard. This is typical of him,' Lily said.

Sebastian was perturbed at how wild her eyes were, how agitated she seemed. The lad was only with his father. She surely couldn't think Denny would come to any harm with him? A darker thought followed: perhaps this was about one-upmanship. Not just on Maxwell's part, but Lily's too – with Denny the prize. Sebastian banished this thought. He was being ridiculous. His wife wasn't like that.

Lily's demeanour changed drastically as they entered Maxwell's affluent estate. She went from angry and defiant to cowed and vulnerable in a matter of moments. Her body language screamed anxiety, her limbs all jagged shapes, her eyes wide and unfocused.

As the car came to a halt outside Maxwell's home, she turned to Sebastian. 'Oh God, Sebastian, what if he won't let us in? What if he tries to keep Denny?'

Sebastian's mind spun as he tried to catch up. 'He won't do that,' he answered, trying to inject reassurance into his voice.

In truth, Sebastian had no clue what Maxwell would do. He would never have guessed that this would be his next move. What was the point? Maxwell worked full-time as a consultant at the Cromwell Hospital in Epsom. He'd need someone to take Denny to school and pick him up … and both his mother and stepfather worked in that very same school. He often worked late into the night, plus some weekends. It made no sense whatsoever for him to go for sole custody. But then it hadn't made sense for him to cut off the electricity either.

Sebastian followed Lily out of the car. He watched her hammer on the door. Inside, the dog barked excitedly. Sebastian wasn't sure how Lily wanted to play this. Was he supposed to go in there, the big protector, and grab Denny back? Or did she want him to be the silent partner, there for moral support only? His thoughts were in turmoil. Why did this have to be so damned complicated? Why couldn't Maxwell just let them get on with their lives?

Maxwell kept them waiting just long enough to frustrate them a little bit more. When he did open the door he feigned surprise at seeing them standing out in the rain, rather than sheltering in the porch. Lily stared at him, chin jutting out, raindrops in her unstraightened hair.

'Give me Denny back. Now.' Her words were slow and enunciated, as if she expected a fight, or at least that Maxwell would pretend he didn't understand.

'Of course. But first…' Maxwell stood aside like a butler, indicating that they should come inside.

The situation seemed to diffuse, the tension unexpectedly departing; but suspicion replaced it. Lily shot a pointed look at Sebastian, who could only shrug. He had no idea where this was going either. She seemed to recover her anger and took Sebastian's hand in an unspoken show of unity. They stepped calmly across the threshold. But Lily's haughty entrance was ruined by the elderly dog, who immediately raced into her legs with the enthusiasm of a puppy.

Despite herself, Lily smiled and let go of Sebastian's hand to pet the animal. 'Hey, Ginny,' she said, obvious affection in her voice.

Sebastian understood: this creature had been her dog, too. He felt even more out of place now.

Maxwell swept to the end of the hallway and indicated his big living room. The door was ajar. Through the gap they saw Denny, still in his school uniform and seated on the plush carpet, poring over his phone, a glass of milk and a plate of cookies to hand. Maxwell gave them a seemingly innocent smile that said, *See, he's fine.*

'Okay, what the hell is going on?' asked Lily, when they reached the kitchen.

She sat down at the table next to Sebastian. Maxwell lounged at the head of the table, one arm slung over the back of his chair. Sebastian squirmed awkwardly. It felt like a job interview.

'I'm sorry. I didn't think how it would look, when you came to fetch him. It's been a … particularly tough day, shall we say.' Maxwell's face seemed open, his expression contrite.

Lily appeared to be on some kind of time delay. She looked like she was sorting through his words. Then realisation appeared on her face. 'You lost a patient.'

Maxwell nodded, sadly. 'Lexi Collins.'

'Oh, no,' Lily muttered.

Sebastian looked at Lily questioningly.

'A young woman Maxwell's been – *was* – treating at the Cromwell for years.'

Maxwell nodded, leaning his elbows on his thighs now. 'Since she was eighteen. Real little fighter that one, going for years. Twenty-three. No age. I really hoped she'd…' His words trailed off as his gaze settled somewhere beyond the window.

Sebastian nodded, discomfort crawling across his neck and shoulders. Yet another link to the past between Lily and Maxwell. Shame followed: was that really his first thought? A young woman had died, for God's sake. It also offered an explanation for Maxwell's impulsive decision to pick up Denny. Of course he'd want to soothe himself by being in the presence of his only child when confronted with such a loss, even if it was mostly professional. Though Maxwell was full of swagger and bravado, it must still affect him to see people die every day. He would have to be a psychopath if it didn't.

'Well, don't do it again,' Lily said, though her tone was softer than her words.

Sebastian decided that saying nothing was the way to go.

Maxwell shook his head. 'I give you my word. I did need to speak to you about something else, though, actually.'

Lily cocked her head. 'Look, I know Denny has a phone now but…'

Her words died away at Maxwell's questioning look. 'That wasn't what I wanted to talk to you about,' he said. 'Look, there's no easy way to say this…' He raised both his meaty palms. 'Denny's been wetting the bed.'

'Jesus, Maxwell, I nearly had a heart attack.' Lily pressed a hand to her chest. Even Sebastian could feel his heart flutter in his rib cage. 'Denny's only six. Kids wet the bed occasionally. You'd know that if you…'

…*Were around more. Were a better father.*

Sebastian saw Maxwell's face darken and was glad Lily had managed to arrest the words on her tongue. He took her hand under the table and squeezed it.

Maxwell sighed. 'It's every single time, Lil.'

Sebastian almost winced at the pet name. He felt sure that was for his benefit.

'Since when?' Lily frowned.

Maxwell's gaze was sad, like he didn't want to have to break this news to them. 'A week or so – since he stayed with me when you were on your honeymoon.'

Sebastian took a deep breath. He'd had no idea Denny was troubled. He'd thought the boy was adjusting to their new lives well. Sure, there had been some teething troubles as all three of them got used to one another, but that was normal, wasn't it?

Lily was defensive. 'Well, he doesn't wet himself at home.'

'Maybe he's hiding it.' Maxwell countered.

There seemed nothing else to say so, with Maxwell's words still ringing in their ears, they announced their arrival to Denny in the living room. The boy seemed in high spirits, bidding a cheery goodbye to his father, and seemingly without a care in the world.

Sebastian was confused. Could he and Lily have been blind to the little boy's distress? Had he been upset by Sebastian being with his mother; had they both been too busy to see it?

As Sebastian drove a drawn, worried Lily and a chatty Denny back to the maisonette, one thought kept returning to him. He was well used to dealing with troubled children; and he knew there was nearly always some kind of marker or sign. Little Denny was no actor or pretender – he was unfailingly open and honest, even to his own detriment, just like his mother.

But there was someone who did like to play mind games – and wasn't above using Lily's concern for their son for his own benefit.

Seventeen

'Can't you see what he's trying to do?'

Sebastian paced. It was awkward in the too-small space of the kitchen-diner. Perched on a stool at the kitchen table, I looked up from the plethora of paperwork in front of me.

'Keep your voice down,' I hissed.

Out in the living area, Denny squatted by the coffee table, doing his homework: he had to colour in and label all the items on the illustration of a kitchen. Every now and again he'd suddenly appear and point at something, wanting to know its official name, even though we kept telling him he had to work it out for himself. I'd told him he could only have his phone back when he'd done it.

Sebastian made an effort to lower his voice. 'Maxwell is inventing excuses to get close to you again.'

Exasperated, I heaved a huge sigh, sending a flutter of papers across the table. I did not need to be in the middle of this, whatever it was. I'd been hit with an extra load of tasks, as well as my usual marking, lesson-planning and work for the upcoming school inspection. Somehow, colleagues had made their heartfelt appeals to my better nature so convincingly, I'd found myself helping to arrange the school fête in just under three weeks' time, thanks to the previous organiser – Sam Miller's normally uber-organised mum – having her baby nearly five weeks early.

'Lily, come on. You know what I'm saying is true.'

Sebastian ran a hand across his face. I could hear the scrape of bristles under his palm. He was nearly always clean-shaven, but today he looked wan and unkempt. Like he still hadn't caught up on the sleep he'd missed, returning from our honeymoon in Mauritius.

'For God's sake Sebastian, what do you want me to do? Denny is having *issues.*' I threw my pencil down. I'd been trying to assign stalls for the fête, but irritation and distraction crowded their way into my brain instead. I couldn't think straight.

'So *Maxwell* says.'

The doorbell sounded and Sebastian's head snapped around. 'Who is that? That better not be him, now.'

'Calm down…' I let out an incredulous laugh but, in truth, Sebastian's manner was unnerving. I gestured towards the oven, where lunch was cooking – the meal I'd got up at eight o'clock on a bloody Saturday morning, after a hard week at work, to make. 'Your mother is coming for lunch, remember?'

Sebastian rolled his eyes. *Of course.* It had even been his idea – to try and build bridges with Fran after the mobile-phone disaster with Denny. When he'd told me he'd invited Fran to lunch, my first reaction had been relief. I'd been trying to think of reasons to get everyone together, without making it seem like a big deal.

Sebastian turned on his heel and clattered down the stairs to the front door.

I grabbed the remote and turned the television off from across the room, much to Denny's annoyance.

'Go and get changed,' I instructed.

Denny huffed and puffed. 'But Mum…'

'Now, please. And don't pull all your clothes out your drawers and wreck the place again.' I warned.

I'd only been to Fran's home once, but I'd seen enough to know she had exacting standards. So we'd not just given the maisonette a lick and a promise, but polished the wooden surfaces, put everything away, even scrubbed the tiles in the bathroom. The air was thick with the smell of beeswax and air freshener.

As I heard Fran's voice in the hallway below, trepidation gnawed at my stomach; we could not afford another misunderstanding or argument. In that spirit, I'd thrown myself into the arrangements for today. I'd wanted to make my signature dish – a fabulous seafood linguine – but Seb reminded me his mother had a life-threatening allergy to seafood. Trying to kill her was probably not the best way to build bridges, he'd advised. I had to agree. Chicken lasagne was her favourite, so I'd sourced top-quality ingredients and spent the morning chopping up lean breast meat, adding fresh tomatoes, basil and Parmesan. I'd not made the dish before and was now worried it might come out dry, or even burnt.

About an hour before Fran was due, the doorbell had rung. Triss had bounded up the stairs, laden with carrier bags. She'd been doing her high-street shopping and needed to use our bathroom. When she returned from the loo, she inhaled the glorious smell of the lasagne filling the kitchen. I had visions of her following the smell from the street below like kids and the Pied Piper.

'Room for one more? Lasagne's my fave.' She'd flashed me a wide grin then pulled something out of one of the bags she'd left on the table. 'I've brought dessert!' She brandished a box of cupcakes.

Caught on the hop, I'd decided deflection was the best tactic. 'Not this time, missus. I'm trying to impress my mother-in-law, not put her off.'

Thankfully, Triss had just made a face and promptly left.

Punctual as ever, Fran appeared at the top of the stairs, at three minutes to one o'clock. I noted that she stood tall, shoulders swept back, stalwart, though she seemed to be holding herself stiffly, as if in discomfort. I knew she would not admit to it though, so I didn't ask whether she was okay. I complimented her on her outfit instead. As ever, she looked immaculate, dressed not in her customary black and red, but a deep peacock blue. Her shoes and handbag matched, as did the shadow on her eyes and the clip in her hair.

'Lily. Wonderful to see you again.' Fran picked her way across the tiles on her blue-suede wedges. She air-kissed my cheeks and presented me with a very expensive bottle of red and a paper bag full of artisan bread rolls. 'Just my little contribution.'

'Thank you so much.' I felt a little wrong-footed. I'd wondered if first we'd have to address what had happened previously, but apparently not. It was as if her last visit and the issue with the phone had been erased. Well, if that was the way Sebastian's family dealt with conflict, fine. I could forget about it and move on, too. Everyone was making an effort, after all.

After excusing herself to 'freshen up' in the bathroom upstairs – it was like Paddington Station up there today – she eventually returned to the kitchen-diner, approached the table and sat down next to Denny.

'This looks delicious, darling.' She inhaled the rich smell of tomatoes from the lasagne on her plate.

As I sat down myself, I beamed, then realised Fran was looking across at Sebastian. I felt sharp irritation that Fran was attributing the meal to Sebastian, rather than me, but decided to let it go. Sebastian was fetching glasses and didn't notice. What was one little misunderstanding over who cooked?

'Quinoa, Fran?' I picked up the bowl to pass to her. I noticed a reaction I couldn't discern flicker across her face. '…What?'

Fran smiled. 'Nothing, dear. Lovely, thank you.'

She took the bowl as Sebastian set the glasses down on the table and laughed at my perplexed expression.

'It's pronounced, "*keen-wah*". Not "*qui-noah*"!' Sebastian chortled.

Embarrassment engulfed me. How was I supposed to know? I'd only ever seen it written down. Besides, it wasn't like I'd grown up with this kind of stuff. The Okenodos' had been a 'meat and two veg' house when my mother was alive. She'd served plain food and plenty of it. When she'd died, my dad hadn't felt much like cooking, so it had been beans on toast or ready meals on trays in front of the TV most nights. He made sure I never went hungry, but I was an adult before I learned to cook for real. It seemed like I still had plenty of culinary blank spots though.

'I bet you think it's "chi-pottle" too!' Amusement sparkled in Sebastian's eyes as he poured me a large glass of red. He took in my blank face. 'You know, chip-oht-lay? As in the Mexican pepper?'

I shrugged, grabbing my glass of wine.

'Oh, don't be horrible to the poor girl,' Fran tutted at her son.

Sebastian at least had the grace to look suitably chastised, though he didn't apologise to me.

As I cleared the plates, I noted Fran hadn't eaten much again. For a moment, I fretted that perhaps she hadn't liked the meal, or the way I had cooked it. Maybe I was a bad cook, as well as an ill-informed one? I banished the thought: she was a thin woman. Perhaps she had never been much of an eater.

Feeling slightly better, I loaded the dishwasher, then brought out dessert. It was just a shop-bought pavlova, but an expensive one: dark-red and purple summer fruits stained the pure-white meringue, which crumbled in thick flakes, a gooey texture underneath. I'd also bought a pot of clotted cream. Everyone loved meringue and clotted cream, right?

Chatting away, I carved crumbly slices onto plates, pushing them towards Sebastian and Denny. As I moved a third one over to Fran, she gave me a tight-lipped smile and held one hand up.

'None for me, Lily, thank you,' she said.

'Oh, go on. Just a little slice?' Perhaps it was because of the quinoa, or the two glasses of wine I'd had with lunch – I wasn't used to drinking during the day – but I passed it to her anyway.

Fran's face seemed to crumple as she took in the small slice of pavlova. Her head bobbed, birdlike towards Denny, who was now shovelling the pudding into his mouth without waiting. She looked next at Sebastian, who nodded encouragement, like she needed his permission or something. This was weird. Finally, almost uncertainly, Fran took the plate.

Wanting to chase away the strange atmosphere, I dug a spoon into the clotted cream. 'Some cream with that, Fran?'

'Oh … no thank you, dear,' Fran said, picking up her own spoon. 'There's quite enough cream in it already.'

'You can't have pavlova without extra cream!' I forced jolliness into my tone, reaching across the table.

'I said no!'

In an instant everything seemed to escalate. Fran grabbed her plate and held it out of my reach, just as I went to dump a great blob of clotted cream where the pavlova had been. As if in slow motion, the cream left the spoon and deposited itself on Fran's lap, all over her beautiful – probably dry-clean only – peacock-blue skirt.

Both of us, plus Sebastian, stared at the cream, as Denny looked on, his smile a mile wide, with the kind of delight only small children can muster in situations where adults are having a socially induced heart attack.

'Not to worry, Mum! We'll soon get that sorted.' Sebastian leaped up from the table, grabbing a sponge from the sink.

Before I could stop him, he'd lunged at his mother with the sponge, dabbing at her crotch with it. Fran grabbed the sponge and gathered her skirt in her hands, hiding the damp patch and the horrible, white stain. There was a dead hush in the room; even Denny's sniggers behind his stubby fingers were silenced by the look of angry mortification on Fran's face. To her credit, she took a deep breath and composed herself, grabbing her handbag.

'I'd better be going,' she said.

Offers of a hairdryer, to pay for the cleaning, or even a new skirt went unheard. I wrung my hands as Fran insisted it was just an accident. Ten minutes later she was gone and I was pouring myself a large gin, with very little tonic.

'Could have been worse,' Sebastian announced airily, sitting down on the sofa next to Denny, who was still trying to finish his homework.

'Are you serious?' I grimaced as the alcohol made its way down my throat. I slammed the glass back down, ready to pour another.

Sebastian shook out the Saturday paper, disappearing behind it. 'Yes. Even Mum has a sense of humour, deep down. We'll all laugh about this, before long. You wait and see.'

I stretched my neck, feeling a *crack* of pent-up stress. Maybe I was overreacting. No one could deny I'd had a lot on lately. Between getting married, trying to get to know my mother-in-law, overwork and Maxwell's campaign to get between me and Sebastian, maybe I wasn't thinking straight. I decided against another gin and screwed the lid back on the bottle.

I couldn't just sit down though, so I started picking up the various things we'd scattered about in the course of the afternoon. Clearing shoes back in the cupboard, grabbing discarded jumpers and toys, I made my way through the maisonette.

Opening Denny's bedroom door to fling his belongings back inside, I stopped in my tracks, wrinkling my nose. A musty smell wafted out at me. Though the bedroom was tidy, as I'd instructed that morning it should be, it was dark; the thick curtains still drawn and the bed unmade. Hadn't I told him to do those things? Obviously not. Denny was too young to look at everything that needed doing; instead he'd taken me literally, putting the toys away as I'd asked. I should have checked.

Sighing, I crossed the threshold and pulled open the curtains to let the early-summer afternoon light in. I opened the top small window, to get rid of some of the musky smell.

The duvet was spilling off the unmade bed onto the floor. I grabbed it without thinking … then stopped. The sheet on the bed was missing. And on the bare mattress was a dark stain. I bent down and sniffed it.

I shuddered. Urine.

'Oh, Denny,' I muttered under my breath.

I glanced around the room: where was the sheet? I noted the closed doors of the wardrobe: an immediate red flag in a child's room. I wrenched one open and, sure enough, at the bottom of the wardrobe was the sheet, a bright-yellow stain – still damp – right in the middle. With it, Denny's crumpled pyjamas, the crotch still wet.

Maxwell's words ricocheted in my skull, even stronger now: *It's every single time, Lil.*

'It wasn't me!'

Caught in the act, I looked up. Denny stood in the doorway, eyes wide with horror. I groaned.

'It's okay, darling.' I took a step towards him, attempting to take him in my arms.

But he thrashed in my grasp like a fish on a line. His little fists were clenched, his face bright red with fury. I'd never seen him like this, but then I'd had no idea he was so upset by everything that had been going on. A sense of trepidation bloomed in my stomach. Sebastian was wrong. Maxwell was right. Oh, God.

'You don't have to be embarrassed. It happens to lots of little boys … Ow!'

I let go of Denny, appalled.

He froze, shocked at his own actions.

I regarded my forearm: indented on it was a row of teeth marks. My son had bitten me. I couldn't believe it. Denny was just like his namesake, my dad: gentle, caring, loving. He'd never hurt me before, not even as a wilful toddler.

Denny recovered more quickly than me. 'It *wasn't* me,' he insisted.

Blinking back tears, I watched him race back out again.

ToTheMax1972 has joined the LIVEchat

Shelly86 has joined the LIVEchat

- Shelly86: Hello, how may I help you today?
- ToTheMax1972: I need some help downloading some software to my son's phone.
- Shelly86: This is no problem for me. Please tell me the name of the software?
- ToTheMax1972: Well, this is it. I'm not sure which is the best one. I need a recommendation?
- Shelly86: I'm good at recommendations. What do you need your son's phone to do?
- ToTheMax1972: I need an app that will keep my son safe, so I can always find him.
- Shelly86: I understand. Do you want free apps or paid-for apps?
- ToTheMax1972: Money is not a problem.
- Shelly86 is typing …
- ToTheMax1972: Actually, no. I need a free one. I prefer no bank record of the transaction.
- Shelly86: Is this android or iPhone?
- ToTheMax1972: First one.
- Shelly86: Is your child frequently away from you, or with you most of the time?
- ToTheMax1972: He lives with his mother.
- Shelly86: I understand. So you will need safe and stable location monitoring by combining GPS, GSM and Wi-Fi hot-spot triangulation technologies?
- ToTheMax1972: If you say so! ;)

- Shelly86: I can recommend iSafeTrack, v4.0. Available on all app stores and for all platforms. You can set up geofences and assign an administrator and users from your own devices, so you can always know your son is where he is supposed to be, even when he is not with you. Total peace of mind.

- ToTheMax1972: Thank you so much, Shelly86.

- Shelly86: You are most welcome. Can I help you with anything else?

- ToTheMax1972: No, that's it.

- Shelly86: Have a great day!

ToTheMax1972 has left the LIVEchat
Shelly86 has left the LIVEchat

PART TWO

July–August

'You never know how much you really believe anything until its truth or falsehood becomes a matter of life and death to you.'
—C. S. Lewis

Eighteen

'Morale is down – having this inspection hanging over us is doing no one any good.'

Monday morning after break, Harry sat in Sebastian's office, tie undone, his expression harassed. 'Raffle tickets aren't selling for the fête. The lead – and the sodding understudy – for the school play both have bloody scarlet fever. What next?'

Sebastian nodded along as Harry ranted next about the system, the curriculum and the 'bloody government'. His deputy had hitched up his trousers in that peculiar way of his, and Sebastian could see the outline of his knobbly ankles. Today's socks had an incongruous pair of reindeer on them – a present last Christmas from his twins, apparently. Sebastian found himself longing for a chilly December wind, or even better, actual snow. An image of making a snowman with Denny and Lily passed through his mind.

'I hear you. Let's hope it all it comes together, eh?' Sebastian said, remembering his leadership training: *Not all problems need solutions. Let your colleagues blow off steam. Make them feel heard.* He hoped that was all Harry wanted, because he didn't have a clue what to do either.

Ten minutes later, Harry left, placated, for his classroom. Opening his desk drawer, Sebastian pulled out a box of hay-fever tablets. He pressed a pill onto his tongue and gulped it down without water. The pollen count was not going anywhere, it seemed. June's muggy weather had extended into July, with only intermittent showers to break it up. The big storm predicted by the Met Office that would clear the air had failed to appear. Sebastian's eyeballs felt scratchy, as did the back of his throat; his chest was wet with mucus. He coughed and spluttered, nose running like it was mid-winter, not the beginning of July. Bloody British summertime. If it wasn't raining, it was bursting with humidity.

Finally, the bell went and Sebastian heard the mass exodus as children hurried through the corridors and out into the playground to their waiting parents, guardians and carers. Within ten minutes, the school was a void, spooky in that way only empty educational institutions could be. Rosanna was already gone, of course – some bunkum about yet another dentist's appointment. Anger suddenly spiked in Sebastian's brain: that was it! She was fired at the end of term. At least over the holidays he would have a little more time to find a new receptionist.

Though it was nowhere near his usual clocking-off time, weariness overcame him as quickly as anger had moments earlier. Sebastian collected up his things, deciding to do his remaining paperwork after dinner. He trundled out through the empty school and across the playground to his reserved parking spot, the words HEAD TEACHER painted across it in red and blue, the colours of Avon-wood's school uniform.

There had been another light shower since the children left but the water was already evaporating off the tarmac in the early-evening glare and had done nothing to break the heatwave. Sweating, Sebastian pulled off his jacket and threw it with the rest of his stuff onto the back seat of the car. As he did so, he heard a sharp whistle behind him. He turned.

Maxwell.

Lily's ex-husband stood there, his head at an angle, a smirk on his face. He took off his sunglasses and put them in the breast pocket of his shirt – a black one this time, with a red-rose pattern. Facing each other, it was clear to Sebastian that the other man was much taller, better looking and broader across the shoulders.

'So, how's married life?' Maxwell drawled.

His hands were free of jewellery, bar one finger. His left hand. He was still wearing his wedding band.

Fury welled inside Sebastian like an eruption of lava. He was sure

Maxwell had not been wearing that the last time they met. He'd put it on specifically as a big fat *fuck you*. Well, it was working! Sebastian knew he mustn't rise to the bait, but seeing the reminder of his own wife's promise to this man was like a dagger through his heart.

'Fine, thank you.' Sebastian's tone was clipped, automatic.

'*Only* fine?' Maxwell seized on Sebastian's choice of word like a predator grabbing its prey. 'Lily already too demanding for you?'

Sebastian groaned inwardly at handing his rival an easy weapon. Maxwell was an educated man with a high price tag; he'd gone to Eton. He would have played the Wall Game, batting a ball in his hands against the corners of those ancient school buildings. Now he had grabbed Sebastian's words and slammed them against the wall, too.

'Everything's brilliant,' Sebastian hissed through clenched teeth. 'There's only been one problem, in fact.'

'And what's that?' Maxwell tutted, though his smirk stayed in place. And Sebastian noticed that, despite having at least a decade on him, Maxwell's mouth was unlined, his forehead wrinkle-free. His smooth features had to be the result of Botox.

'You.' Sebastian liked the look of momentary uncertainty that crossed Maxwell's expression now. He was recovering the upper hand. 'We know what you did.'

Maxwell's face was stony. 'I don't know what you mean.'

'What kind of man trashes the house his own child lives in, eh?' Sebastian felt a kind of grim satisfaction bloom in his stomach. 'Or disconnects the electricity? Some dad.'

Maxwell flexed his large hands. 'I didn't do those things.'

Sebastian stifled a laugh. Lily was right: this guy *was* deluded. He was probably so caught up in his own lies, he believed himself. Maxwell shifted from one foot to the other as he took in Sebastian's incredulous expression.

'Bye, Maxwell,' Sebastian said, his tone deliberate.

But the other man was not ready to end the conversation. He leaned on Sebastian's open car door, getting in the way.

'Been seeing a lot of Triss lately, I bet.'

'What's that supposed to mean?' Sebastian responded. And as he did so, he could feel his advantage slipping away. He resisted the urge to push the door closed, slamming Maxwell's surgeon fingers in it.

Maxwell shrugged. 'Just saying. You must know by now Triss and Lily come as a package deal? I bet Lil was on the phone to her the moment you came back from honeymoon. Then they're cosying up in the staffroom … more coffees and drinks after work. Hanging out at weekends. Am I close?'

Maxwell's words rankled more than Sebastian would have liked to admit. He'd always known Lily and Triss went back a long way; they were like sisters. Or so Lily said. He'd never got an inkling of anything else from his wife. But what if it was something more for Triss? Sebastian had previously been struck by the fact he'd never seen Triss with a steady boyfriend, the whole time he'd been with Lily. Sure, she talked about men and dates … but could it be just a front, to stay close to Lily, sail under the radar? And now with what Maxwell was saying, Sebastian couldn't help wondering if he should reassess Triss's constant shadowing of Lily.

But he wasn't about to admit it to Maxwell. 'What are you trying to say?'

'I'm not *trying* to say anything.' Maxwell looked bored now, clearly aware his jibe had landed home.

Sebastian was weary of these mind games. 'I don't have time for this,' he said, pushing against Maxwell to shoulder him out the way, so he could clamber into the car. 'I'm going home. To *my* family!'

But Maxwell's hand snaked under Sebastian's armpit, clenching the top of his bicep. Before Sebastian could react, Maxwell slammed the car door across his shoulders. It was not that hard – Sebastian was not fully inside the car – but the shock stung enough to bring a blue edge to his vision. Maxwell let go, allowing Sebastian to windmill around in an unruly circle, making a grab for his rival's collar.

'What the hell are you playing at?' Sebastian roared.

But Maxwell did not attempt to hit him again. He flashed Sebastian a grin.

'Hey, she tell you yet how she likes to be fucked? Or she playing nice for you? Cos you should know, girls like Lily like it rough.' Gone was the suave, expensively educated man. Maxwell was playing the part of a drunken lout in a bar, as if a switch had flipped inside him.

Sebastian glowered. 'Don't talk about her like that.'

Maxwell bumped his chest against Sebastian's, a clichéd move designed to flood his adversary with more antagonism. It was working. 'It's the chav in them, those working-class girls. You pin her down next time and you'll see. Dirty little slut…'

With a howl of rage, Sebastian let loose with his fist and felt it connect with Maxwell's face. Maxwell went down straight away, and Sebastian felt a rush of gratification. But then he became aware of an intense, stinging sensation in his knuckles. He turned his hand over and was surprised to see blood. His own? Definitely: the skin was punctured, but not just by the force of the blow; he could see the indentation of Maxwell's teeth.

On his hands and knees on the wet tarmac, Maxwell looked up. He didn't seem surprised, or even particularly shocked. Puffed and red, a shadow was already forming above his cheekbone. Blood had sprung up from his split lip, colouring his white tombstone teeth a weird pink.

He breathed through the pain as he staggered to his feet. 'You're gonna wish you hadn't done that.'

Sebastian already did. As well as the throbbing in his fist, there was a deep ache stretching its way from his elbow and up his bicep, into his neck. Even so, he raised both fists again, ready to land another blow on Maxwell.

But his rival merely winked at him and turned his back.

It was over, just like that.

Shocked, Sebastian watched Maxwell meander out of the car park towards his ridiculous car, which was parked across the road.

Had he won? wondered Sebastian, feeling slightly elated now. He'd won! Holy shit!

He slumped into his oven of a car. He rolled his sore shoulders, sending more tingling waves of pain down his spine. Raw anger had enabled him to land a good blow on Maxwell, square on the jaw, just like in the films. While the resulting pain was not something the movies had prepared him for, he felt he could chalk himself up as the victor. Maybe this was the turning point? Perhaps an alpha male like Maxwell just needed a show of dominance to put him off. Sebastian cracked his knuckles, winced, then started the ignition to drive home.

Back to Lily and Denny.

Nineteen

By Tuesday lunchtime, I was ready to fall down. I'd had another terrible night, courtesy of Sebastian. He'd tossed and turned, crashing around the bedroom to the bathroom and back again – attempting to creep around, yet making more noise, like only men and the very drunk can.

He'd been in a weird mood since he got back from school that evening. Initially, I'd been pleased that he'd come home early for dinner, but he had picked at his food before going for a run for over an hour and a half, leaving me to my own devices once I'd got Denny to bed and done my marking.

Giving up on any hope of romance, or at least a glass of wine together on the sofa, I'd been about to go to bed with a paperback when Triss turned up. She had some kind of life crisis she needed to talk about. About three times a year Triss would float the idea of travelling; or changing career; or getting back in touch with her waster parents. Each time I would encourage her to do what she felt was best and each time she did nothing, saying it was better to leave it as it was ... until the next time she had to dissect everything.

Coming up to nine o'clock, Sebastian had reappeared, red in the face and soaked in sweat. He'd stopped dead at the top of the stairs as he saw Triss at the kitchen table with me. Triss raised her glass.

'All right, boss. Bet you see enough of me at work, right?' She cackled.

I smiled. Sebastian didn't.

'Something like that,' he'd mumbled, before disappearing into the shower for another half-hour.

Now, as I made my way into the staff room just before the lunch bell, having let my class go two minutes early, I felt a little guilty, but

I needn't have bothered: Triss was already in there, flicking through a travel magazine. She'd kicked off her shoes and was reclining on the old, grubby sofa.

Looking up, she answered my unspoken question. 'They're on the computers; too hot for anything else. Technician's watching 'em.'

'Bloody maths specialists get away with murder,' I grumbled, though I wasn't really bothered. I was too busy searching for a clean cup. There was a host of dirty ones in the equally dirty sink. Some of them had been there for so long there was mould in the bottom. The work surface was covered in coffee and sugar granules, plus there were used tea bags everywhere and teaspoons stuck to the counter as flies crawled over every available surface.

'This place is minging,' I shuddered, reminded of Sebastian's – *Sorry*, I told myself, *home*.

The housework had slid right off the agenda; just three days after Fran's visit, the place looked once more like a bomb had hit it. I supposed I could have tidied while I was waiting for Sebastian to come back from his run the previous night, but why should I? I'd been at work all day as well. Plus, I was the only one who seemed to notice the state it was in, or even tried to sort it out and put stuff away. Sebastian was neat at work, but as soon as he walked through the door at home, he became as bad as Denny, leaving dirty socks and pants everywhere like a weird Hansel on his way to the Gingerbread House.

I finally located a cleanish mug and, pouring the last of the stewed coffee from the glass jug into it, I glanced at the calendar on the wall. Someone had ringed the last day of term with red marker and scrawled '*SCHOOL'S OUT!!*' beside it.

'Bit late for booking a holiday?' I indicated Triss's magazine.

Triss rolled her eyes at me. 'Duh. This is for *next* summer. Some of us aren't lucky enough to have a *second* rich husband who's already taken us to Mauritius.'

I made a face at my best mate and laughed, but I was stung. Triss knew what I had gone through with Maxwell. He might have been rich, but I had never experienced the benefits, and neither had Denny. Like so many well-off people, Maxwell was tight with his money. When I was home on maternity leave, Maxwell had kept me so short of cash I'd had to go to him, cap in hand. Even now, he was not paying what he should in child maintenance. Sebastian told me that it didn't matter, but it was the principle of thing – Denny was Maxwell's child, so he should have been contributing to his upkeep.

That said, I hadn't had to fight him to get an appointment for Denny with the child psychologist about his bed-wetting. I'd told Maxwell we were going private and that he was paying. Expecting objections, I was surprised when he had readily agreed. The three of us had an appointment the following week.

'What's going on down there?'

I looked up. Triss had drifted towards the window. Next to the Venetian blinds, she was just a tall, lean silhouette; her piled-up top-knot of red hair made her look like she had a pineapple for a head. I joined her at the window and parted the blinds for a better look.

A group of schoolchildren were gathered below, on the play-ground that backed onto the staff car park. Even through the glass, I could sense the pack mentality: it was evident in the way the kids were holding themselves. Elbows sharp and jostling, shiny eyes, rictus grins. They surged forwards, hungry for scandal. As a teacher, I could recognise this straight away: I'd seen it plenty of times before, usually accompanied by chants of *Fight! Fight!*

But this time, there was no brawl. At the heart of the throng were two police officers, both female. They were both large in stature, broad-shouldered, with big hands. Clad in their shirtsleeves, their vests over the top, radios in the top pockets, they were overdressed for such a sweltering July day.

One grabbed her radio and spoke into it.

The other placed a hand on the shoulder of the much shorter man standing next to her. She was muttering something, her visage almost blank; it was an automatic spiel she must have delivered countless times before. I guessed exactly what she was saying: '*You do not have*

Twenty

Sebastian could barely take in what the police officer was saying. He was aware of the children in his peripheral vision, but confusion swirled in his brain. An adult playground monitor, her face a picture of concern, seemed to be keeping her distance, as if trouble with the police might be contagious. Then she remembered herself and started to call the kids away, gathering them to her like a shepherd rounding up sheep. As kids began to fall into line, a couple of others had to be yanked away by their elbows by their friends.

'What's going on?'

Sebastian's heart lurched with dismay as the crowd of kids parted. Lily appeared from the back of the art block, her expression incredulous. Triss trailed behind her as always, though she at least had the good grace to help the playground monitor. It didn't stop her casting a questioning eye over to the pair of them though, clearly desperate to know what was happening.

Sebastian sighed. 'It's okay, Lily.'

'It is not!' Lily went on the offensive immediately, but to Sebastian's relief, it was not directed at him. She turned her attention to the police officers. 'I asked you a question. What is the charge?'

His reprieve was momentary. Both the police officers looked at Sebastian, waiting for him to explain himself.

'It's Maxwell. He says I hit him.'

Lily opened her mouth, but then closed it again. Then she rounded on the police officers, eyes flashing. 'You couldn't have waited until the end of the day? Sebastian has a duty to these kids!'

'We're under no obligation to arrest anyone at a more convenient time, madam.' The younger of the two police officers proffered a sarcastic smirk. 'Now, if you would step aside?'

Lily shouted something about calling his mother, a lawyer and even the PTA as he clambered into the police car; Sebastian simply nodded.

The ride to the police station was a blur. He'd been in one before, but only on school open days when the police would show the children their equipment and talk them through the lighter parts of what they did. Sebastian had never expected to be on the wrong end of their work. The notion of criminality had been a concept to him; its consequences were something that happened to other people, not him. Besides, it had just been a tussle with Maxwell. Sebastian had seen far worse at boarding school; and coming from that world too, so would Maxwell. How the hell could that silly scuffle have led to this?

Sebastian was booked in by an older, male desk sergeant with short, tightly woven dreadlocks and a weary expression. Sebastian had to hand over his belt and shoelaces, plus his phone and wallet, just like in the movies. He'd expected to be shown straight through to an interview room, but the desk sergeant said he would have to wait. There was a race meet on at Epsom, he explained, so they were full to the brim with pickpockets and scam merchants. Great.

The metal clink of the door slamming behind him made Sebastian want to vomit. A hot feeling coursed through him and his vision was a little blurred. Sebastian felt as if he had left his body: he was staring down at a hollow-eyed, sunken-cheeked pallid man in a six-by-eight dingy cell.

Then, he was back.

The stench of stale urine and body odour assaulted his nostrils, making him feel woozy. He sat down on the bunk, which creaked under his weight. Sebastian could not bring himself to lie down. He sat forwards, head in hands.

Finally, after what felt like years, the door opened again. A woman in her forties appeared. Instantly, he could tell she was not police, but a lawyer. She was dark, like Lily, but she had a creased brow, as if everything disappointed her. She wore jeans and an unironed top, like she'd thrown her clothes on in a hurry. In one hand she had a tatty notebook and a chewed biro; in the other, a roll of quilted toilet paper.

'Here you go; what they give you in here is like tracing paper.' She chucked the toilet paper onto the bunk. 'Well, this is a pickle, innit?'

The lawyer's accent was more street than Sebastian expected. She sat down on the bunk with him, introduced herself as Soraya Campbell and confirmed that Lily had called her. Apparently, she'd found her on Facebook.

Soraya took him through the charges. And to his surprise, she told him to deny everything.

'But I did it,' Sebastian said.

'Sebastian – I can call you Sebastian, right? – what do you reckon is gonna happen if you plead guilty to assault? Goodbye to your headmaster's job; goodbye teaching. That's what. Now, I've already spoken to your wife and she says Maxwell has been gunning for you both since you got married, probably before. So what's the point of falling on your sword?'

Sebastian finally acquiesced. Afterwards – it was impossible to tell the exact time, though it must have been night by then – he and Soraya were shown into an interview room. Two plain-clothes detectives – one white man, one female and east Asian – were waiting for them. Soraya appeared to recognise them, which was somehow reassuring. She must have done a lot of business at that station.

'Thought you guys would have bigger fish to fry.' Soraya's tone was half joking, half serious.

'It's been mad today. Just trying to clear the decks.' The man yawned, tugging at his crotch absentmindedly as he crossed his plump thighs.

He nodded at Sebastian. 'I'm Detective Meyer, this is Detective Inspector Su.'

'Okay,' said Soraya. 'My client wants to get out of here. He's a model citizen, pillar of the community, blah, blah, blah. And we all know this other guy is making it up, cos he's jealous. C'mon.' Soraya flashed Meyer and Su a brilliant smile.

Su's gaze alighted on the lawyer. 'I'd like to hear from Mr Adair.' There was a trace of an accent to her speech; Geordie or Liverpudlian, perhaps.

Soraya did not break eye contact. 'He has nothing to say.'

'What a pity.'

Sebastian's gaze moved from one woman to the other. He could sense the antagonism coming off them both in waves. Soraya was the type to go in fighting, no matter what. Su was not much different. They were alpha females, determined to make a difference in their respective worlds, clashing like stags.

Some three hours later, Sebastian was finally bailed and released. Soraya went out with him into the vestibule and gave him her card. She told him she doubted very much he would be called back in for more questioning, but not to go anywhere for the time being.

He'd expected to have to pay a bail fee. He'd started to take a credit card out when he was given back his wallet, but according to Soraya, that was only in America, or for the most serious of charges in the UK. Feeling embarrassed and considerably less worldly than he had that morning, Sebastian put his wallet away and bid Soraya and the weary desk sergeant goodnight.

He emerged into the night air and breathed it in, grateful to be free. Even the orange streetlight glinting on a Coke can lying in the police car park seemed beautiful. His roiling stomach began to calm down at last. What was he going to say to Lily? He recalled Soraya's words. There was no point throwing himself on his sword. He'd tell her Maxwell was a liar. It wasn't so unlikely, after all.

'Over here, darling!'

The familiar voice pierced his thoughts. Sebastian turned to find his mother standing by her car. She was smiling, no judgement on her pale face. This made him feel worse. Under the light of the streetlamp she looked small, frail. She shouldn't have come out to get him in the middle of the night. Unexpected tears welled up in his eyes. He strode into her outstretched arms, burying his head in her shoulder as he wept.

She stroked his hair, her soothing words washing over him. 'There, there,' she cooed at him, like he was a little baby. 'Let's get you home, darling.'

Twenty-one

'Look. I'm just saying what we're all thinking.' Sadie, Madison Taylor's yummy mummy, and head of the PTA, sat her yoga-sleek form back in her chair, folding her perfect, snow-white arms. 'Our very own head teacher arrested … at school!' She took in the shocked faces, held rapt by her words, then fluttered a weak apology towards my husband. 'Sorry, Sebastian. I'm just thinking of the children here.'

My hands clenched around my cold coffee mug. I didn't trust myself to let go. I might just start screaming and never stop. Or worse, break down and cry. I couldn't believe what was happening. *Damn you, Maxwell.*

'We're aware of your opinion on the matter, Sadie,' Harry said, adjusting his Homer Simpson tie. He was feeling the pressure, too. With Sebastian in the hot seat, it had been decided Harry should lead the meeting.

Across the table, Sebastian's gaunt face seemed to sag under all the scrutiny. Several governors were openly hostile, staring angrily at him. Injustice flooded my insides.

Sebastian's expression had been earnest when he'd finally arrived home, past midnight, from the police station. 'I swear Lily, I never touched him,' he'd said.

I'd cast my eyes down towards his hand. There were scratches on the back of his knuckles. I'd spotted them at dinner the previous night, before he'd gone on his run, but he said he'd caught them on the car door. He was telling the truth; he had to be. Maxwell probably hit himself somehow, trying to set Sebastian up. It wouldn't be outside the realms of possibility. Nothing was when it came to my ex-husband. Sebastian couldn't lie.

Not to me.

'Let's approach the situation logically, shall we?' The voice at the back was clear, not a sign of a tremor in it.

Everyone's heads turned. Fran was sitting a small distance away from the table, in a chair beside the window. She'd become a governor of Avonwood shortly after Sebastian became head teacher, but she did little other than turn up to meetings. Today she was dressed in black, her long, thin hands folded on top of the blood-red patent leather handbag on her lap. Her shoes matched her bag perfectly. She looked out of the window at the common as she continued to address us.

I felt a rush of optimism at the sound of authority behind her words. If anyone could help call the governors to order and make them see sense, it was Fran. Despite her physical frailty, she was commanding and unflappable in the muggy room, especially in comparison to Sadie. The other woman scowled at my mother-in-law.

'There have been no charges—' Fran began.

'Yet,' Sadie added sourly.

My mother-in-law pursed her lips. 'In the absence of a witness, or even a charge, then I think we can all agree Sebastian is innocent until proven guilty, no?'

There was a moment as the room digested this.

'Sadie's right. They arrested him in front of the kids, for God's sake!' Another woman sat forwards. Simon Tucker's mum. She looked just like him: fleshy lips and floppy hair.

'That's hardly Sebastian's fault,' Fran pointed out.

'It is if he thumped the guy!' Simon's mum shot back.

'*If* is the operative word.' Fran folded her arms, waiting for the counter-response. There wasn't one. She smiled, victorious.

Harry blew out his cheeks as everyone turned to look at him again. He raised his hands in the air. 'Let's hang fire, shall we? It's nearly the summer holidays, just ten days to go.'

There were murmurs of both agreement and discontent. I looked questioningly at Sebastian – did this mean the board of governors wasn't suspending him? Seeing the relief shimmer across his face was enough. My stomach unknotted itself.

Harry rose from his seat. He clapped one hand on his superior's shoulder, showing his support – not just for Sebastian's benefit but the whole room's. Small smiles were shared around the table. Sebastian was generally well respected by the teachers, parents and governors, not least because he was such a young man in such a senior position. Sadie didn't share the positivity though; her face was like thunder, her mouth screwed up tight like she was chewing wasps.

'This will all be resolved by September,' Harry said, 'you wait and see.'

As the rest of the governors, teachers and PTA members filed out, I decided to catch Fran before she left. Standing apart from the others, aloof and calm, she was a stark contrast to Sebastian, who was huddled with Harry again, muttering.

When I touched the older woman's arm to gain her attention, her gaze alighted on me, surprised, as if she'd thought herself alone.

'Fran, thank you so much for going in to bat for Sebastian there. We really appreciate it.'

Fran smiled and momentarily the lines around her lips and eyes betrayed her real age. 'My dear girl, what else would you expect me to do?'

I felt wrong-footed. 'I mean, thank you for believing Sebastian. That he didn't hit Maxwell, I mean.'

Fran's smile dropped from her face. She cast a furtive glance to the few other members of the PTA still chatting nearby. She lowered her voice and took a step closer to me. 'You're not telling me you *do* believe him?'

There was a sharp tone to her words that cut through my trust in my husband's innocence in an instant. It felt like a physical blow. My shoulders sagged under the weight of the truth.

Of course Sebastian had hit Maxwell. Who wouldn't have? Maxwell's behaviour had been despicable and relentless. Sebastian would have had to have the patience of an angel to withstand it, especially if Maxwell had baited him on purpose. Which he likely had done. Everything that Maxwell received, he had asked for. That did not bother me.

What did was that Sebastian had lied to me.

Fran must have noted my stricken expression because she leaned even closer. 'Don't be too harsh on him, dear. He's just trying to adjust to this new situation of yours, just like you and the boy.'

Then she patted the back of my hand sympathetically. I smiled, grateful, wanting to hug her for stepping in and helping us again. Instinctively, I knew she wouldn't like that, so I held back.

Across the room, still besieged by Harry, Sebastian stared after his mother then back at me, a question in his eyes. It was clear he was trying to gauge whether or not I knew about his transgression.

I had a split second to decide: did I let on that I knew my husband had lied to me about hitting my ex? While I wished Sebastian had told me the truth, part of me felt like Maxwell deserved everything he got. What a mess. Besides which, if this came between us, then Maxwell would win again – just like he had when he'd taken Denny from after-school club.

Finally, I returned Sebastian's gaze and smiled.

Relieved, he smiled back.

- *Welcome to iSafeTrack, v-4.0! With bug fixes and greater stability, this is the best version of iSafeTrack ever! Total peace of mind for all parents – keep your precious angel safe, always. Do you wish to continue?*

➡ *YES*

- *You can track up to three profiles on the free version. Do you want all three activated?*

➡ *NO*

- *That's okay. You can always activate your other two profiles later! Name your profile:*

➡ *Denny6*

- *Profile Denny6, activated. You can activate up to five geofences on the free version of iSafeTrack v-4.0. Don't know what a geofence is? <CLICK HERE>.*

  - A geofence means you can set up a virtual protective boundary around your child by nominating landmarks where you expect your child to go; a text message will be sent to you when the child goes beyond the perimeters of that boundary. Thanks to the exciting new features on iSafeTrack v-4.0, you can also assign an avatar to your child's profile, so you can see where s/he is within the boundary.

- *Do you wish to continue?*

➡ *YES*

- *Set geofences and assign names – you can have to up to five on the free version. Enter now…*

➡ *The maisonette*

➡ *Avonwood School*

➡ *Epsom Common*

➡ *Epsom High Street*

➡ *The Cromwell Hospital*

- *Congratulations! You are all set. iSafeTrack v-4.0, putting your child's safety first. Follow us on Twitter, Facebook and Instagram.*

<LEAVE SET UP>

Twenty-two

'Typical!'

The alarm rang at six-thirty, as we'd agreed the night before. Sebastian was already awake. Groggy, I rolled over in the direction of his voice. It was far too early for a Saturday morning, especially after yet another hectic week. Still, we were into July now and the summer holidays were five days away. I couldn't wait.

'It's been good weather for weeks, so of course the storm arrives the day of the fête.'

Daylight spilled into our bedroom. He stood next to our bed, at the window, already dressed, his back to me. The dormer window in our bedroom looked out onto a brick wall, and he was craning his neck so he could see the sky, the dark black clouds rolling overhead. I could see and hear the cause of his dismay: raindrops slammed against the windowpane and wind rattled the frame.

I sat up and rubbed sleep from my eyes. 'It'll be okay.'

'People stay in when it's shitty weather. We need the funds! This is all we want – especially with that bloody inspection any day now.' Sebastian's posture slumped.

I stretched and rose to my feet too quickly. The blood rushed to my head and I tottered forwards a step. Finding my voice, I said, 'We'll move most of the stalls under the football canopy. The bouncy castle can go in the upper gym. We can do the majorettes and the other demos in the lower gym.'

I was glad now I had paid attention during the fête meetings and had seconded a suggestion for a bad-weather contingency plan.

Sebastian turned towards me, impressed, and grabbed me around the waist. 'This is why I married you. You keep your head in a crisis.'

'I hope that's not the only reason.' I kissed him on the lips. 'Now make me some coffee while I get in the shower.'

Sebastian gave me a mock salute. 'Yes, ma'am!'

As I padded into the bathroom, I logged in to the school website on my phone. On the front page of the blog was a poster for the fête. As I waited for hot water to reach the shower through the maisonette's ancient pipes, I updated the blogpost with a short message in bold: *STILL GOING AHEAD DESPITE BAD WEATHER.*

Then I dragged myself under the spray of water, as hot as I could stand it. Drying off, I dressed for comfort: jeans and a T-shirt, zip-up hoody, ponytail. It was going to be a long day. Feeling refreshed and more awake, I joined Sebastian in the kitchen.

'Hi, Mum.' Denny was already seated at the table, swinging his stick legs and flicking through a comic.

'Hi, sport.' I ruffled his hair. There was jam around his lips. 'Looking forward to today?'

Denny nodded, wide-eyed. Like most kids, he loved school fêtes. Sebastian had warmed some croissants through and one sat on a plate next to a large mug of black coffee. Blackberry jam sank into the buttery pastry. Realising I was ravenous, I picked it up and devoured it in a few bites.

We arrived at school at about quarter to eight. In the staffroom, a bunch of teachers' kids perched on small chairs, drawing and colouring at an undersized red plastic table. Kelly from after-school club sat with them, wrapping gifts for the lucky dip. She attempted coolness as I caught her eye; she was still embarrassed about letting Maxwell take Denny. I decided to be the bigger person.

'Thanks Kelly, you're a star,' I told her as I took Denny over.

She smiled. 'Don't mention it.' An overpowering smell of antiperspirant wafted from her and there was old mascara smudged under her eyes. I wondered if she'd even been home yet.

Triss was waiting in the upper gym to meet the bouncy-castle man. She had a mug in her hand and a sour expression on her face. She did not say hello as I approached, preferring a good whinge instead: 'Can't believe I'm at work on a Saturday! Remind me why I'm a teacher?'

'To inspire and educate young minds / to give something back / to keep you out of trouble – delete as appropriate.' I grinned, handing her a small float of coins in a plastic ice-cream tub.

'Wait, wait. Don't tell me I'm doing the bouncy castle!' Triss's eyes were wide with horror. 'All that screaming! Can't I do the tombola or something?'

I laughed. Triss was a reception teacher, screaming kids were her forte. 'You can handle it. I'll see if I can swap you halfway through the day.'

'Fine…' Triss grumbled, her face as dark and surly as a petulant teen's.

Moments later, the double doors of the hall opened and a man with a pot belly and a rolled-up bouncy castle appeared, whistling. I left them to it.

I consulted my clipboard as I walked down the school hallways, the rubber soles of my flat shoes squeaking on the lino. That had been one of Sam Miller's mum's top tips: *For the love of God, don't wear heels. You'll be on your feet, running around all day.*

Sebastian appeared carrying bags of plastic cups and paper plates to the kitchens. We would be serving chips, burgers and hot dogs: hot food always did well at fêtes, especially on colder, miserable days like this. As we passed each other, he gave me another cheery salute and I grinned, turning to watch his cute butt saunter away.

Under the canopy on the tarmacked mini-football pitch, the stall-holders were amassing, putting up their trestle tables and unpacking goods. The school's stands were on the left: tombola; pin the tail on the donkey; guess the number of sweets in the jar; second-hand books and toys; plus a spot for Kelly's lucky dip. On the right were craft and food traders who'd donated to the school in return for a stall: a chocolate fountain; a maker of wooden toys; a jeweller; a guy selling bubble swords and beach and garden goods. There wasn't enough room for all of them, though.

'Where do you want this?' To my relief it was Jackson, my cousin Maya's other half, carrying a large rolled-up canvas gazebo across his huge shoulders. Maya would be home with little Clyde, but I'd already spotted her girls, Jasmine and Amy, with Kelly in the staff-room, so I'd been waiting for Jackson to arrive with the gazebo for the stalls that wouldn't fit under the canopy.

I instructed him to put the gazebo up as close as he could to the canopy, so people could escape the weather as much as possible. Jackson gave me a meaty thumbs-up and wandered out into the rain. He didn't even flinch as the bad weather hit him, even though he was dressed only in a T-shirt and shorts.

The next two hours of prep time rocketed by in a blur. Before I knew it, it was ten o'clock. As I predicted, Sebastian needn't have worried. There was a small queue by the school gates at five to the hour.

The fête was declared open by the local mayor, decked out in all her traditional regalia. She shook hands with both Sebastian and me, then we posed for photographs for the local gazette. Her smile fixed in place, the mayor allowed a duo of year-five kids to lead her to the lower gym for a selection of songs sung by the school choir. Some parents followed the children and the mayor, others swarmed under the canopy and through the doors into the main building.

I wandered around the stalls outside and inside the school, checking everyone had what they needed. Then I peeked through the doors to the upper gym. Despite her protestations, Triss was now barefoot and in her element on the bouncy castle. She was bossing kids around and jumping into the inflatable, sending giggling kids into the air.

I took stallholders cups of tea, coffee and water; I fetched and carried, chatting with parents, who all seemed jovial and to be enjoying themselves; and I cleaned up as I went, picking up wrappers, lolly sticks and used napkins, depositing them in the black bin liner I trailed after me.

About an hour in, I walked past the lower gym on my way to

the kitchens, dragging two full bags of rubbish with me. The beats of a Beyoncé track boomed through the hall: I could see little girls in leotards twirling batons. I smiled as one of the little ones at the front dropped her baton, but then simply shrugged and chased after it under one of the benches.

I shouldered the kitchen's door open and shoved the rubbish in the backroom. Across the tiles, Sebastian stood at the serving hatch, wielding a scoop over a metal tray. He was wearing a hairnet and deposited chips into paper bags for one of the lunch ladies, a woman in snake-print leggings with a frizzy eighties' perm whose name I'd forgotten. I could see the queue on the other side extending all the way down the corridor, towards the back doors of the main building.

I sidled up alongside my husband. 'Need a hand?'

'In a word, yes.' Sebastian threw a hairnet at me and another scoop. I caught them up with a laugh, and took my place next to him at the serving hatch.

It was all going so well.

I should have known it wouldn't last.

Twenty-three

'Sir, sir!'

The first Sebastian heard of any problem was when a year-six, Jack McAllister, burst through the kitchen double doors.

'What is it, Jack?' An experienced teacher, Sebastian was not concerned by the urgency of the boy's voice at first. If adults took every kid's freak-out seriously, they would be in a permanent state of high alert.

The boy was breathless. 'It's Mrs Stevens.'

'Oh?' Sebastian dumped the last lot of chips from the deep-fat fryer into another metal tray. The sound of Lily's old name still rankled him, though he knew it shouldn't.

'She can't find Denny.'

Sebastian was still unconcerned. There were lots of children milling about at the fête, so it was not inconceivable that one little boy might be difficult to locate.

'He won't have left the building. If he isn't with Triss – I mean Miss Lomax – he'll be with Kelly from after-school club.'

The little boy clenched his fists, radiating frustration. 'No, sir, you don't get it. *Nobody* can find him!'

Now panic seized Sebastian. It felt cold, as if claws had seized his ribcage, stopping him from breathing properly. Frozen, he looked up at the lunch lady next to him.

She nodded and took the tray of chips from his arms. 'Go, go,' she urged.

Jack sped off ahead of Sebastian; he had to race to catch up with the little boy. Adrenaline surged through Sebastian's veins, yet his legs felt heavy. As he ran down the tiled corridor, he scanned the atrium and the sports field beyond the windows. Thoughts clamoured through his head with the thundering speed of a freight train. What had Denny been wearing? He couldn't remember. As Sebastian passed the door to the playground, he was comforted to hear various parents yelling his stepson's name. Then disturbed: if all these people were searching, that meant Denny had not been found yet.

'I can't believe this!'

Sebastian arrived in the gym to find the bouncy castle deflated and Triss and Kelly at each other's throats. Or rather, it looked like Triss had turned on Kelly; the younger woman stood with her arms wrapped around herself in a protective stance. Triss's pale skin was flushed with fury and black mascara tracked her cheeks with uncharacteristic tears.

'I haven't seen him since before the fête started, when he came up here.' Kelly was grim-faced with guilt, but defiant. She was not accepting the blame for this. 'You were the one who saw him last!'

'He left the bouncy castle about twenty minutes ago … I thought he'd gone back to you!' Triss snarled.

'That's hardly my fault. I'm not a bloody mind reader!'

'Ladies, please. This is not helping.' Sebastian appeared next to them, gesturing to the doors as Lily appeared in the gym. Now was not the time for accusations. They had to find Denny. Triss withdrew, head bowed.

'He can't have been gone that long, then?' Lily's eyes shone with fervour, but not with tears or panic. Good – she was still in teacher mode, yet to go to pieces.

Sebastian took over, directing Triss and Kelly to join the search outside. He told his wife to wait with the bouncy castle. If Denny was nearby, he said, and had simply wandered off, then he was most likely to return to the last place he'd been. Lily and Sebastian both ignored the subtext of his words: *if* he had wandered off. Neither of them wanted to entertain or even imagine the alternative.

Sebastian kissed her on the lips. 'We'll find him.' He sounded more certain than he felt.

Lily gave him a hasty nod, unable to speak.

Sebastian had heard about the horror of lost children: the fear that gripped a parent in your gut; the terror that surged through your limbs to the extremities, making adults feel like they were shaking all over. The breath catching in your throat; the bargaining that rolled over in your mind in a never-ending loop: *pleasebeokaypleasebeokaypleasebeokaypleasebeokaypleasebeokayplease.* Sebastian had thought it all hyperbole.

It wasn't.

As Lily waited in the upper gym, Sebastian searched with the other teachers and the volunteer parents. Under the benches; in the gym lockers and stationery cupboards; in every classroom. In the upper- and lower-school toilets; in the playhouse in the kindergarten playground; even under the stage in the lower gym that doubled as a drama hall.

Every time someone said 'Not here', Sebastian's belief the little boy was still there was shaken. Yet still they all pushed forwards, the triumph of hope over experience; everyone seemed to have decided to be sure he must still be there, in the school. It was simply unthinkable he was not.

They were in the last room – the science room nearest the upper gym. The tables and chairs were all clear: no one hidden under the metal legs. At the back of the room was a large store cupboard for all the science equipment. Sebastian hesitated. He looked to Jackson, who'd trailed along with him. He could read the expression on the other man's face, because it was probably on his own, too. It said, *If we open that door and Denny is not in there, it's time to call the police.*

Then the next horrifying instalment would have to kick off: the authorities would sweep in, with interviews, statements, sniffer dogs and accusations. Every parent would be quizzed; allegations would take precedence. An image of the inevitable headline in the papers burned its way across Sebastian's brain: 'CHILD SNATCHED AT SCHOOL FÊTE'. Its subheading, below: 'Clueless adults let him go, right under their noses'. Sebastian banished the critical words, hating himself for thinking of the bad publicity for Avonwood at a time like this.

He took a deep breath, then strode across the classroom and wrenched open the store cupboard door. Though he braced himself, there was still a part of him that expected to see the little boy curled up inside. Perhaps exploring; or fallen asleep; or trapped in there accidentally; maybe all three.

But Denny was not in there.

Dismay stabbed Sebastian in the belly. He turned, shoulders slumped, towards Jackson. The big man already had his phone to his ear.

Someone on the other end answered. 'Police please...' said Jackson.

Then, a sudden commotion in the corridor, beyond the science room.

'Denny! Denny, thank God!'

Lily.

Sebastian raced out of the room, towards the sound of his wife's voice. There was a small crowd circling around her. He pushed his way through. As people recognised him, the throng parted to let him in.

Sebastian blinked, unsure if the sight was just his brain showing what he wanted to see. But no, the little boy was very much there. Sebastian could see a crying Lily; she knelt on the floor of the gym, her arms around the neck of a very confused, but very much okay, Denny.

'Oh, Jesus. Oh, thank God.' Relief flooded through Sebastian now. He felt lightheaded; the room spun.

Lily sat back on her heels, her hands still on Denny's shoulders, unwilling to let go. 'Don't you ever do that to us again, you hear?'

Denny nodded, wide-eyed. He looked up, to the side. Sebastian followed his gaze, towards the window of the sports hall. Though there was nothing to be seen there except the street beyond, Sebastian was sure there was a sudden movement, just on the periphery of his vision. His brow wrinkled in confusion.

Had someone just ducked out of sight?

'Sorry, Mummy.' Denny's mouth formed the words, but again the little boy glanced sideways, back towards the window.

Lily was too relieved and grateful to notice, but though he saw no movement through the glass this time, Sebastian was sure of it now. Someone had been outside, prompting the boy.

Twenty-four

The release I felt when Denny trotted in to the upper gym, alone and bewildered, was indescribable. The pain in my chest that hadn't allowed me to breathe properly for the last hour dissipated. The adrenaline that had been keeping me upright suddenly swept through me even harder, making my vision swim. The hubbub of voices gathered around us seemed deafening, joy and relief swelling outwards from every adult in the room.

I found myself on my knees, at my son's height, my arms wide open. Looking stunned, Denny allowed me to fling my arms around his neck.

Tears pricked my eyelids as grateful fury followed. 'Don't you ever do that to us again, you hear?'

But I was too relieved to want to spoil this moment with more rebukes. I looked up and saw my husband watching us, his expression difficult to read.

Sebastian turned away and murmured something to Jackson. The big man nodded and clapped his gnarled hands together. This seemed to restore real time, which had been on pause during the crisis. The throng broke up and began to drift away. There were mutters of *So glad it worked out* and *Thank God for that,* as other parents dragged overexcited, sugared-up kids away, leaving wrappers and detritus in their wake.

Jackson shot me a sympathetic look. 'Better clean up and get all the stalls taken down.'

I groaned. Sam Miller's mum was going to go postal. I'd assured her absolutely nothing would go wrong at her precious event, yet here I was somehow losing my own kid.

'I'll handle things here,' said Sebastian. 'You take Denny home, Lily. I'll call you a taxi.' He fished his phone from his pocket.

I opened my mouth to argue, but then fatigue surged through me all over again. I picked Denny up, his eyes rolling back in his head, as worn out as me by the morning's events. I grabbed our stuff from the staffroom and went outside to wait for the taxi.

It was only much later, as I prepared to put an exhausted Denny to bed with his numerous cuddly animals, that I remembered Sebastian's strange expression when we'd first found Denny. He'd been looking towards the gym window, unbridled fury contorting his face. I had an inkling I knew why, because on the taxi ride home I'd had the same thought: Denny had never really been lost at all.

Maxwell had taken him, from right under our noses.

As I moved back into the living area, I found Sebastian, finally home from the fête. He was slumped on the sofa, can in hand, flicking through the TV channels, every one of them showing some kind of reality show: *Swap a Wife, Live with the Poor People, Find Love on an Island, That's Entertainment.*

Sebastian looked terrible, much older than his twenty-nine years. His skin was grey, his clothes crumpled, the stress evident on his face.

He looked up as I appeared. 'So, Denny tell you where he went?'

I shrugged. 'The loo, apparently.'

Sebastian furrowed his brow. I tried to make sense of it, too: how did a little boy avoid being seen for an entire hour, while about sixty adults were looking for him?

'You thinking what I'm thinking?' Sebastian's mouth was a grim line, as if daring me to disagree with him.

I sighed as I sat down. 'Yes. It was Maxwell. I know.'

Sebastian clapped his hands together. 'I told you! This shit has been him, all along!'

I could not resist. 'So, he beat himself up?'

Sebastian seemed to deflate. Exhausted, strung-out, it appeared as if he could not lie to my face a second time. 'The lawyer you sent told me to deny everything.'

'To the police. Not to *me*, Sebastian!' I could not keep the hurt out of my voice. Then something else occurred to me: Fran's impeccable, completely unflappable form in the emergency governors' meeting; her unwavering belief that Sebastian was guilty. 'Did you tell your mum you'd hit Maxwell?'

Sebastian's sheepish expression confirmed he had.

'God!' I stood up, trying to pace away the fury. 'We're supposed to be partners, Seb. You're not supposed to be sharing stuff with your mum rather than me!'

Sebastian held up his palms in a placatory gesture, getting to his feet too. 'I'm sorry, okay? I didn't mean it to happen. She was just there, to pick me up from the station…'

'Because she has a car! And because they let you go in the middle of the night. I couldn't leave Denny.'

Sebastian took my anger in his stride. He did not raise his voice in return. 'I know, I know. I'm an idiot. I guess I was worried, you know? I just didn't want you thinking I was, well, like him.'

My anger melted away in an instant. I pulled Sebastian close, hugging him. 'You are an idiot. I could never think you were like Maxwell.'

I could feel relief spreading through his stressed body, unravelling through his back and limbs. 'What are we like, eh?' he said.

Lying in bed later, my husband snoring softly beside me, I thought over the events of the day. Despite Sebastian's lack of honesty over hitting Maxwell, I couldn't deny he was on the money this time. But Maxwell hadn't turned up with Denny, playing the hero in front of an audience, as I would have imagined he would if he'd wanted to make a show. And it couldn't be about seeing his son – he had regular access to Denny – I'd never stopped that. So his covert abduction this afternoon made little sense.

I knew Maxwell, though: he liked to play games. But he would only bother if the odds were in his favour, and only if there was a clear objective – one that benefitted him. Try as I might, I couldn't put my finger on what exactly my ex-husband was aiming for with this one.

What was I missing?

Twenty-five

'The Mum Mafia is having a field day, Seb.'

Harry paced nervously around Sebastian's office. Watching him go back and forth was making Seb feel ever so slightly seasick. Harry was only about forty but had the lines of a much older man. He was a glimpse of Sebastian's future, if he let stress take its toll.

Sebastian looked back at the printouts in front of him. 'I know. Sadie says the PTA has had at least five parents saying they're pulling their kids out, as of September.'

'Arseholes!' Harry blustered, though whether his interjection was aimed at the parents, or the situation itself, was unclear.

The school inspection had fallen in the final week of term, as they'd all realised it would. People outside of teaching could have been forgiven for thinking the never-ending paperwork and preparation should have paid off; in reality, old-fashioned nerves had counted against them. The staff at Avonwood had overcompensated, somehow drawing attention to, rather than away from, any deficiencies. Sebastian loathed the whole system: how could the inspectors gauge a teacher's effectiveness from observing just fifteen minutes' worth of lessons?

'Every school loses pupils when it gets a report like this,' Sebastian reminded his deputy. 'Some parents will always chase that "outstanding" rating, regardless of whether their kids are happy in school.'

Still pacing, Harry didn't hear Sebastian's reassurances. 'All the bloody parents can see is that damned report.' He read out from his own printout: '"Teaching is inconsistent across the school and is not good enough to secure good outcomes for pupils".' He rounded back on Sebastian, eyes shining. 'I know it's not fashionable to say it, but teachers are human beings! Some are brilliant, some are good, some are average. If the bloody government sacks all the average and good teachers in the country, what schools would be left?'

Sebastian raised a palm. He didn't need a lecture on the short-sightedness of league tables, nor on middle-class parents' obsession with them. 'I hear you. Look, we just have to wait it out. It's not like there's going to be a mass exodus.'

Sebastian also didn't want to hear how his own brush with Maxwell in the school playground – or Denny getting lost at the school fête three days before – had made a dent in the Avonwood parents' confidence. He'd heard the mutters at the school gates that morning. It had taken no time at all for rumours and yet more condemnation to spread.

The meeting over, Sebastian sat back in his chair and massaged his temples. He admired his colleague's passion for the job – that was why he'd chosen Harry as his deputy and right-hand man – but sometimes his fervour and idealism drained him.

The clock read half past two. Sebastian was considering packing up early and surprising Lily, when there was a soft knock on his door. Rosanna appeared, her shoulders hunched, obvious resentment at actually having to do some work on her round face.

'Erm, Mr Adair? Someone to see you.'

Sebastian glanced at his open appointment book. The section for that afternoon was blank, as was customary on the last afternoon of school before the six-week summer holiday. Must be a parent – and probably bad news at that.

He sighed. 'Send them in.'

Moments later, a tall woman with impossibly broad shoulders swooped into the room. She was about thirty-five, with the grace of a catwalk model. Her clothes didn't match her demeanour; she was wearing worn jeans, scuffed trainers and a top with a ditsy flower pattern.

She grinned at Sebastian, taking his proffered hand. Her grip was stronger than he expected. 'Mr Adair. Thanks for seeing me at such short notice. I'm Hina Bokhari, Social Services.' She held up the card ID that hung from a lanyard around her neck.

Dread like concrete sank in Sebastian's belly. 'I see.'

Hina glanced around Sebastian's office, taking it all in. 'Lovely school. Kids look happy. That's how you tell a good school, I reckon.'

'I wish everyone thought the same,' Sebastian replied. 'So, what can I do for you?' He indicated the chair in front of his desk.

Hina threw herself into it, dug in the bag that hung from her shoulder and pulled out a clipboard. 'Don't look so worried. There's been a complaint of reckless endangerment of a minor. As I'm sure you realise, we just have to follow up on these things.'

The words dropped on Sebastian's head, as if from a great height. *Reckless. Endagerment. Minor.* Each one sent his senses reeling.

He felt the tension in his jaw grow. 'A complaint from…?'

Hina bowed her head in mock deference. 'Ah. Well, that is confidential, I'm afraid. As I'm sure you also realise.'

Sebastian nodded. 'I understand. Is this about the school fête?'

'It is.' Hina consulted the clipboard in front of her, thumbing through some papers. 'Apparently a child – a Dennis Stevens, aged six – was missing for almost an hour?'

'A misunderstanding,' Sebastian declared. He'd decided to stick to the party line the school had put out on the blog, Facebook page and as a text to parents. 'Denny was never actually missing. He was here the whole time.'

Hina took in Sebastian's explanation and appeared to consider it, before dropping her bombshell. 'That's not what our complainant says.'

Sebastian gritted his teeth. 'And where does the complainant say Denny was?'

Hina flicked through another form. 'On the common. On his own, apparently. For at least twenty minutes.'

Sebastian shook his head, incredulous, though he knew he shouldn't be. The audacity of that man… 'Is the complainant Maxwell Stevens?'

Hina smiled. 'You know I can't confirm that.'

So, yes, then. Sebastian puffed out his cheeks. 'Can anyone else confirm Denny was alone on the common that day?'

'Again, I can't comment on that. But do you have anyone who can confirm that Denny *didn't* leave the school site on Saturday?'

Sebastian considered the odds. There was a strong chance Maxwell was bluffing them. It had been raining on Saturday, so it was likely that he and Denny would not have seen anyone if he had taken the boy off-site as he and Lily suspected. But they had not called or gone to see Maxwell after the fête, feeling that was what he'd have wanted. Now Sebastian wondered if that had been a mistake.

'I can confirm I had sixty parents looking for Denny, as soon as the alarm was raised. Plus, the child won't admit to being off-site. And even though it was pouring with rain that day, he was dry when we found him. So, I *believe* he never left.'

He expected her to say something in return, but she didn't. Sebastian watched Hina scribble on her forms. Then she shut her clipboard and slipped it in her bag, standing as she did so.

'Well, that's all for now. Thank you, Mr Adair.'

Sebastian ushered Hina towards the door, reaching to open it for her. As he did, Hina stopped, as if she'd only just remembered something. Sebastian recognised the technique at once.

'Dennis … he's your stepson as well as your student, right? Bit strange you didn't mention that.'

'I just assumed you would have known that, that's all.' Sebastian could feel the breath, shallow in his chest. He felt light-headed. It was obvious she wanted him on the back foot.

'That's all?' Hina echoed. There was a sense of anticipation in the air. Then she grinned her Cheshire cat smile again, shattering the feeling like glass. 'Well. If there's anything else, we'll be in touch.'

The door shut behind her.

ME: *So, safe to say they bought it, then?*

OUR MUTUAL FRIEND: *Now what?*

ME: *We wait* 🖐

OMF: *I don't like it.*

ME: *You've done the hard part.*

OMF: *Tell me about it. This is getting out of control … It feels too risky. What if they make the connection?*

ME: *They won't. Besides, he who dares wins and all that…*

OMF: *I'm the one who'll get it in the neck first when they find out. I could lose everything!*

ME: *Just keep your nerve.*

OMF: *Easy for you to say.*

NO REPLY

OMF: *Can you at least make it worth my while? Come over to mine tonight?*

NO REPLY

OMF: *Come on. You owe me. We can have some fun.*

NO REPLY

OMF: *Fine. Fuck you.*

NO REPLY

OMF: *I'm sorry. I need you. PLEASE reply.*

NO REPLY

Twenty-six

'But I *didn't* wet the bed!'

Denny's face was painted with dark, six-year-old fury. His little arms crossed, legs spread wide, his body language screamed hostility. He abruptly threw himself down on the floor next to the sofa, rolling under the coffee table. Typical kid response to stress: *I am not here … You can't see me if I can't see you.* I felt like joining him under there.

'He keeps saying that.' Maxwell's voice was apologetic.

I bit my tongue. I could not pretend I wasn't relieved to get an appointment so soon, especially after what had happened at the fête the previous week. But I hated the fact I was here with Maxwell, even if he was Denny's father. As I'd agreed with Sebastian, I had not mentioned our suspicions to my ex-husband, or the fact we were rattled by his sending Social Services to the school afterwards. Even so, the sight of the bruising cut on Maxwell's cheekbone, the legacy of Sebastian's tussle with him, made me want to hit my ex-husband myself.

'Come on now, darling.' I attempted to grab Denny, pull him back out from under the table. 'We're not angry with you, I promise.'

But he writhed out of my touch, as if he hated me. Discomfort rankled through me, made worse by the humidity in the office. I could taste sweat on my upper lip and I was self-conscious: there had to be perspiration marks under my arms. In contrast, Maxwell looked as if he'd wandered off a Caribbean beach. He was wearing all white and flip-flops, his perfect, pedicured toes on display.

The psychologist, Sally, looked up from her notes, just in time to see Maxwell place a hand on mine, as if to comfort me. I jerked it away automatically.

'I'm noting some tension.' Sally spoke quickly and succinctly, as if someone had pressed her fast-forward button. 'Could that be a contributory factor to Denny's … *issues*, do you think, Mum?'

Sally was probably in her late forties, but called us *Mum* and *Dad*.

'Could be.' I fought the urge to shrug like a recalcitrant teen. I was conscious of Denny grabbing at my feet from under the coffee table.

We were seated on a ridiculously low and overstuffed sofa, in a room that was supposed to put children at ease. Posters on the wall proclaimed this a 'safe space', and basically it was a paradise for kids. Everything was at child height. There was an easel, with paints and chalks and felt tips. There was a box of plastic games; a deep bin full of cuddly toys. Various board games; modelling clay; a box of musical instruments. There was even a games console. They'd thought of everything.

But despite Sally's open invitation to play with whatever he wanted, Denny remained where he was, under the table. Despair welled up within me, tears not far behind. What the hell was going on?

'Also, we should mention … Lily remarried recently.'

Maxwell shot me another contrite look as Sally's eyes seemed to light up at this new titbit. She scribbled some more on her clipboard.

I felt the familiar anger pool itself in my belly. I couldn't let Maxwell get away with this – using our son's issues to get between Sebastian and me. What kind of mother would that make me? I had to get a grip. Okay, Denny had obviously been having a harder time of my remarriage than I realised, but bed-wetting was a phase many kids went through. That was why we were at the appointment: we would get Denny sorted and he would be happier. I could not let Maxwell sabotage my relationship.

'Sebastian and Denny get on very well,' I told Sally.

More scribbles. 'Have you and – sorry, Sebastian, is it? – have you been together long, Lily?'

I started to say, 'Since last September,' but Maxwell jumped in with, 'Not long.'

Now I really did want to punch him. I glowered at him.

'So, coming up to a year. But Denny knew Sebastian before this?'

'That's right. Sebastian is the head teacher at Denny's school. I work there too.' I eyeballed Maxwell. 'I would *never* just bring a stranger into the house.'

'Well, technically you moved into *his* house.' Maxwell picked an imaginary piece of lint from his white linen slacks. He caught my vitriolic gaze and raised both palms. 'I'm just trying to help paint a picture, that's all.'

I counted to ten. Then I glanced up at Sally, eager to continue, but the older woman was not looking at me. Denny had emerged from under the table while I was busy shooting daggers at his father. She started moving her pencil across the paper now, as if sketching him. Perhaps she was. He moved a toy car across the floor, then crashed it into an action figure.

'He's dead!' Denny announced as he sat back on his heels. 'Flat as a pancake!'

He laughed, his face almost demon-like. A shudder made its way down my spine as I considered his behaviour. I always checked his YouTube history and not found anything other than his usual super-hero cartoons and toy unboxings. Denny played soldier games on the Xbox, but I tried to vet them, looking out for extreme kinds of violence. Before now, I'd certainly never seen him delight in violent games with his toys. He was the type of child who served imaginary tea to his dinosaurs and cried if someone pretended to steal his nose.

Before I could confess my fears, though, another woman came in. This one was petite, but with a round, tight drum of a belly, like she'd swallowed a basketball. Pregnant. I felt jealousy leap out of me, shocking and unexpected. She folded her hands over the top of her bump and smiled at both Maxwell and me, beatific.

Sally raised one tanned arm in the pregnant woman's direction. 'This is Anna, our play specialist.'

The rotund Anna gave us an absurd little wave. I swallowed an incongruous smile. How much was Sally assessing me? Maybe she already had and it was written down on her little clipboard: *Mum is clearly neurotic and a negative influence on her child.*

Sally gave us a shark-like smile. 'Now, if you could give me, Anna and Denny a moment, please?'

I blinked. 'Yes, of course.'

We shuffled out, like chided kids leaving the headmaster's office. I'd expected the room to have one of those one-way windows, so we could see in, like in police interrogations. Instead, we were shown to a little waiting area further down the corridor. Maxwell collapsed into a chair with a sigh. I paced up and down the small hallway. A female receptionist with tightly cropped blue hair and a nose ring asked us if we wanted a drink. We both declined, so she turned back to her workstation.

'Sit down, you look exhausted, Lil.' Maxwell leaned back as if he were on a throne, not a plastic orange chair.

'Oh, shut up,' I snapped.

Maxwell regarded me with his big blue eyes, his feelings supposedly hurt. 'You see, all this acrimony, it's not good for the boy.'

'Then maybe you shouldn't be playing your stupid games.' The words leaped out and I cursed myself for showing our hand.

'Like I told Sebastian, I'm not playing games,' Maxwell said the words slowly, as if he was talking to a child.

'When did you tell Sebastian this?' I demanded.

Maxwell raised an eyebrow, pointing to the bruise on his cheek-bone. 'When he did this.'

'When you *made* him do it, you mean,' I hissed.

'You're excusing violence now? Wow.' Maxwell sat back in his chair, shock on his face. 'I know we've had our differences, Lil, but you know I would never raise a hand to you or Denny. I can't believe you'd be with a man who might. I'm scared for you, but you're a big girl and it's your life. It's my son I'm worried about.'

I couldn't believe how he'd twisted my words. I didn't trust myself to say anything else, in case he used it against me, back in the room with Sally. Was this Maxwell's endgame – taking Denny away from me? I felt my mouth quivering, and ground the heel of my hand into my eye to stop frustrated, angry tears from spilling out. Maxwell mustn't see me cry. I didn't want him thinking he was getting somewhere.

About twenty-five silent minutes later, the door opened again. Sally appeared and crouched beside my chair. Normally I would feel the need to move away, or even mimic her and crouch too. But I was bone-weary with it all, so I stayed where I was. Sally's position was weird, but no weirder than anything else about this situation.

'So, Denny's been quite forthcoming,' she said.

I felt trepidation bloom in my chest. '…Right…'

'He is adamant about the bed-wetting not being him. He's not even blaming someone else: a cat or dog, a friend or a sibling…'

'He's an only child,' said Maxwell. 'And they don't have any pets.'

Sally swivelled towards Maxwell, still in her crouched position. I wondered if he could see up her short skirt.

'Yes, I understand that. But sometimes only children will invent friends or people as being at fault, rather than them … an imaginary friend, if you like.'

I raised a sceptical eyebrow. 'So, he's strange because he *doesn't* have an imaginary friend?'

Sally tipped her head at me, like an admonishing parent. 'I didn't say that.'

She stood up and led us into the playroom. We saw Denny sprawled on the floor. The games console was on. Despite her enormous stomach, Anna had somehow got down on the floor with our son. They were engrossed in a racing game.

'As you can see, Denny seems happy enough now,' Sally said.

'But that's kids – they bury stuff. They don't know what they're bothered about, deep down.' I knew I was teaching my grandmother to suck eggs, but I didn't care whether Sally was bothered or not. I had to know what was troubling my boy enough to wet the bed. He'd been dry through the night since he was two. It *had* to be all the change, or at least the upset and stress with Maxwell.

But Sally just indicated Denny: his posture was no longer rigid, nor was his attitude spiky. His back to us and unaware of our observation, Denny chatted to Anna, his tone light and happy. You wouldn't realise he was the same child. His behaviour was in stark contrast to half an hour earlier.

But rather than being pleased, I felt despair sink through me. This was obviously deeper than I thought.

Now what?

Twenty-seven

'Child *endangerment*?' Triss said, agog.

I shifted on the grass and rolled over onto my side to get a better view of my best friend. It was finally the start of the school holidays, the last week of July. Triss had turned up that morning with a picnic, demanding we go out with her. Being the head teacher, Sebastian still wasn't able to tear himself away and had already left for school, but I was only too happy to oblige. We were now in Webb's Folly, one of the most popular recreational areas for families on Epsom Common. My friend lay on an old blanket, her leggings rolled up, her red hair piled on top of her head.

She shook her head in dismay. 'Oh, God. Kelly was right. This is all my fault!'

'It is *not*,' I countered. 'You thought Denny had gone back to Kelly. Besides, Sebastian told Social Services that Denny was never on the common. If they could prove otherwise, they would have said. It's not likely we will hear from them again; they were just ticking a box. No harm done.'

Triss narrowed her eyes. 'There's something else you're not telling me…' She knew me too well.

'Look, we can't prove it,' I said, 'but we think it was Maxwell. He's been baiting us for weeks. Practically since the wedding reception.'

'Where did Denny say he was when he went missing?'

I shrugged. 'He *said* he was in the toilet.'

'Little bugger. He was not!' Triss leaned forwards, fervour in her eyes. 'I checked in there, like, a billion times. Are we supposed to believe Denny was trotting around the school, just ahead or behind everyone who was looking for him?'

'Exactly.' I sighed. 'Denny worships Maxwell, too. I can't get him to admit it. I think he's still angry with me for taking him to the bloody play therapist.'

There was a pause as we both contemplated this impasse. Triss grabbed a can of spray-on sunscreen from her bag; it was already time for her to reapply. She rubbed the green lotion into her pale calves. 'This is all a bit weird though. Why would he steal his own kid, then bring him back in secret? What the hell is he playing at?'

I adjusted the rim of my hat. 'Maxwell likes to play the long game. This is all adding up to something, somehow. I'm just not sure what yet.'

I could almost taste the coconut smell of the sunscreen. It was all over my hands. Denny had begrudgingly allowed me to put some on his face and neck before running off across the common with a little friend he'd spied from school. That boy's mother sat to our left, her nose in her Kindle, underneath a parasol. Next to me, Denny's clothes were neatly folded, his phone tucked into one of his trainers. I hadn't wanted to bring it, but he'd insisted.

Nearby, I could see Denny and the other boy in their shorts, little stick legs. They poked at something in the long grass with a branch. I recognised the boy, if not his mother: Owen Keller, from year two; he was always at after-school club. There were other kids too, marking out goalposts with T-shirts, or running around in circles, arms punching the air. Mums and dads chased toddlers across the still-lush grass.

I decided to change the subject. 'Six whole weeks off school…' I stretched with forced delight.

But Triss rolled her eyes as she lay back down, her arm over her eyes to block out the sun. 'Holiday's only just started and I'm already on a countdown to going back.'

I laughed. Triss had always been a glass-half-empty type. 'Get a new job!'

Triss scoffed. 'Yeah, right. Doing what?'

I tutted. We'd been through this so many times. 'I dunno. A shop. Start your own business? You're a maths teacher, for God's sake, you have transferable skills.'

Triss chuckled. I knew what was coming next: a joke. 'Hey, I got one for you. What does a mathematician do about constipation?'

I braced myself. 'I dunno. What?'

'He works it out with a pencil!' Triss cackled.

I groaned and grabbed a handful of mown grass, throwing it at her. Triss laughed even harder, then chucked some back at me. Returning to reality and parental duty, I checked on Denny again. I was panicked when I couldn't make him out among the other bodies wandering about on the common … for about three seconds. Then I spotted him again, now near the Greater Stew pond off to our right near the trees. He was chucking pebbles in the water.

'Oi, Dennis Stevens!' I adopted 'teacher voice' and boomed at him from afar. Startled, he turned in my direction, arms raised in mock innocence.

But I was not fooled for an instant. 'Don't come it with me, I saw you. No throwing stones!'

Denny and his friend legged it towards a small copse of trees.

'And stay where I can see you!' I yelled after them.

They stopped dead, making their way back towards the play park instead.

'Scary Mummy…' Triss winked at me.

This rankled me, and I wasn't sure why. 'I'm not scary.'

Triss sat up again, hugging her red knees. 'Pfft. If you were my mum, I'd shit myself.'

I smirked. 'You try having a kid, show me how easy it is.'

Triss's mouth dropped open, in a perfect 'o' of horror. 'Me, have a snot-nosed brat? No, thank you.'

'You just work with them instead.'

'At least I can give 'em back.'

I'd ribbed her enough times about this. It was all good-natured fun. Two old pals. It was good to do absolutely nothing for once, just stop the hectic roundabout of life and get off. Just *be*.

'So, where's Sebastian? You never said.' Triss stretched her long legs up in the air, a parody of a yoga pose.

'He had a few things to do at school.'

'God, does he ever take any time off?'

I shrugged. I'd been annoyed too when Sebastian had announced at breakfast that he was going to tie up some loose ends. We had weeks for that. But I'd let the irritation pass. Maybe he simply thought it best to get it over with, then we could concentrate on enjoying ourselves for the rest of the holiday. Besides, it was good to spend some time with Triss outside school after the nightmare of the last few months; the dynamic would have been different if Sebastian had come too – not that I'd ever confess that to him.

'How's he doing, anyway?' Triss nodded at Denny, who was now running at the head of a pack of other children, chasing a light-weight, neon-pink football. 'He seems okay … No more wet sheets in the cupboard?'

I frowned. I'd told Triss about the bed-wetting, of course, but I didn't recall telling her how Denny had tried to hide them from me. I dismissed the thought; it didn't matter.

'He's much better.'

My boy laughed as a small girl nipped ahead of him and dribbled the ball through his legs. There'd been no wetting the bed over the last ten days – at mine or at Maxwell's, apparently. Nor had he bitten me again. We had a second visit to the psychotherapist coming up over the holidays, but now I wondered if it was necessary. Maybe Denny's resentment was greater at what he saw as my interference?

Always the teacher, I noticed Owen was no longer playing with Denny. My line of sight wandered towards his mother, to check the little boy had made his way back to her. There he was, but he was crying, as she packed up their things and struggled with the parasol. He didn't want to go, poor lad.

Denny's friend was making such a racket, I didn't even hear the first shout. It was only when the children started running towards the copse of trees again that my attention was grabbed.

I clambered to my feet and called for Denny. Triss did the same.

But the kids didn't even look back. They moved like a shoal of fish, slipping out of our reach.

'What the bloody hell are they all doing?'

They were rocketing towards something beyond the long grass, on the peak of the common. My heart leaped up into my mouth. Triss stood up too. Foreboding gripped my chest.

I burst forwards, leaving my shoes, my book, even my wallet and Denny's phone. I didn't think or care about any of our stuff. Triss fell into step with me. As we neared the children, I realised they were standing in a circle, their eyes on something.

Someone.

I could make out an adult body on the ground, now being helped up by a crouching form.

'Who is it?' Triss said.

I pushed my way through the small crowd, my brain taking a second to catch up – to realise it was Fran.

She looked pale and drawn. And, after a moment, I saw why: unusually, she was not wearing any make-up. I didn't think I'd seen her without her scarlet lips before. But more than that, her hair looked tousled, unbrushed. She did not seem herself at all. An earnest, serious-looking young man had one arm around her shoulders, the other holding her elbow. I'd never seen him before. The older woman smiled at the sight of us and attempted to stand, but then lurched forwards, as if she might faint again.

'She just collapsed,' the serious man said.

'Really, I'm fine. I'm just a little light-headed. I was going for a walk,' Fran said in that clipped, assured way.

But the serious man was not taking 'no' for an answer. 'Easy, easy…' He guided my mother-in-law back to the bench, forcing me to follow.

'Oh, I can't abide such fuss,' Fran mumbled, her eyes shiny. Despite her bravado, it was clear it was all she could do to contain her emotions. I could empathise; she was roughly the age my own mother would have been, had she lived. Women of their generation were so proud. This had to be mortifying for Fran.

I turned and moved the crowd back, teacher voice coming out again. 'Give her some air, please, everyone!'

Triss took my lead and cranked into action, moving the kids away. Other adults had joined the throng now, looking for their children. Kids safe, the adults started to drift away from the spectacle, a couple of them watching from a safe distance. Triss and Denny hovered nearby, though Triss distracted my boy as best she could.

'Are you okay now?' I leaned down over Fran.

She blinked. Even sitting, it was clear she was not at all well: she swayed, side-to-side, with wooziness. 'I do feel a bit faint.'

'It's so hot. It'll be dehydration,' the serious young man said, in an authoritative tone.

Despite my shock at seeing my frail mother-in-law like this, there was a horrible inevitability to it. The image of her struggling down the stairs at the maisonette came back to me. Unsatisfied with the serious young man's diagnosis, I grabbed my phone from my back pocket. 'We need to take you to hospital, Fran.'

'No, no…' Fran objected; the idea appeared to horrify her.

'You have to get checked out,' the serious young man insisted.

Fran seemed more willing to accept it from him. 'Oh … well if you're sure,' she said.

'I'll call 999.' I took out my phone.

'Take her to the Cromwell,' Triss said, appearing beside me. 'You'd prefer it there, wouldn't you, Fran?'

Fran smiled weakly at Triss.

I thought A&E at the General was better, but I made the call to the Cromwell. Then I rang Sebastian. It went straight to voicemail. I told him to call me urgently.

Triss took Denny for me along with my doorkeys, saying she'd wait for us back at the maisonette. By now, nearly everyone else was gone or packing up their stuff. The late-afternoon sun was starting to slip behind the trees. A cooler evening was on its way.

As we waited by the bench, I proffered a quick smile to the serious guy, who still stood next to us. 'Thanks for helping.'

The young fellow shook his head. 'Don't mention it.'

'I'll take it from here, okay?' I took Fran's hand in mine; she let me. Her palm felt cold, papery. The skin on the back of her hand was translucent.

Looking a bit miffed, the man wandered off, though only after he'd given me his number, insisting I update him. I smiled as I took it.

Fran gave me a weak smile, and then said in a small voice: 'I want to see Sebastian.'

My automatic smile did not reach my eyes. 'He'll be here soon.'

But where was he?

Twenty-eight

Sebastian had woken that morning stiff-limbed and aching from yet another interrupted night. Lying to Lily about the tussle with Maxwell was well and truly behind him, but Denny's disappearance and then the Social Services visit were adding to his deep discomfort. He couldn't shake the unease. As he had patrolled through Avonwood's deserted corridors, even the sight of the children's colourful artwork failed to cheer him. Without children, a school was a building devoid of purpose. The forgotten desks and chairs looked forlorn, even with sunlight streaming through the window.

Sebastian returned to his office, powered up the computer and opened up some of the spreadsheets he had to get through. But his heart was not in it. He drifted towards social media instead, updating the school's Facebook page and Twitter feed. He noted a couple of the photographs from the fête were tagged with parents' profiles, so he allowed himself to scroll through those. Jackson, Lily's cousin Maya's husband, had been caught in a couple of them. In the first, he raised a tattooed arm in a strong-man pose as he prepared to pack up a stall. In the second, he was running across the muddy sports field, his daughters under each arm, like footballs. All three of them were laughing, their joy at playing together evident on their faces.

A weird feeling stabbed Sebastian in the chest, almost like a physical pain. He'd felt such things looking at the pictures of ex-girlfriends in the past, but never a man with his children. Yet there was no question in Sebastian's mind; he sat back in his chair and knew that he was jealous.

Sebastian had never known his father; he'd been barely three months old when he'd died. Exhausted from a long shift and home late from the hospital, Jasper Adair had been calling for roadside assistance from an emergency phone when another car had come off the road and hit him. The bastard had then driven off, leaving him to die; a hit-and-run. Sebastian could recite all this, by heart; his mother had told him the story again and again when he was just a kid. What a waste. His father had been barely older than he was now.

Fran had tried hard to fill Sebastian in on what his father was like; there was a whole wall of photographs of him in her living room. There were pictures of him in every conceivable pose; Fran must have always had a camera in her hand in her youth. Formal portraits were contrasted with more informal ones, of picnics, Christmas dinners and walks along country lanes. Sebastian's favourite was a picture of his father on a beach, bare-chested and holding the infant Sebastian's tiny toes in the water as the tide came in.

His parents had met when Jasper had newly qualified as a doctor and was beginning his journey to become one of the most renowned surgeons in the area. Fran told Sebastian they'd met at a family friend's christening. Aged twenty, Fran had not wanted to go, complaining to her mother she wanted to see a film that afternoon instead. Her mother had insisted – and thank goodness she had.

'I know we only had a short while together, but at least I still have *you*,' Fran would say, misty-eyed as she reminisced.

Sebastian wondered what his father would think of him. By Fran's accounts, Jasper had been a high-flyer at work and a great provider for his family. He'd been excited his child was a son, Fran said; he'd had big plans for them both. So, was Sebastian successful enough? He'd settled into the role of class clown at school because he'd never been the sporty type, or into the sciences, as Jasper must have been to become such an accomplished surgeon. Sebastian was a hard worker: organised, dependable, ambitious. But despite his hard-won status and position, he wasn't exceptional. Would Sebastian be a disap- pointment to his father? A hollow feeling spread throughout his body.

Sebastian grabbed his phone, wanting to hear Lily's voice. But it seemed Lily had already called him: he had a voicemail notification.

And there was a text notification too, Lily's name beside it. He opened this first.

It said, simply: *Your mum's ill. Hospital.*

Sebastian went into autopilot. He grabbed his keys from his desk and ran out towards the car park, only just remembering to lock the school doors after him. In what seemed like a flash he was in his car and driving, guilt and fear roiling in his stomach. He tried to calm himself; stop his thoughts from spiralling. Fran was at the Cromwell, not the local NHS hospital, so she had to be conscious at least, as the Cromwell didn't have an Accident & Emergency department.

He parked his car haphazardly outside the Cromwell's main building and crashed through the double doors into reception. To his relief, Lily was standing beside a vending machine, paper cup in hand. Sebastian ran straight over to her.

'Sorry … sorry! I missed your call. What happened?'

Seated in the soft reception chair into which Lily had pushed him, Sebastian listened, grimly, as she calmly repeated what had taken place at the common. He hadn't been able to take it all in the first time around. But now his heartbeat was finally beginning to subside, the adrenaline washing from his veins.

'She was with it enough to request to come here; so that's good, don't you think?' Lily said.

It was apparently a throw-away comment, But Sebastian felt its significance like a punch to the stomach. 'What do you mean? Do you know something?'

Lily seemed to shrink away from him. She could barely hold his gaze. 'You should talk to the doctors.'

This was enough to make Sebastian jump up. 'What room's she in?'

They sped down the corridor together and into his mother's private room, Lily putting a hand on Sebastian's back as he stopped dead.

Fran was sat up in bed, a painted smile on her face, brave and stalwart. She regarded her son with watery eyes. Sebastian's shoulders slumped, knowing somehow, straight away, that he was about to hear bad news. He didn't want to. Yet he knew they all had to go through the motions anyway, beat by beat.

'I'm so sorry, darling,' Fran said. 'We … *I* … have something to tell you.'

Fran patted the bed beside her. But Sebastian did not move. He hovered on the threshold, as if not sitting by her would stave off what was coming next. His eyes alighted on Fran, then the man standing by the bed, an iPad in his hands.

Sebastian rounded on Lily, who was standing beside him now. 'What's *he* doing here?' He couldn't keep the accusation from his voice.

Lily took a deep breath. 'He works here, remember?'

Standing beside the bed, Maxwell proffered an unconvincing smile. Though he was as immaculately turned out as ever, he lacked his usual, easy-going swagger. He looked as wary as Sebastian.

'Yes, I know.' Sebastian's voice was clipped, harsh. 'What … what kind of doctor – I don't recall.'

Lily closed her eyes, as if she did not want to say it. 'Oncologist.'

'Right.' Sebastian cleared his throat, as if something was stuck there. Tears sprung into his eyes. A flickbook of images seemed to pass through his mind – all the times he'd thought Fran had looked weak and brittle recently, older than her years.

'I wish we could have met again under better circumstances.' Maxwell was careful to keep his tone neutral.

Sebastian seemed to snap out of his reverie. He took a seat on a chair near the bed and grabbed his mother's hand, staring at her hard.

'Don't worry, Mum. It will all be fine. We'll get you the best treatment. Whatever needs doing, let's do it. We've got the money.'

Fran smiled sadly. 'I'm afraid it's a little late for that, sweetheart.' She looked to Maxwell, giving him a tiny nod.

Maxwell sighed and turned the iPad around, presenting the

picture to Sebastian. Lily moved sideways slightly, placing her hand on Sebastian's shoulder, as if to help him brace for impact.

He stared at the screen momentarily, not taking in what was displayed there. Then his eyes began to discerning the black-and-white image: a grey ribcage; the faint outline of lungs.

The huge, dark shadow on the right.

Maxwell's manner was awkward. 'I'm afraid it's much too large … It's, um, inoperable.'

Sebastian emitted a low moan as his brain finally allowed him to process this news.

Fran gripped her son's hand. A single, valiant tear made its way down her pale cheek. 'He means it's terminal, son.'

'How long?' Sebastian murmured.

'It's difficult to say, every case is different—' Maxwell began.

'Your best guess?' Sebastian interrupted, meeting Maxwell's gaze. 'Please?'

Maxwell sighed, as if going against his better judgement. 'With chemo? Perhaps we could hold it off a year or so. Without it … weeks, I'm afraid.'

'Then chemo it is!' Sebastian clutched both his mother's hands now, nodding and blinking, trying to sound positive. 'Right, Mum?'

Fran nodded. 'Right you are, darling. That's what we'll do.'

ME: *We're all set* ☺

OUR MUTUAL FRIEND: *Oh, you're talking to me now?*

ME: *Don't be like that.*

OMF: *Like what? Sometimes I think you're just using me.*

ME: *Don't be silly. I couldn't do this without you, could I?*

OMF: *That's true. I just feel you sometimes take me for granted, that's all.*

ME: *Absolutely not. I adore you. You know it, really.*

OMF: *So, what next?*

ME: *We wait.*

OMF: *This is taking too long!*

ME: *I know, I know. I hoped we'd have made more progress by this point too. But this part of the plan is bound to take us to the next level. How can it not?*

OMF: *Yes. It IS a great plan.*

ME: *When I'm not tied up here, why don't you come over to my place?*

OMF: *Maybe.*

ME: *Aw, you're still sulking.*

OMF: *Maybe. I'll let you know.*

ME: *Wear the blue, I like you in that. I'll see you at the usual time, then.*

OMF: *Maybe…*

ME: *I will.*

Twenty-nine

'It doesn't make a lot of sense, moving her into the maisonette with us.'

Sebastian looked across at Lily. He took in the worry lines on her usually blemish-free forehead; it was obvious she didn't want to fight him on this. Behind them, there was a red car hugging their bumper as they made their way to the hospital again. Uncharacteristic rage flowered in his chest, though whether it was directed at Lily, the car, or his mother's situation, he was unsure. Maybe all three.

Sebastian gritted his teeth and flicked the indicator. It started to tick, like a metronome or a countdown. 'I want to look after Mum.'

'I understand that, but…'

Sebastian gripped the steering wheel. 'She can't go through chemo on her own! What if she faints, or is sick? I'll clear out my study, make her a bed in there.'

Lily pursed her lips, clearly choosing her words carefully. 'Yes, of course. I just mean the maisonette is poky. She'd be more comfortable in her own home, her own bed. Plus, think of the stairs, Sebastian. It's the only way in … It won't be long before she can't get up them.'

Her point landed. Sebastian felt a weariness fill his bones, as heavy as concrete. Lily was right; it made no sense to move Mum into the maisonette with them. Sebastian realised Lily probably meant they should go and check on Fran every day at her own place. But a better idea bloomed in his brain.

'I'll go and stay with her. Keep an eye on her.'

Sebastian watched the red car finally overtake them, resisting the urge to flip the driver the finger.

He glanced over and saw Lily's eyes bulge. 'Wait, that's not…' She stopped herself, took a deep breath. 'Yes, of course. If that's what you want.'

Sebastian removed his hand from the gear stick and placed it on her thigh. 'Thanks. Look, I know this is difficult, especially with us not being married that long…'

Lily forced a smile. 'Don't be silly. This is your mum. Besides, I know what all this is like.'

Of course she did. Lily hadn't shared the whole story about her mother's death with Sebastian, but she'd told him enough for him to recognise it had been a defining aspect of her childhood. How could it not be? All those moments, watching friends and classmates taking pictures and cards home to their mums; meeting them at the school gates. Lily had told Sebastian once that her dad had always been working, so from age nine onwards she was a latchkey kid, taking herself home and putting noodles on to boil, or baked beans in the microwave. It was one of the reasons she and Triss were so close. With Triss's parents so neglectful and Lily motherless, at that young age they'd turned to each other. And had been like the closest of sisters ever since. If he hadn't known their history, he might even have felt threatened by their tightness.

'I won't neglect you and Denny,' Sebastian promised. 'I'll see you every day, just like I do now. I'll just be sleeping at Mum's, so I can stay on hand … In case she needs me.'

Lily smiled back at him. It did not reach her eyes though. 'Of course,' she said.

Inside the Cromwell, Fran was sitting on the bed, ready to go. She was fully dressed, her small case beside her, hands folded on her lap. She looked tired and small, but visibly brightened as Sebastian rounded the corner and appeared in the doorway, Lily and Denny beside him.

The little boy trotted into the room. 'Hi, Mrs Fran.' He flashed her a gap-toothed grin.

Fran laughed. 'Well, that's an improvement on Mrs Adair, at least.' She dug in her handbag and brought out a bar of chocolate. 'I'm afraid this is just from the vending machine. Is it okay if he has this, Lily?'

Denny regarded Lily with pleading eyes. She'd already told him back at the maisonette there were to be no sweets before lunch today. Sebastian was relieved when she made no mention of this.

'Yes, of course,' she said.

Denny's smile widened as he took the chocolate. Fran sighed happily and ruffled his hair. The boy's attention was short-lived, though: movement behind Lily drew his notice.

'Dad!' he bellowed.

Maxwell came in, leaning down and catching Denny as the little boy barrelled straight at him. 'Hey, sport! You ready for some fun this afternoon?'

Denny nodded his little head energetically. Sebastian took in his wife's ex-husband, the rivalry returning even as he stood next to his dying mother. Shame blossomed inside him – he couldn't help appraising Lily's ex. Maxwell's teeth were impossibly white. He was dressed casually, his collar open, exposing the dark hairs underneath. His lightweight jacket was draped over one arm. Studied chic, effortlessly cool. That was Maxwell.

As if remembering what he was really there for, Maxwell held something out towards Sebastian. But did not meet his eye; instead he winked at Fran. 'Home today then, Fran!' he said.

Fran closed her eyes in affected bliss. 'At last.'

'And the pharmacist has come by?'

With a visible effort, Fran held up a bulging plastic bag. Inside were a variety of pills and potions.

Sebastian peered at what Maxwell had given him. It was a clear folder of leaflets and helpline numbers. As Sebastian smoothed a thumb across the plastic, he could read the top one: *What To Expect when on Chemotherapy.*

Sebastian indicated the folder to his mother. 'I wish you had let me sit with you during your first treatment.'

Fran shrugged. 'Oh, it sounds worse than it is. The cannula was a bit painful, but that was it. I just sat in a little room, with all the other brave souls.'

Maxwell hoisted Denny onto his hip. 'Well, if that's everything, then?' He looked to Lily, expectant.

Lily regarded him with a stony, impassive expression. Sebastian could read the loathing and suspicion in her stance. An old saying sprang into his mind: *There's a thin line between love and hate.* He blinked, banishing the thought. That was playground bullshit.

'Back at six o'clock, please,' Lily said, her arms folded.

Maxwell gave her a mock salute, swung Denny onto his back and piggy-backed him out the room. Sebastian breathed deeply at last, letting his unease go. Lily believed in him, not Maxwell. Besides, they had to put all that aside now for his mother's sake. Cancer trumped rivalry, for God's sake! Even Maxwell realised that; he'd not made a single dig at them since the diagnosis. Sebastian was being juvenile. He had to follow suit and let it go.

There was a lull, as if none of them knew what to say. Sebastian tried to inject some positivity back into the room. 'How about we go out to lunch on the way home? Somewhere quiet, of course.'

But Lily gave him a barely discernible shake of her head. 'Your mum probably just wants to get back, Sebastian…'

Sebastian felt out of his depth. He floundered on. 'Okay, well maybe we could get some nice meats and cheeses from that deli in town? Have a quiet one, back at the house.'

But Fran sighed. 'To be honest darling, I'm feeling rather the worse for wear. I don't think I'm up to eating much. I just want to get back, have a sit down.'

'Of course.' Sebastian took his mother's arm. It felt bonier than ever under his grasp. But now, there was something else. Knowledge of her illness made her seem frail, old. Fran had always been such a big personality, a huge presence. To see her reduced like this created a hard ball of pain in his throat. Once again, he recalled all the times he'd noticed how fragile and feeble she'd become in recent months. Why hadn't he insisted she have herself checked out? He forced it down, fixed a smile back on his face.

'Let's just get you home, then.'

Thirty

I sat Fran down on the sofa and plumped up some cushions around her. Fran sighed, closing her eyes and patting my arm. 'You're a good girl.'

I was absurdly touched. I remembered my own mother saying the exact same words when I had done the same thing for her. Tears welled up. I blinked them back. Fran was old school. It wouldn't do to break down in front of her. It would alarm and pain someone like my mother-in-law and the last thing I wanted to do was bring her more discomfort.

As I looked around the palatial living room with its chrome and glass, I couldn't help but compare it to the two-up, two-down terrace I'd grown up in. We hadn't been exactly poor, but we weren't well off, either. My school uniform and books had been second-hand, and Mum and Dad had had to save all year round for a holiday to Padstow in Cornwall. After Mum had died, Dad and I hadn't gone again. It was like that part of our lives had disappeared with her.

I shrugged the thoughts away. 'Can I get you anything?'

Fran proffered a weak smile. 'Just the remote, please.'

I leaned over the shining coffee table to hand it to her. There was an awkward pause as both of us dug for something to say. When she turned her head to the side as she pointed the remote at the television, I realised I was standing in her way.

'I'll, er, just be in the kitchen.'

The theme tune of *Deal or No Deal* was my answer.

Unsure what else to do in the pristine house, I washed up the cafétière and the tiny espresso cups. I wondered when it became normal, rather than a treat, to have such things at home? Perhaps the likes of Fran had always had them, but back when I was a girl, we'd just had instant, served in a motley crew of mugs with the names of chocolate bars on them – the ones that came free with Easter eggs.

The front door slammed and a moment later Sebastian appeared. He had three or four bags with him and a slightly crazed expression. He dumped the carriers on the counter top and started to pull items out.

'We need to sterilise this house,' he declared.

'Remember what they said at the hospital?' I prompted.

Maxwell had taken us through all this, already. Though he'd recommended Fran stayed away from pet faeces, he'd stressed that we didn't need to take any other special precautions. Deep-cleaning or sterilising the house were not necessary. He'd even said that if Fran felt like eating, she should eat whatever she wanted, no matter how odd it might seem. Food wouldn't taste the same, now, he'd warned: what she'd loved, she might hate and vice versa. He had told us about a cordon-bleu chef who'd eaten nothing but McDonald's when he was on chemotherapy.

Sebastian blinked at me. It was clear he didn't remember. Or that he'd decided what was best, regardless of what the professionals said. Or maybe because it was Maxwell who had said it. I couldn't blame him.

'I've been reading up on the internet. Her white-blood-cell count will come down with the chemo, which means she'll be more susceptible to infections,' he insisted.

I took a deep breath, not bothering to argue. It would be a cruel reminder that whatever he did would not influence the outcome of his mother's treatment. I recognised Sebastian's need to feel like he was doing something for his mother. I remembered my nan doing exactly this for my mother, nearly thirty years ago, before anyone had the internet. She'd descended on our home, vacuuming and scrubbing in bright yellow rubber gloves and pink fluffy slippers.

So I gave Sebastian a hand.

As I scrubbed at the carpet and aired rugs, my thoughts tumbled around my head, making me clench my teeth. Bloody cancer. It felt like it was everywhere, sometimes. There was always a mum, gran or guardian at the school gates, every single year, wearing a headscarf and a pained smile. Now it was our turn, it seemed. And my turn again.

This wasn't fair, we'd only just got married. Horror followed this thought. I was being selfish, just like the parents at the school gates who avoided people with cancer, anxious not to hear the prognosis. I'd always made a point of talking to the parents who were going through this, taking an interest in the child whose mum was ill. No one had with me, so I felt like I was giving something back, balancing the universe somehow.

Though cancer had been a death sentence for my mother and history was repeating itself for Sebastian, people did recover. I'd seen more than one mum reappear at the school gates, pale but enduring, the fuzz of her hair growing back on her scalp. She'd leave it uncovered, a badge of honour. The other parents would relax enough to approach her at last. She would be showered with congratulations, even by parents she'd never spoken with before. *Well done*, they'd say, *you beat it!* They would call her a warrior, pat her on the shoulders, or even hug her.

Other times, though, that mum would simply disappear from the crowd at the school gates. The gathered parents would make murmured enquiries or speculate, then someone would finally confirm the truth.

She's gone, they'd say.

As if she'd turned to vapour and been filtered away, to be spat out again into a new body at some point.

Those poor kids, they'd follow with; then: *How's the father holding up?* They'd suck their teeth: *Not good.*

Being the kid whose mum was dead was a hard cross to bear. Dads, you might take or leave. Your mum might have chucked him out, or perhaps he went of his own accord. Perhaps you never had one. These things happened.

But a mum was the very least a child should have.

When we were in the last year of primary school, Triss always introduced me with: 'This is Lily. Her mum is dead!'

It was always like I wasn't even there. Instead there was a red mark on me I couldn't rub off and everyone could see it.

'How come?' the other kid would say.

'Cancer,' Triss would reply, eyes wide. 'In her guts.'

Then, when the other kid inevitably drifted away, alarmed at the description, Triss would put her arm around my waist, holding me tight to her.

'They don't understand,' she'd say. 'But I do. You've got me. Forever.'

It was a comfort back then. And it was now. I knew Triss was there for me – I knew at some point later today she would be hugging me close like she always had.

I sat back on my heels and looked at my watch. It was half-five. Denny would be back at the maisonette soon. I could smell the cleaning products in the air, not just lavender but lemon-fragranced, plus the sharp tang of bleach. It was enough to make my eyes water. I wondered how many of these man-made chemicals contained carcinogens. How was that for irony?

From across the hall, Sebastian, mop in hand, must have seen me check the time. Before I even asked, he said: 'I'll drop you back in the car.'

'It's okay, I can walk,' I said. 'I'll just about make it if I go now.'

'Mum will be okay for ten minutes, I'm sure…' he began, but as if on cue, his mother's panicked voice cut through from the living room.

'Sebastian! Come quickly!'

He dropped the mop and went running.

Thirty-one

'Mum? Oh, God!'

Sebastian appeared in the doorway to see Fran sitting forwards, a hand clamped over her mouth. He dithered. What would his proud mother hate least: shuffling to the toilet, or being sick into a receptacle? He didn't know what to do!

Lily appeared and made the decision for him. 'I'll get a bucket.'

Fran shook her head, vigorously. 'No! I can make it.'

She held out a hand for her son to help her up. Sebastian grasped her forearm, pulling her towards him, his other arm gripping her shoulders. Lily hovered behind them, hopping from one foot to the other.

Sebastian chivvied his mother along, his body tense, expecting her to suddenly lurch forwards and vomit on the floor. She didn't. They picked their way over the fallen mop and made it through the hallway, to the downstairs toilet.

Fran broke away from Sebastian, pushing her way through the door. She shut it after her and turned the lock, preventing him from coming in after her.

'Mum!' Sebastian pounded on the wood. 'What if you faint?'

'It's okay,' Lily muttered. 'It's one of those safety locks. We can open the door from this side if we have to.'

But Sebastian still pounded on the wood. 'Mum!'

'Sebastian, don't,' Lily said quietly. 'Just let her get on with it.'

The sound of retching and spitting filtered through the door. Then the thick, fluid sound of vomit hitting the water. Sebastian looked at Lily, then shuddered, casting his eyes skywards, unable to believe what they were hearing. Lily gave him a sympathetic smile and gave his shoulder an *It will be okay* squeeze. But they both knew it wouldn't be.

Finally, Fran gave a loud sigh, as if she'd finished.

'I'm okay.' Behind the door, Fran's voice sounded tiny and vulnerable. 'I just don't want you to have to see me like this, Sebastian. Just … go drop Lily off. She needs to see to Denny when Maxwell brings him back.'

'No, I'm not leaving you.' Sebastian was outraged at the thought. He turned to Lily. 'Do you mind…?'

Lily's voice was apprehensive. 'No, of course not. But I'll have to get a taxi. It's ten to, now. I won't be back in time.'

'Take a cab then,' Sebastian replied, knowing he sounded gruff.

But he didn't care. His mother's need was greater right now. He heard Lily's feet as she walked across the hall tiles, into the kitchen.

He was still keeping vigil by the toilet door when the taxi arrived and the front door closed after her.

Fran finally opened the door and allowed Sebastian to help her back to the living room. As he turned the television back on for her, he noted she was shivering, teeth chattering after her vomiting ordeal. Though it was late July, the weather had taken a turn for the worse, as if autumn had already arrived. The skies were white and oppressive; a harsh breeze rattled against the window pane.

Sebastian retrieved a quilt from the spare room. 'There you go,' he said as he tucked it around his mother's knees like she was an octogenarian.

The cold reality pierced him like a dagger through the heart. She was only in her early fifties; no age at all. This wasn't fair!

'I do wish you wouldn't fuss.' Fran stifled a yawn behind her hand.

Sebastian couldn't help smirking. His mother had always liked fuss, no matter her protestations to the contrary.

'How about a cup of nettle tea? I got some for you from that health-food shop in town. The internet says it's good to settle the stomach after chemotherapy.'

'It sounds ghastly.' Fran gave a heavy sigh, both hands held to her midriff. 'But go on, then. I'll try anything.'

Sebastian shuffled into the kitchen and flicked on the kettle. He looked at the clock: it was barely six o'clock, but it felt much later. Days seemed to be longer now. Time always seemed to slow down around serious illness. There was a sense of marking time: day by day; hour by hour; minute by painstaking minute. Sebastian felt trapped, as if a force field had formed around his mother and all of them were orbiting around her. Life had suddenly shrunk: when once Sebastian might have been concerned with the world around him – work, politics, religion, sport – now it all seemed to be suspended. There was only the spectre of death, waiting to make its claim, to spirit his mother away.

Fran was right: the nettle tea did look ghastly: a deep brown-green colour, like seaweed in liquid form. It didn't smell much better. Sebastian brought the tea through in one of Fran's best cups and saucers, a shining teaspoon balanced on it. In his other hand he carried the sugar bowl, in case she wanted to add some. He had no idea if you were supposed to or not.

Sebastian placed both in front of his mother then glanced up and found her gaze upon him. 'What?' he asked.

Fran's eyes were glassy with tears, yet a small smile pulled at her thin, bloodless lips. She averted her eyes, uncharacteristically exposed. 'Oh, nothing, darling.'

Sebastian forced a smile. 'Go on,' he prompted her.

Fran rolled her eyes as if exasperated, but it was just a front. Sebastian could always tell when his mother was play-acting. Then she leaned forwards and grasped his hand.

'Just … this. I'm so grateful to be spending my last days with you.' Fran brought two of her fingers to his cheek, pinching his flesh. 'You're my boy.'

A ball of pain appeared in Sebastian's throat; it barely allowed him to force three small words out.

'Me too, Mum.'

Thirty-two

The taxi pulled up near the bank, dropping me a few doors down from the maisonette. As the car stopped, I could see both Denny and Maxwell up ahead, waiting on the street just beyond the side alley that led through to our home. Maxwell carried a plush soft toy in his left hand: a sheep. That was new. Denny was on his father's shoulders, looking out to the junction.

Someone else was with them.

Triss.

Denny held up both hands, counting on them. I recognised what they were doing immediately: the yellow-car game. You got a certain number of points for red, green, blue or black cars, with yellow the highest (being one of the most rare). It was a game that Maxwell and I had introduced to Denny when we took him on our last family holiday to Center Parcs. Now, here was Triss playing the same game with Denny and my ex … like happy families? My brow furrowed as I took in the odd scene. Triss had always struggled to be in Maxwell's company.

'That's four sixty,' the taxi driver prompted.

I passed a five-pound note to him and without waiting for change, pulled open the door and spilled out onto the pavement.

The three of them turned to look at me.

'Sorry, sorry.' I hated being late, especially when Maxwell was likely to hold it over me.

'Don't worry. Triss has been keeping us company.' Maxwell indicated to his left.

'I can see that,' I said, careful to keep my tone neutral.

Even so, it felt awkward. 'Found them on the doorstep.' Triss shrugged. 'Thought I'd come over for a catch-up?'

She had a rucksack over one shoulder and a bag dangling from the other hand. I could guess what was inside: wine, crisps, chocolate. My heart plummeted. We hadn't arranged this. I'd wanted a quiet one tonight, not a booze-up and heart-to-heart. But I smiled, anyway.

'Well, I'd best be getting off. It's a school night for some of us.' Maxwell leaned down, letting Denny hop off his shoulders.

I felt the familiar resentment curdle in my stomach. Typical Maxwell, going on as if teaching was a dosser's profession just because we got a summer holiday. If he spent his time in the classroom too, he'd soon need it. Besides, though he might have done his time in the trenches as a junior doctor, he had a pretty cushy number going on up at the Cromwell these days, what with half days, picking his own hours, his own patients…

'Can't Dad come in?' Denny pulled on my arm.

'It's fine, Denny. Your mum's had a long day.' Maxwell handed over the new sheep toy.

Denny grabbed it, a pout on his round little face. '*Pllllleeeeeease*, Mummy!'

A look passed between me and Triss. My heart sank. I could sense we were perilously close to the tantrum danger zone.

'No, I don't think so,' I said firmly.

'But I want to show Dad my room,' Denny whined.

I could sense how exhausted he was; Maxwell had told me by text that he was taking him out to a local farm park. That meant Denny had spent the whole day getting what he wanted. He'd also undoubtedly had sugar galore, as well as that new toy. Denny was a good boy, but when he tantrummed, he went nuclear. Unlike some kids, who go in fast and hard and blow out quickly, Denny's infrequent tantrums were epic and could last hours.

I made a split-second decision. 'Oh, go on, then.'

I ignored the triumphant grin on my son's face and led the small procession down the side alley to our front door. I slid the key in the front door.

'Five minutes,' I warned Denny.

He and Maxwell traipsed up the stairs ahead of Triss and me. As they disappeared out of our sightline, Denny chattered nineteen to the dozen about his posters and his new cabin bed. I knew Sebastian would hate the idea of Maxwell being in the maisonette when he wasn't there, but I was exhausted and I just needed a quiet life. If Denny went off on one that night, I might just start screaming and never stop myself.

As we made it into the kitchen area, Triss set her bags on the table. I found myself welcoming the clink of bottles, after all.

'Wine?' she asked. 'You look like you need it.'

'Is it that obvious?'

Triss pulled open a drawer, selected a corkscrew, then plunged it into the top of the bottle. 'I could just put a straw in it for you?'

'Don't tempt me!'

As we touched our glasses together, I could hear Denny's giggles from the other room. Despite Maxwell's faults – and he had many – our son sounded so relaxed and at ease with him.

Denny liked and looked up to Sebastian, that was not in question. And Sebastian would never let Denny down or leave him waiting. Even so, I recalled Maxwell's words to the psychologist: *Lily remarried recently.* Sebastian assured me before we married he would treat Denny like his own child. And I'd had no reason to doubt him on this – before or now – but suddenly I felt like I'd failed to consider Denny's own feelings towards Sebastian. Could Denny love Sebastian like he loved Maxwell? Probably not. It hadn't been long enough. But would he? How long did it take for a child to love his stepfather?

I had no clue.

'I'm starving,' Triss announced. She opened a big pack of wasabi crisps and the fridge at the same time. Inside were my yoghurts, a load of vegetables, milk for Denny's cereal. All healthy stuff. 'You never have any food!'

'You mean I have no food you want!' I corrected her. I opened a drawer, pulling out a selection of takeaway menus. 'Pizza or Chinese?'

'Neither. I want fried chicken.' Triss shoved a crisp in her wide mouth. 'Or Indian. Actually, maybe both…'

I took in my skinny friend, her red hair a mad contrast to her milky-white skin. She had barely any breasts to speak of; she was just elbows and knees and shoulders. 'How the hell are you not the size of a house, with the amount of crap you eat?'

'Natural talent.' Triss affected a pose, then strode across the kitchen, as if she was on a catwalk.

Maxwell appeared in the kitchen and Triss's demeanour changed instantly. She turned her back on him, giving her attention to her crisps instead: a snub so obvious it was schoolgirlish – and seemed completely at odds with the friendly little scene I'd witnessed on the street just a few minutes before. Much as I loved her, sometimes Triss was a complete puzzle. But I didn't have the energy to solve it right now.

And Maxwell was unconcerned. He had his hands in his pockets, arms drawn towards his body.

'Well, I'll be off, then,' he smiled.

As Denny slunk in behind his father, I suddenly felt that I was being horribly churlish. Denny looked so disappointed his dad was leaving. Would it really kill me to let Maxwell stay?

I sighed. 'Look, why don't you stay? We're having takeaway. You can do bedtime with Denny, if you like.'

Denny's little face lit up, but he stopped himself … It was not confirmed yet. Triss looked from me to Maxwell to Denny, a crisp halfway to her mouth. I could almost see the cogs spinning in her head as she waited to see how this would play out. But I wasn't doing this for me, or even for Maxwell, but for Denny. He should have at least one memory of his biological father tucking him in at home, of his parents being able to speak to each other. It was not much to give a kid.

But Maxwell looked undecided. He shifted from one foot to the other. In that microsecond, I actually willed him to stay, to not let our boy down. Then he smiled and a feeling of relief flooded through me; I found myself grinning back as Denny jumped up and down on the spot, emitting a squeal.

I glanced at Triss, expecting the usual sour expression she reserved for anything to do with Maxwell. But she simply dug in her carrier bag for another bottle. 'Well, we'll be needing more wine.'

I shrugged at her and presented my glass for a top-up.

Thirty-three

As August rolled in and the initial shock of Fran's diagnosis wore off, so did the numb feeling that had marginalised all the other considerations in Sebastian's head. He began to notice the strained look in Lily's eyes when she came over, the plastic smile pinned to her face. A dull ache rolled around the pit of his stomach as he realised how hard this was for her, seeing someone wither in front of her a second time.

Each time, Lily brought treats to tempt his mother: handmade dark chocolates, topped with salted caramel; plump Brazil nuts; salt-and-vinegar kettle chips. On every visit, Fran thanked Lily for her thoughtfulness, but then put the gifts to one side, leaving them untouched. She claimed nothing tasted right; or that there was a metallic taste in her mouth; or of waves of nausea. Though both Sebastian and Lily tried their best to cajole her, Sebastian knew it was pointless: even before the chemo, her appetite had seemed to be shrinking dramatically. For the umpteenth time, Sebastian wished he'd paid attention to the signs of illness earlier. Perhaps they could have done something.

Sebastian and Fran fell into a daily routine. She rose at seven and showered. Sebastian prepared her a light breakfast of black coffee and dry toast, which she usually nibbled at before leaving it to go cold on the plate. If she felt well enough, they might walk to the common and back. In the afternoon, she might look at her iPad, or watch a film, while Sebastian saw to the chores around the house. In the evening, he would make a light supper – pasta, beans on toast, tomato soup – something his mother's poor stomach could cope with. She was usually in bed again by seven, watching her soaps from under the duvet.

Fran was on weekly cycles of chemotherapy, but just like the first treatment, she didn't want Sebastian to go in with her. He drove her to the Cromwell each Tuesday, dropping her off outside, so she could shuffle in at her own pace. Sometimes Maxwell would wait outside for her, that bright-white tombstone grin on his face. Sebastian would find himself curiously resentful as he watched his wife's ex-husband take his mother's hand, placing an arm around her slight shoulders. It seemed so unfair that Fran should allow Maxwell to see her vulnerable, yet not him. But he arrested these thoughts each time. His mother had always been a fiercely private woman. It was not Maxwell she was favouring; in her mind, it was Sebastian. Fran would never want her precious only child to see her like this.

Each morning, Sebastian would go back to the maisonette to spend some time with Lily and Denny as a family, alone. But it never seemed to work out that way. Outside of the cocoon of his mother's home, he was always fetching and carrying, racing from one place to the next. His wife and stepson would fill him in on what had been going on during his absence. Lily put a brave face on, but Sebastian felt stretched between two roles, two lives: son and husband. After a couple of weeks of toing and froing from his mother's, Sebastian realised that Triss was now ensconced almost permanently at the maisonette.

'Here again?' he couldn't help saying, when he arrived one morning.

'Just keeping Lily company.' His wife's friend's tone was airy, nonchalant. Like she belonged there. Or worse, like she had replaced him…

This is still my house, he thought.

Sebastian looked around the room. Lily was nowhere to be seen. Neither was Denny. The whole place was still. He noted the dishes in the sink, on the countertop. A selection of takeaway boxes balanced on a pile of recycling that had not been put out. The washing machine was full of wet clothes. Lily wasn't usually this sloppy. Through the skylight, the grey light of another wet British summer. Rain beat on the glass. September was around the corner.

'Where is she?'

'Just popped out. Be back soon.' Triss flicked through a magazine at the kitchen table. She was acting as if she owned the place, stretching both her long legs out across the kitchen chairs.

Sebastian reached out, knocking her legs from the chairs. She dipped forwards, surprised, almost overbalancing and falling. She regarded him, eyes blazing.

'Don't get too comfortable, will you?' he said.

Triss cocked her head at Sebastian. She smiled. 'Worried, are we?'

Sebastian chose his next words carefully. 'Why would I be worried?'

Triss sat back in her chair and folded her arms. 'You tell me.'

Irritated, Sebastian turned his back on her and swept through to the living area. He ignored her as she called after him.

'Cor, touchy, aren't we!'

He saw Triss's things scattered on the sofa: her bag, her duvet, a pillow. But that could be just for show. He marched out into the hallway, up to the second storey. He cast an eye over the bedroom he was supposed to be sharing every night with Lily. Everything looked in the right place. There was none of Triss's stuff up here: none of her clothes on the floor, not even so much as a stick of unfamiliar deodorant on the dressing table.

Sebastian sat down heavily on the made bed, head in his hands. He was being ridiculous. Again. Triss was Lily's best friend. That was all. He was letting Maxwell's comment from the day he hit him get inside his head.

After forty minutes of waiting, Sebastian gave up and went back to his mother's. As he walked up to the front door he found it was ajar. He was certain he'd shut it behind him when he left.

Someone else had been here in the short time he was out.

Dread pierced through him as a number of different scenarios sped through his brain. Burglars? Had Fran been taken ill, suddenly? Maybe she'd had to call an ambulance, while he was gone?

Sebastian checked his phone, expecting to see a missed call. Nothing. The anxious flutter in his chest calmed. Maybe Fran had just answered the door to the postman, then forgotten to close it properly. He'd noticed she'd been less focused than usual. Maxwell had warned them all of this: 'chemo brain', he'd called it. He'd said forgetting things, or even doing mad things, was a common side-effect of the drugs, not to mention the stress.

'Mum?' Sebastian called as he went inside.

Nothing. Sebastian moved swiftly through the hall. As he made it into the living room, his panic renewed its surge: the room was empty. The curtains were drawn, even the long ones over the patio window. The long swathe of fabric wafted towards him: the door to the garden behind it was open. Sebastian could smell rain, mown grass and earth.

Sebastian floundered against the long curtain, almost wrenching it off the pole in his hurry to make it outside. He was certain he would find his mother on the wet grass, collapsed. The rain still pattered down, less heavy than earlier, though it pasted itself to his thinning hair in moments.

The small back garden was deserted.

'Mum!'

As Sebastian turned back into the living room, Fran's surprised features swam into view on the stairs beyond. She moved slowly, her second foot joining her first on each step. She seemed like a woman twenty years older. She stopped halfway down.

'What on earth are you bellowing about?' she said, peering at him through the bannister posts. 'And why are you back so early?'

Her skin seemed even more translucent, as if she was slowly beginning to disappear. A blue scarf was wrapped tight around her head, the ties of the bow at the back trailing over one shoulder. It had said in the medical literature Maxwell had given them that her hair would start to drop out approximately two weeks after her first chemo treatment and sure enough, Fran had reported hers was thinning, even coming away in the hairbrush. Sebastian had comforted her as she'd presented a clump of it to him a few days earlier.

'I was worried when you weren't on the sofa,' he said, relief taking hold of him: a warm sensation that filled him head to foot, making his fingers and toes tingle. 'And the front door was open.'

He strode forwards, into the hallway. He joined his mother on the stairs and threw his arms around her. She stiffened, surprised at his uncommon show of affection. Then she relaxed, allowing him to embrace her fully.

'I must have left it open. Forgetful, you know. And don't you worry, I'm not going anywhere just yet,' she said.

Thirty-four

'You just missed Sebastian. He was in a right mood.'

I felt irritation work its way through me as I entered the kitchen to find Triss still seated at the kitchen table where I'd left her nearly an hour and a half earlier. Denny trailed by my side, his body uncomfortably close in the muggy August heat, his head under my elbow. Thankfully, he'd stopped crying now. His high-pitched wail all night had set my teeth on edge. I felt like I'd been awake for years.

'Why was he in a mood? Didn't you tell him we were at the doctor?' I ripped open the paper bag from the pharmacy and took out the bottle of amoxicillin prescribed for Denny's ear infection. I drew the medicine into the syringe provided.

'Yeah.' Triss looked up at me from her magazine, then her brow furrowed as she reconsidered her answer. 'I think so, anyway.'

'Well you either did, or you didn't.' I tried to keep the exasperation out of my tone as I presented the syringe to Denny. He screwed up his face in a scowl, turning his nose up at the antibiotics. Weariness filled my bones like concrete.

'I did. I'm sure I did.'

I took my phone from the countertop where I'd left it charging while we were out. No messages or missed calls. A pang of irritation and hurt bloomed. Sebastian could at least have sent me a text when he heard Denny was ill. It was like he could only concentrate on his mother at the moment.

But then I caught myself. It was understandable. His mother was dying. Denny was not. But Denny was just a child. No! I had to pull myself together. Things were hard for everyone. And I could've sent him a message to tell him about Denny. I tapped one out now:

Sorry I missed you, doctor took forever. Denny OK. See you later? XXX.

Triss leaped up from the table, giving Denny a bright smile. 'C'mon soldier. Take your medicine for your mum.'

'Don't want to.' Denny's lip jutted out.

'Do you want your ear to fall off?'

I nearly dropped the syringe. 'Triss!'

'What? Could happen. How do you know it won't?' Triss winked at me. 'I get it, it's horrible. But if you take that icky stuff, I'll buy you some sweets. How about it?'

'I don't want him eating all these sweets…' I began, but I knew I was already losing the battle.

'Let's get his ear sorted. Then we can fix his teeth if we need to.' Triss took the syringe from me and advanced on Denny. 'Now, open wide…'

His medicine taken, we put a DVD on for Denny and he lounged on the sofa for the rest of the afternoon, under his Batman blanket, his expression morose. Finally, around five, he fell asleep.

With him comfortable, I found myself suddenly irritated by the state of the kitchen and began cleaning up. Triss perched on her stool and scrolled through her various feeds on her phone as I tidied and wiped around her.

'So, any news on how the mother-in-law is doing?' Triss asked.

I'd seen Fran the day before, taken her some flowers. She'd seemed stalwart and brave, but also vulnerable and sad, just like my own mother had all those years ago. 'She seems okay. But it must take a toll on your body, right? Chemo, I mean.'

'Well, it's essentially poison, isn't it?' Triss's expression was grim.

A picture of my mother flashed into my head – in the wingback chair in the bay window of our house. She spent a lot of time in that chair, watching the world go past. Red figured a lot in memories of my mother from that time: the curtains; the buses that swept by outside; the postbox on the corner of our street, all visible from her vantage point. And the red beanie hat she'd wear that accentuated her pale skin, the wide white expanse of her forehead, her eyes seeming too big for her head.

I'd come straight home after school to show her my pictures, or read with her, resting my head on her bony lap. I realised now that I could barely remember Mum healthy. In the vast majority of my recollections of her, she was ill.

As this thought fluttered through my mind, I saw my mother's face move away from her window, to look at me, dead-on. Her moon-like face drew me further into the memory and I felt an irritating niggle in the back of my head, just like when I attempted to leave the house, but was struck by the notion that I might have left an appliance on. What could it be?

'Lil?' Triss's voice crashed into my daydream.

I blinked, brought back down to earth.

'Someone's at the door,' she laughed.

I reached over and pressed the intercom.

'It's me.'

I raised my eyes towards the skylight and the fast-approaching dusk beyond. Only Maxwell was arrogant enough to announce his presence like that. I said nothing in reply, but pressed the button again. I heard the front door open, then his heavy, swaggering footfall on the stairs.

'Evening,' he said as he appeared at the top of the stairs. He leaned against the top of the bannister, clocking Triss lounging at my kitchen table. He nodded to her. 'Beatrice.'

Triss attempted to give him the side-eye, but I noted that she was fingering the silver chain around her throat.

'What are you doing here?' I asked, hands on my hips. Maybe he thought cosy takeaway dinners were going to be a regular thing now.

Maxwell raised a quizzical eyebrow. 'It's my night to have Denny…'

I groaned. In all the palaver, I'd forgotten. 'Denny's ill. He's been up all night. Sorry.'

I braced myself for Maxwell's anger at being let down, but he was uncharacteristically sympathetic. 'Don't worry. I know how stretched you are with … everything. Can I…?' He indicated the sofa, where he'd now spotted Denny asleep.

I nodded.

Maxwell wandered over to the living area, his face softening as he took in his son, bundled up under his blanket. When he looked up at me I couldn't help but be touched by the fatherly concern in his eyes.

'He's fine. Just an ear infection,' I found myself reassuring him. I felt unreasonable all of a sudden. Perhaps Maxwell wasn't all bad. I must have seen something in him once, after all?

'Can I put him to bed?' He hovered over Denny, his strong arms ready to pick him up.

Out of habit, I almost said no. But Maxwell was strong enough to carry Denny to his bed, without disturbing him. Which, in turn, meant I might get a good sleep, after the torture of the previous night. Besides, it wouldn't be the first time Maxwell had done such bedtime duty that week.

'Sure. I'll turn his bed down.'

Maxwell scooped up Denny, who murmured in his sleep, opened one eye, saw his father, smiled, then dropped off again.

'He's still in his clothes,' Triss observed from the kitchen table.

'Doesn't matter.'

I walked ahead of Maxwell and opened Denny's bedroom door. I pulled back his duvet and Maxwell carefully laid our son down on the bed. It creaked. We both winced at the sound, seemingly loud in the quiet bedroom. But Denny did not stir. Next, I undid the drawstring of his shorts and pulled them down. I balled them up and chucked them towards the wash basket. They went in first time, like a basketball hoop.

Maxwell smiled. 'You've done this before.'

Denny stretched out on the bed in his T-shirt, pants and socks. Then he turned over onto his front and buried his face in the pillow. I pulled the duvet up to his shoulders.

'Night, night,' I whispered, kissing the top of his head.

I straightened up and Maxwell and I regarded our sleeping son for a moment.

Maxwell's voice was wistful as he broke the silence. 'You're such a good mother. Denny is lucky to have you.'

I looked up, surprised. Maxwell had never complimented my parenting skills before, even in the years we were married.

'We were happy once, weren't we?' he said.

As our eyes met, I thought I saw something shimmer in his. Apology? Regret? I couldn't decide. I sighed. All of this crap had been so unnecessary. I noted all his usual bluster was gone and there was a vulnerability in his expression that in an instant transported me back nearly a decade. I saw myself in bed, waking up from a marathon sex session. Shirtless and newly showered, Maxwell was presenting me with a breakfast tray, a little box next to my eggs Benedict, the same uncertainty in his eyes as I saw before me now:

'Marry me?' he'd said back then.

I'd opened the box to find a ring he'd had made for me. He knew I didn't like diamonds – they reminded me of the one on my mother's gaunt finger. So he'd designed me one in white gold, with a pink sapphire. Pink was still my favourite colour, even though the ring had long since been returned.

'Of course I will!' I'd squealed, throwing my arms around his neck.

Standing over our son's bed now, I felt a sharp pang of sorrow that it had turned out so badly.

From the doorway came two short, sarcastic barks.

'Well. Isn't this cosy?' Triss said, observing Maxwell.

I was torn: I was pleased to have her support before things got awkward, but irritated Triss had thought I needed rescuing. What did she think would happen – that I'd let Maxwell jump my bones with our kid in the room?

I painted on an automatic smile. 'I'll call you when he's better,' I said to Maxwell.

He seemed to deflate, shooting a look at Triss. 'Sure,' he said.

I saw Maxwell out and returned to the living area to find Triss now splayed across the sofa, some reality show on the TV. On the coffee table was the bottle of good red I'd been saving for the weekend, plus two glasses. I was both annoyed by her presumption and relieved she'd opened it already.

Triss poured, then held up one of the full glasses. 'Here's to new men,' she said.

We clinked glasses.

Thirty-five

'Have you tried turning it off, then turning it back on again?' As ever, Sebastian sounded distracted at the other end of the line.

I counted to ten again. The landline to my ear, I swept a finger across the useless phone screen. Denny had dropped it on the bathroom tiles that morning.

'Of course I have! The swipe function won't work, either.'

Though it was not smashed, the phone was unresponsive. On it was the vacuous, faraway look of some YouTuber, frozen mid-rant. It was not someone I recognised, but then I'd grown up in the eighties with four channels and no internet.

Sebastian sighed. 'Bring it over, I'll see what I can do.'

I looked at the calendar on the wall. It was the last Tuesday in August, a chemo day. Sebastian had told me he planned to escort his mother to the Cromwell and sit with her throughout the treatment, whether she liked it or not.

'Bring it to the hospital?'

'No. We're at the house.'

'How come? It's Tuesday.'

'I'll tell you when you get here.'

I strode through to the living area where Denny was working hard on a drawing. Triss was gathering her stuff together, shoving dirty clothes into her rucksack. She'd more or less become a permanent fixture over the past few weeks. I'd given up trying to send her home to her cramped, damp flat on the other side of town. And besides, I'd been grateful for some adult company, if Triss could be counted as a real adult.

'Can you keep an eye on Denny?'

Triss froze. 'Sorry, I would, but … I've got a … a *thing*.'

I noticed she had a make-up compact in her hand; she'd put on lipstick. Triss only ever wore make-up on dates, and it was barely midday.

I narrowed my eyes. 'What's going on?'

Triss looked so stricken, I burst out laughing.

She smiled, relieved. 'Look, it's just a blind-date thing, off that app I use. I'm meeting him for lunch, scoping him out. I can rearrange, no problem.'

'No, no! It's fine, don't worry. I'll take Denny with me; he could do with the fresh air, anyway.'

'Don't want to go out,' he mumbled, choosing another coloured pencil.

'We're going to get *your* phone fixed.' I indicated the clock on the wall. 'Five minutes: teeth and shoes, please.'

👁

Getting off the bus, we cut through the parkland by the side of Stew Pond, crossed the busy, tree-flanked road near the massive green WELCOME TO SURREY sign and slipped into a cul-de-sac of more modern builds, all red brick and sandstone. Just beyond the housing estate was a small, green copse of trees. Five tall, white, palatial homes were built like a toadstool ring around an ancient oak tree. Fran's was the nearest. The oak itself was dead, hollowed out by centuries of rot caused by the rain and wind. It was an awe-inspiring sight, held up by a single baluster, to stop gravity claiming the ancient tree.

Sebastian looked strained as he opened the door and ushered us in, taking Denny's broken phone from my outstretched hand before it was forgotten.

'All right, mate?' Sebastian's face lit up at the sight of Denny, but he just got a shy, tight-lipped smile in return. 'We've got some chocolate biscuits in the living room.'

Denny didn't need telling twice. He raced through.

'How is she?' I asked, my enquiry automatic. I'd hated hearing people do this when they came to visit my mother when I was a child. I'd wanted one of them to come up with a solution; to save her; or at least make her happy. But now, in the world of grown-ups, I realised why they'd all fallen back on polite enquiries and platitudes.

'Oh, you know Mum.' He looked even worse than at the end of term; his complexion was pallid, dark circles under his eyes. He looked completely done in. And he made no effort to kiss me, even on the cheek.

'Lily? Is that you?' Fran's voice sounded shockingly frail.

'Hi Fran,' I drifted through to the living room, fixing a smile on my face before I saw her, in the hope it wouldn't falter. 'I thought it was chemo today.'

'It is, it is.'

As I crossed the threshold, I discovered Denny on the sofa next to Fran, several biscuits in his hand already. His glance challenged me to take them away.

I looked to Sebastian, who shrugged. 'Apparently, Maxwell decided to switch Mum to oral chemo, so she can take it at home.'

I leaned down and kissed Fran's cheek. Her skin was cold and clammy. She stiffened, as if she didn't want me touching her. I couldn't blame her. Being ill meant having your space invaded by all and sundry.

'I did tell you, darling. Last week. And the amount I'm paying, I should get the best service,' Fran murmured. 'You don't get this on the NHS.'

Sebastian chuckled halfheartedly. The disrespect for one of our country's greatest institutions set my teeth on edge, but I let it go. I took in the red turban wound around Fran's head and a flash of my mother's translucent moonlike face seared through my memory again, taking my breath with it.

'Red suits you,' I said, but again, that niggling feeling sprang up in the back of my head. It travelled down my neck, into my spine, making me clench my fists.

'Thank you, dear,' said Fran, her eyes closed.

'Tea, Lil?' asked Sebastian.

I was about to turn in his direction, when realisation cracked open inside my skull. But first I had to check.

My eyes followed the line of Fran's jaw; her sharp cheekbones; the folds of her neck. My mother-in-law was older than my own mother had ever been and she looked nothing like her. Fran had always been long, thin, tapered; some might have called her 'willowy' in her youth. Mum had been all soft edges, even retaining that round face of hers as first cancer – and then the chemo had ravaged the rest of her body, taking her hair, eyebrows and even her eyelashes with it.

And Fran still had hers.

Task	Objective	Task status	On track?
Whisper Campaign	*Undermine Sebastian's credibility as head teacher, before school inspection*	ONGOING	YES
Interrupt wedding	*Spoil the big day / ensure marriage gets off to a bad start*	COMPLETED	YES
Cut off electricity	*Reminder of who is in charge here, even in their own home*	COMPLETED	YES
Trash the maisonette	*Punishment for marriage / honeymoon / leaving me behind*	COMPLETED	YES
Assault charge	*Get Sebastian arrested / charged*	ONGOING	YES
Denny – unexpected pick-up from school	*Reminder of who is Denny's REAL father / come between Sebastian and Lily*	COMPLETED	YES
Install GPS tracker app on Denny's phone	*Surveillance*	COMPLETED	YES
Install GPS tracker app on Sebastian's phone	*Surveillance [especially important regarding the ultimate plan; be sure that OMF does not know about this]*	COMPLETED	YES
Install GPS tracker app on Lily's phone	*Surveillance [NB. Haven't been able to get hold of Lily's phone. Can proceed without this]*	INCOMPLETE	NO
Denny [bed-wetting]	*Invented issue to create friction between Sebastian and Lily*	ONGOING	YES
Therapy for Denny	*Use parenting of Denny to remind Lily of times past*	ONGOING	YES
Denny – missing	*Bring in Social Services; bonus – undermine Sebastian's credibility as head teacher*	COMPLETED	YES
Cancer diagnosis and treatment	*Trauma to come between Lily and Sebastian*	ONGOING	YES
Our Mutual Friend	*Wind up our involvement; implicate Sebastian instead re: ultimate plan*	ONGOING	OVERDUE

Thirty-six

Sebastian stalked into the kitchen, slamming Denny's phone down on the countertop.

Lily followed him in, her posture defensive: shoulders squared off, arms folded across her middle.

Fury bloomed in him, red and fiery as lava. 'What the hell was all that about?' He took a deep breath, trying to keep a lid on his anger as he indicated her to shut the kitchen door.

But Lily didn't, she just chewed on the inside of her cheek and shrugged.

Sebastian sighed, still trying to keep his anger in check.

In the living room, moments earlier, Lily's bombshell had been in the form of a question: 'I would have expected Fran's eyelashes and eyebrows to have gone first, wouldn't you?'

Still on the sofa, Fran's eyes had sprung open. Sebastian had frowned, unable to understand the question at first.

'Lily, what are you saying?' he'd said.

Lily had looked as if she felt the carpet under her feet was shifting, but she stood her ground. 'I was just pointing out that Fran still has her eyebrows and eyelashes.'

Sebastian felt his voice drop an octave. 'So?'

Lily swallowed. 'I'm just surprised, that's all. Mum lost all of hers straight away.'

Sebastian was confused. His wife had read the leaflets Maxwell had given them. 'Lily, you know everyone responds differently to chemotherapy. Some people don't even lose their hair at all, never mind their eyebrows or eyelashes.'

Yet Sebastian could see fierce anger burning inside Lily's eyes. What he couldn't fathom was why. What did she think was going on, here? Sebastian recalled that there had been a head teacher at the first school he'd worked at, Mrs Bennett, who'd had breast cancer for two years. She'd not lost her hair.

Now, Sebastian reached around Lily and shut the kitchen door himself. Out in the living room, he could hear Fran distracting her stepgrandson with cartoons on TV.

'What's going on, Lily? Talk to me.'

Lily sighed, as if she couldn't decide whether or not to part with her thoughts. 'Don't you think … don't you think it's a bit weird that Maxwell happens to be the one treating your mum?'

'Well, not really. He's an oncologist. She's got cancer. She's not one to go to an NHS hospital, so the Cromwell is the best in Epsom. And it's not like they're actually related, so there's no real conflict.'

Lily took a step towards him. 'Yes, but has she?' Her expression became earnest.

'Has she what?' Sebastian couldn't believe what he was hearing – couldn't yet articulate the thought to himself.

'Look, Maxwell did everything he could to get between us … Then he suddenly stopped – at the very moment your Mum *apparently* developed cancer…'

'Apparently?' Sebastian echoed, backing away from his wife. 'So … so you think she's … *faking* it?'

'No, no … I reckon Maxwell is!' Lily grabbed at Sebastian's hands, but he pulled them away. 'Think about it,' she pleaded. 'There must be ways of faking chemotherapy … Do you even know what chemo looks like?'

'No,' Sebastian admitted.

'Maxwell could have been hooking Fran up to a bunch of saline solutions in there, for all we know! Would Fran know the difference?'

Lily managed to grab his hand now. Sebastian wrenched it away.

'She's not stupid,' he said. 'My father was a doctor as well, remember.'

'And I was married to Maxwell! But I don't know the ins and outs of chemotherapy. Not really.' Lily looked earnest. Her accusations were confusing him now. 'Neither do you. Why would we? But now suddenly he's switched her to oral chemo … just like that?"

Sebastian quickly sorted through his thoughts. It was true Maxwell had behaved terribly, using Denny as a pawn. But all that was over now. Sebastian could not believe he would abuse his position as a doctor to fake a cancer diagnosis. It made no sense; the plan couldn't go anywhere. Unless … he was giving Fran real chemo, killing her off slowly? No, that was ludicrous. As horrible a person as Maxwell was, he had sworn the oath all doctors must – *'primum non nocere'*: 'do no harm'.

'If what you're saying is true, he could be struck off. No, he wouldn't risk it. And what for, anyway?' Sebastian was certain Lily was mistaken.

'But that's Maxwell all over; he loves risk. And he's so arrogant, he'd never imagine he'd be found out!'

Sebastian felt sorrow surge through him as he regarded his wife's fervent gaze. The past few months had been so tough. It was true Maxwell had been difficult, but he couldn't fault him now. Lily was jumping at shadows. He could hardly blame her, either. They'd all been pushed as far as they could go.

Sebastian placed his hands on his wife's shoulders. 'Is this because I'm not home much at the moment?'

Lily twisted from his grasp. 'I'm not a child, Sebastian. I can cope alone.'

Sebastian raised his hands. 'Look, I know this is not ideal. But I'm doing my best…'

'I never said you weren't!' Lily clenched her fists, but kept them at her sides, as if to stop herself from lashing out. 'But don't you see – this is what Maxwell wants?'

'I don't need this right now.' Sebastian shook his head, as yet more frustration and resentment came bubbling up. On a knife-edge for weeks after a difficult half-term followed by the new stress with his mother, Sebastian suddenly could not deal with this tantrum from Lily – and he was sure now that this was all it was.

'Need *this* ... or need *me*?' Lily challenged him.

Sebastian paused for a fateful beat.

Lily stepped backwards, sardonic smile on her face. 'Message received, loud and clear, Sebastian. Thanks a lot.'

'Oh, Lily for God's sake...' Sebastian began, but she wrenched open the kitchen door, swept through the hallway ahead of him onto the porch.

He had just enough time to grab at her arm as she opened the outer door. 'Come on, let's talk about this.'

Lily tilted her head at Sebastian, then indicated Fran's house. 'Actions speak louder, Sebastian.' Then she jerked her arm out of his grasp and stormed down the path and back towards the road beyond.

Sebastian sighed and turned, only to find Denny standing behind him in the middle of the hallway, seemingly unconcerned at being left behind.

Thirty-seven

My trainers hit the pavement, the rubber soles scuffing against the slabs. I was at the traffic lights, just beyond the common, before I realised I'd left Denny back at Fran's.

Momentary guilt arrested me in my tracks, but then I ploughed on. It wasn't as if I had left him at a stranger's house, for God's sake. He was with his stepfather, my husband. The man I married, for better or worse, for all the good it seemed to have done us. I pressed the button on the pelican crossing, waiting for the little man to flash green. Our fledgling marriage appeared to have faltered after only a few hurdles ... More shame heaped on me now. There couldn't be many newlyweds who had had to face so many obstacles in their first few months of marriage. First Maxwell, then Fran ... *If* her illness was real. No, surely Sebastian was right. Maxwell couldn't be that much of a sociopath that he'd fake Fran's diagnosis...

Could he?

Cars came to a halt just as the crossing beeped. I didn't look at them as I usually would have, but marched across the road, sights set straight ahead. I didn't have a destination in mind, but as the incline steepened, pulling at the backs of my calves, I recognised I was on my way to Maxwell's. I didn't have a plan, but I knew I needed to confront my ex-husband.

This couldn't go on.

Rage coursed through my veins once again. Thoughts and accusations flickered through my brain like light through a hall of mirrors. No, I was right: Maxwell *had* to be behind all our problems. Besides which, how could Sebastian trust that Maxwell had Fran's best interests at heart, just because he was a doctor? He'd got Sebastian arrested! He'd tried to ruin Sebastian, make him lose his job: first via the assault charge that was *still* ongoing, then by reporting him to Social Services over 'losing' Denny at the fête. It wasn't much of a jump to suppose Maxwell could have seen an opportunity when Fran fainted at the park. Fran had been a patient at the Cromwell for decades; he could have looked up her records with ease.

Maybe he'd even got to her before all that. Fran had been sickly for some time – I'd noticed it, and I knew Sebastian had too. Maybe she'd gone to the Cromwell to see what was up, and then, somehow, Maxwell had slipped her a drug of some kind, made her faint? It wasn't like he didn't have access to any medicine of his choosing. Maybe he'd been planning it all along. I shuddered. I'd always known Maxwell was ruthless, but maybe even I had underestimated him.

The further I walked, the more I was certain of it: Maxwell was lying about Fran's cancer. As this conviction took shape, becoming solid in my mind, anxiety pierced through my thoughts. Could he be giving Fran *real* chemotherapy? Was he that much of a psychopath? She had been throwing up … I heard it.

No, I reminded myself: *Fran still has her eyebrows and eyelashes.* The nausea was probably stress, brought on by a supposedly terminal diagnosis. Who wouldn't be traumatised by being told they were about to die?

As well as that, Maxwell had switched my mother-in-law to 'oral chemo' at home. Hopefully, some kind of placebo. This must have meant someone at the Cromwell had been asking inconvenient questions. Even in a private hospital, as a consultant, Maxwell would still have to answer to someone.

Within half an hour, I was standing outside Maxwell's lavish home. I'd barely broken a sweat: it was like dark fury alone had carried me there.

Denny and I had never lived here; Maxwell moved in just after our divorce. With its three storeys it was far too big and incongruous for a single man. But, like everything Maxwell did, it was a statement – not only of the size of his bank balance and his status in the world, but also his bottomless well of self-belief: it said, *You and Denny will both return to me.*

Well, fuck that.

I undid the latch on the garden gate, stormed towards the porch, opened the outer door, put a finger on the bell and left it there. Inside, Ginny howled in disharmony with the noise.

'Okay, okay!' I heard Maxwell's irate voice float down the stairs.

Bored of pressing the bell now, I grabbed the ostentatious lion-shaped door knocker and starting rapping. I heard Maxwell lower his voice and say something, but it wasn't directed at me and I couldn't catch what it was.

'Coming! Jesus…' Maxwell's shadow appeared behind the glass. He pulled the door open, the aroma of lemon shower gel accompanying him.

I took him in: he was bare-chested, wet from the shower. A white towel was slung low around his hips. It accentuated, rather than covered, his crotch, as it led the eye towards the dark pubic hair there. He met my gaze with a smirk, as if to say, *See anything you like?* It was true, Maxwell was an attractive package – on the outside – but I had no time for his games now.

I was just about to start on my accusations, when I heard laughter floating down the stairs behind him: bell-like, unmistakably female.

'Hey, you coming back or what?' came the call.

So, he had a woman up there. But that wasn't what twisted in my gut as I made the connection.

'Hey!' Maxwell called halfheartedly after me as I shoved my way past him.

I raced towards the stairs and grabbed the oak bannister. He made no move to pull me back or manhandle me out of his house. He could have, if he'd wanted to; he was just three or four steps behind me, a good foot taller and much broader across the shoulders. Instead he trailed after me as I ran up the stairs two at a time.

I faltered as I made it onto the landing, momentarily disorientated. Maxwell was still a few steps behind but, weirdly, he still didn't make a grab for me.

'Lil.' His voice was low, carrying a warning, but I didn't turn in his direction.

I had to see it to believe it. I looked left, down the palatial landing: the doors were all closed. I looked to the only door ajar, on the right. I couldn't bring myself to cross the threshold, and hovered outside instead.

I pushed the door and as it swung open, I could see an unmade double bed, the sheets rumpled. The unmistakable musty smell of sex still hung in the air. Betrayal pumping through my veins, I digested the sight of her clothes on the floor, her bag on the dresser.

Inside the bedroom, next to built-in wardrobes, another door opened: the en suite bathroom. Though I wished with all my heart not to see her, inexplicably she was right there in front of me, naked, groping for a towel off the bed. As she saw me in the doorway, she brought it away from her face, her expression stricken.

I recalled all of the events of the past twelve weeks, her part in all of it: spying for him, covering for him, lying for him. Setting Sebastian and me against each other, getting between us, metaphorically and literally. Had she been the one to trash the maisonette? Had she swiped the electricity bill so Maxwell could phone to have us cut off? I realised she'd not been at the meeting that first day back at school. And did this all mean she hadn't been on my side at all when she'd seen him at my flat. Had she just been *jealous*?

Her words of just a few months ago came to my own lips, almost unbidden, as a thousand synapses fired into life inside my brain: 'Wouldn't mind a crack at that, myself.'

And now she was frozen beside the en suite door, guilt etched all over her pale face, the towel now covering her modesty.

Triss.

Thirty-eight

Sebastian waited for Lily to return to his mother's all afternoon. When it became clear that she wasn't going to, he called her on her mobile, then at the maisonette. Both lines just rang, and he didn't leave messages – he didn't know what to say.

Unease prickled through him as he stood in the kitchen, his fingers drumming on the pristine countertop. Was this the end of them … already? A hard ball of fear formed in his throat; his stomach twisted. He couldn't lose her. Not now. Not when they'd barely begun!

Sebastian had always thought marriages ended up exploding with the same kind of fanfare with which they began. The idea that his marriage to Lily had limped its way to failure within twelve weeks, withering away and dying quietly, just seemed wrong.

As Lily's phone went to voicemail over and over again, Sebastian found himself spinning like a top, his mood flying through emotions one by one, from abject despair to quiet reproach and back again. He beat himself up, too. He was being ridiculous! He and Lily had gone through so much, there was no way a stupid argument about his mother's eyebrows was going to finish them off. The thought raised a smile to Sebastian's lips. Eyebrows. For God's sake.

Sebastian just needed to sit tight. Lily had left Denny with him, after all. He was reading it all wrong: leaving the child was a sign of her regard for him as her husband and Denny's stepfather. Lily was an exemplary parent. There was no way she would abandon her son and go off to … well, where?

He took in several deep breaths. He had to be logical, rational. Lily lived at the maisonette, with him. She had given up her small flat on the other side of Epsom about three weeks before they had married. She had nowhere else to go, unless she wanted to sleep on the sofa at Triss's or her cousin Maya's. They also shared a bank account, so he knew she had not taken out any large sums that afternoon: he had an app on his phone that would have notified him.

Sebastian finally managed to calm the twisting knots inside his stomach. The past three months had taken their toll on all of them. Lily had been so strong through all of this. She just needed to blow off some steam. Sebastian was panicking without good reason. This was a blip – granted, *another* one – but they would get through it.

They had to.

He ambled back from the kitchen to the living room. He watched Denny and his mother from the doorway. His mother was teaching the little boy how to play Happy Families. She'd taken the pack of cards from the small bureau next to the magazine rack and now they were engrossed in a game.

'You have the card I want,' Fran prompted the little boy.

But Denny just stared at her, swinging his little legs on the chair next to the card table. His gaze wandered over to the television, where a colourful game show still played with the sound off.

'Dennis, pay attention. You have to give the card I want to me,' Fran tutted in exasperation; then, as if she felt Sebastian's gaze on her, she looked up and smiled. 'Honestly, this one doesn't catch on any quicker than you did.'

She smiled and got up, walking stiffly to the windows. Sebastian watched Denny match all the colours of the cards instead, the official game forgotten. They were ornate and beautifully illustrated. Each one was embossed on the back with gold leaf. Fran's grandfather had brought them back for her from a trip to India when she was a child. Sebastian recalled his mother dealing the cards every rainy day after dinner when he was home from school. She was always meticulous in ensuring both of them had an equal number. As Sebastian grew older, he'd wanted to play different games, but his mother would purse her lips and do that little shake of her head. They were *her* cards, she would remind him.

One day, when he was about eleven, Sebastian brought his own cards home. They were part of a cheap pack bought from the local shop with his allowance when he was at boarding school. He'd delighted in playing games like Go Fish and poker with the boys after lights out – torches on, voices low to avoid detection by their house supervisor.

He'd wanted to teach his mother these games, but she'd listened to his suggestion, her face blank, then she had simply taken the cards and placed them in one of the bureau's slim drawers. She had not brought them out again. If he'd been a gambling man, Sebastian would have bet real money they were still there, untouched and covered in dust, the best part of twenty years later.

Suddenly, Sebastian couldn't wait any longer. He looked at his watch: nearly eight o'clock. Even if Lily didn't want to speak to him just yet, she would need Denny back for bath and bedtime. He called his stepson to him and, after assuring his mother he'd be back in half an hour or so, bundled the little boy into his car.

☜

'Hello? Lily!'

Sebastian turned the light on in the dim hall. As usual, Denny bounded up the stairs ahead of him. The little boy was showing no signs of slowing down for the day. Sebastian heard the clatter of Denny's shoes on the tiles above him before he made it to the top.

'Mummy!'

Denny's exclamation made Sebastian's stomach settle somewhat. So, she was here. Sebastian emerged into the dim light of the small kitchen-dining area, where the grey fingers of dusk protruded through the skylight. Lily sat at the table, a bottle of wine in front of her, a half-empty glass in her hands.

'You finally made it home, then?' Her voice echoed his own thoughts, though it was loaded with sarcasm.

'I told Mum I'd be back in half an hour.' Sebastian tried hard to keep his tone level. He didn't want her to think he was ready for a fight.

It didn't work.

'Yes. Can't keep *mummy dearest* waiting!' Lily brought the large glass to her lips, knocking back the wine as if it were a vodka shot. Then self-loathing seemed to hit her full on; her face twisted in disgust at her own words. 'Sorry. I didn't mean that. None of this is Fran's fault. It's … *his*.'

As Lily poured another glass, Denny regarded her with a tiny frown. It was clear the little boy had never seen his mother like this before, all sharp edges and bitterness. Lily seemed to realise and looked up, smiling. She held out her arms for the boy, who immediately folded himself into her embrace. She hung on to him like a lifebuoy.

'Hey, sport, go get your PJs on.' Sebastian kept his voice light and gave his stepson a reassuring smile.

Denny glanced towards Sebastian, suspicion written all over his little face, shoulders hunched. He opened his mouth as if to argue, but then decided better of it. He traipsed off in the direction of his bedroom.

As soon as he was gone, Sebastian attempted to take the bottle of wine away from his wife. 'Come on, I'll make you some coffee,' Sebastian said in what he imagined was his most soothing voice.

'You will frigging *not*.' Lily grabbed the bottle back. 'How drunk do you think I am?'

Sebastian just shrugged.

Lily shook her head at him in disbelief. 'This is my first one!' She sipped her full glass, then, obviously remembering she'd just necked the first one, said, 'All right, second. But it's been a shit day. For Christ's sake, Sebastian, I knew Denny would be back tonight. I'm not going to get paralytic, am I?'

'If this is about earlier…' Sebastian sat down on one of the kitchen stools. He was disappointed Lily was still so angry; he'd thought she would have calmed down by now.

But Lily barely looked at him. 'God, it's always about you, isn't it?' Her tone was final, rhetorical. As if there was nothing to discuss.

Perhaps she really had had enough of all this? Maybe she wanted out. Sebastian wanted to fall on his sword, so he could know one way or the other, but he couldn't bring himself to conjure up the words.

Lily glanced up from her glass, taking in his stricken expression. 'You didn't believe me.'

'You didn't believe *me*,' Sebastian countered, though a pang hit him as he said it: she had never lied to him, like he had to her.

A sad, sardonic smile pulled at his wife's lip. 'Maxwell's really done a number on us, hasn't he?'

'We can get past this.' Sebastian sounded stronger than he felt.

Lily blew out her cheeks. 'Can we?'

Dread settled, brick-like, on his shoulders. That familiar ball of pain flowered into life, travelling its way into his throat. 'Of course we can.'

Lily brought her hands to her face. For a moment, Sebastian thought she was crying. That would be promising; that would mean she still cared, surely? But when she took them away again, he saw her eyes were dry. She was just weary. Which was far worse.

Denny appeared again, in his pyjamas. Lily forced a smile and abandoned her wine. 'Hey, champ. Let's get you to bed, shall we?'

Sebastian understood; he was dismissed. With a heavy heart, he got up from the stool and made his way to the top of the stairs. He looked back to see Lily piggy-backing Denny towards the bedroom, his legs and arms around her waist and neck like a baby monkey.

Before she could disappear from sight, Sebastian called after her: 'Lily … I'm sorry.'

She stopped and turned. Denny's head was buried in her shoulder. She flashed Sebastian a grim smile.

'Yeah, me too.'

Thirty-nine

I'd barely got Denny into bed before the doorbell rang again. Denny had been drifting off, but at the sound of the bell, he sat bolt upright in the bed, eyes bright and beady. I swore under my breath as he bounced straight out of bed and started rummaging in his toy box.

'Denny! Get back in bed.' Even as the words passed my lips, I knew they were futile.

'But, Mummy, I'm not tired.' Denny pouted.

If I wanted any peace, I knew I would have to just let him get on with it. After all the events of such a horrific day, I wasn't likely to get any sleep anyway, so what harm would it do? I made an executive decision, moving back to the bedroom door, towards the hall.

'Okay, fine! Stay in here, though, or you're in trouble. Understand?'

Denny nodded happily, pulling toy cars and his race track from the toy box.

I didn't bother answering the doorbell with the intercom. I didn't want to let her think she could just wander up the stairs and back into our lives. I passed through the kitchen-diner and went down to the dim hall leading out to the front door. It had no glass in the front, so I couldn't see for sure who it was, but I just knew: Triss. The fury I'd felt earlier was still buzzing in my veins, I had to say my piece.

Opening the front door, there she was – under a pool of orange light shining down the alley from the streetlamp by the betting shop.

She was wearing clothes this time: purple converse with a denim jacket over a short day dress decorated with neon pink pineapples that clashed with her red hair. Her shoulders were hunched, her arms folded, both her feet facing inwards like a sulking teen. Her eyes were puffy, like she'd been crying.

'I can explain…' she whined.

I matched her cliché with one of my own: I slammed the door hard in her face, leaving her on the other side.

'Lily! Please, let's talk about this?' Triss's pale fingers appeared through the letterbox, a childish plea.

'It's too late!'

As I said the words, I felt the weight of history between us unravel, falling into a tangled heap: we'd been like sisters. No, we'd been more than that: we'd found each other in the chaos of childhood and held onto each other throughout the decades, without needing to rely on the bond of blood.

'You've got the wrong end of the stick…' Triss wailed. She left her fingers in the letterbox, trusting me not to slam the metal down on them. She knew me as well as she thought; I would never do that.

'So, you *didn't* have sex?' There was an absurd part of me that hoped it was all some kind of big mistake: I hadn't found my best friend, naked, with my ex-husband or involved in his ridiculous plot. 'How long have you been reporting back to Maxwell?'

Triss gulped back more tears. 'Look, if you just let me in…?'

'Was it worth it?' I spat.

A trite old saying appeared in my brain: *Friends are the family you choose*. I'd chosen Triss, I'd cherished her. I thought she'd felt the same way about me. Yet all Maxwell had had to do was click his fingers and she'd fallen into his bed and betrayed me, even helping him come between me and Sebastian as part of his sick plan.

'Please … listen to me!'

'Listen to your excuses, you mean.'

I suddenly felt bone-weary. We were acting out some kind of scene, courtesy of Maxwell. I was overwhelmed by it all. What was the bloody point? We might be back at school in a week or so, working together, but other than that, I was done with Triss.

I moved away from the door, back towards the stairs. She must have heard my footsteps on the creaky old steps.

'No, no Lil! Don't go. Please. We have to talk … tonight!'

Though I'd resolved not to look back, I couldn't resist: Triss was now beseeching me through the letterbox. Even so, I didn't take the bait.

'Piss off, Triss.'

I turned my back on my oldest friend and walked heavily upwards, all the while Triss's pained pleas landing on my back.

'I'll fix this, Lily. I swear to God, I will fix it…'

As I reached the top, I turned the light off, plunging the stairwell into darkness.

Forty

Sebastian returned to his mother's home in a daze. Hearing the abject weariness in Lily's voice at the maisonette had really shaken him. There was a sharp pain in his chest; his head banged in rhythm with his heartbeat; the back of his mouth felt dry and sour. Was this what heartbreak felt like? The realisation that he'd let his marriage slip through his fingers, without seeing the signs, the opportunities to turn things around. Disappointment, dread and devastation lanced their way through Sebastian's body one after another.

Anger came next in the kaleidoscope of thoughts swirling through his mind. How could Lily have let Maxwell come between them like this? It was true her ex's vendetta had been sustained, and his mother's cancer had been a dreadful blow coming so soon after it. But Lily had pledged her vows to Sebastian, *for better or worse.* Okay, neither of them knew it would be worse before it got better, but they could not be the first married couple in the world to get off to a rocky start.

Sebastian strode through to Fran's living room, grabbing his father's crystal decanter off the shelf. He poured himself a large measure of whisky, then stepped over to the large patio window. He glanced at the clock: it was coming up to ten p.m. The immaculate garden was dark; he could see only his reflection in the glass. He looked dishevelled, five-day old stubble on his cheeks. His clothes were rumpled, his hair hadn't seen a comb in days. His shoulders were hunched and there was a deep crease in his forehead. Everything about him yelled stress and frustration.

It was like looking at his father's photograph in its silver-plated frame on the mantelpiece. It was the only one not on the wall. He moved over to the picture, picking it up. Sebastian could not remember a time he hadn't looked at this picture, trying to feel a connection with the man he'd never known, trapped under the glass.

It was Fran's favourite for some reason. Perhaps she thought Jasper looked authoritative, commanding. To Sebastian, his father looked as bad as Sebastian now felt. He was staring directly into the camera lens; his expression seemed to be one of suppressed anger. He was trying to smile, but it looked more like a grimace. Sebastian had often wondered why his father seemed so unhappy in this picture. Was it marriage? Was this the one lesson he could have taken from his dead father, if he'd paid greater attention to the lines on his face, his pain captured in a photograph?

Don't get married, son. You'll regret it.

As soon as this thought surfaced, Sebastian chuckled. He was seeing things that weren't there. His father had worked long hours as a surgeon; maybe he'd just been exhausted. Or maybe he'd just not wanted his photo taken at that particular moment. His mother had always said they'd been very happy together.

Sebastian and Lily could be again, too. All he needed to do was not pressurise her. That was kryptonite for all relationships recovering from a crisis. Sebastian just had to show himself as worthy, steadfast; prove to Lily – and Denny – that they could depend on him again. And what better way than to do something for the boy?

He ambled back into the kitchen and retrieved Denny's broken phone from where he'd placed it earlier in the day on the countertop near the bread bin. In the furore, it had been forgotten. Sebastian smiled to himself. All he needed to do was fix it and he could legitimately go over tomorrow, after Lily had calmed down. She would be glad to see him, relieved that he wasn't staying away.

Outside, Sebastian could hear a fox barking and the faraway swish of traffic out towards the common. He turned the phone over, noting its frozen screen. It was the same make and model as his own, so he pressed down on the large button and held it there for ten seconds, forcing a hard reboot. The phone beeped and the start-up animation began. Sebastian smiled to himself. Lily was so impatient, ten seconds was probably more like five to her. No wonder it hadn't rebooted.

He put his whisky glass in the dishwasher as the screen's various sections and features came back to life. When it was ready, he swished a finger across the screen as it prompted him to choose the date, its language, region and backup status. Sebastian followed the prompts. Then he pressed OK, expecting that to be the end of it. But now another screen popped up straight away:

RESET GEOFENCE? Y/N

Sebastian liked to think he had his finger on the pulse, but he had no clue what a 'geofence' was. Perhaps it was something to do with one of the forest of apps on the phone? Sebastian noted Denny had downloaded more than twenty, most of them games in primary colours and with cartoon faces.

Sebastian pulled his own phone from his pocket and googled the term. The definition flashed up:

A geofence is a virtual barrier. Programmes that incorporate geofencing allow an administrator to set up triggers so when a device enters (or exits) the boundaries defined by the administrator, a text message or email alert is sent.

Sebastian thought for moment. To all intents and purposes, this was a stalker app. As a head teacher at a school, Sebastian had heard about these. Some parents installed them on their kids' phones, but he couldn't see Lily doing that. Not only did she not have the technical know-how, she was a fierce believer in trusting kids to do the right thing.

Sebastian pressed *Y* on Denny's phone. It took him to yet another screen and that was when a feeling of trepidation descended on him. The app was connected to a street map. On the map were various locations:

- *The maisonette*
- *Avonwood School*
- *Epsom Common*
- *Epsom High Street*
- *The Cromwell Hospital*

Plus, there were dotted lines; he realised they were journeys – to and from these locations. And each was labelled with a date. The earliest was three months ago.

Fury leaped into Sebastian's throat. Now it was obvious who'd installed the stalker app: Maxwell. He'd had them all under surveillance, via Denny! Unbelievable. No wonder Maxwell had seemingly been able to ambush them at various intervals and get away unseen, like he had at the school fête!

Sebastian's anger travelled from his throat into his chest. At the bottom of the map was a button: ADMINISTRATOR.

Sebastian tapped on the screen, expecting to see the administrator's details: Maxwell's name and number – clear digital proof of his guilt.

But he didn't.

Instead, he saw a number he knew off by heart.

His mother's.

Sebastian did not stop to digest this information. He raced out of the kitchen and up the stairs. He was on the landing before his scrambled thoughts could catch up with him. He cleared the small hallway and burst through his mother's bedroom door, crashing inside without knocking.

As he staggered in, breathless, his outrage died on his tongue, and a second wave of shock replaced it.

He took in the sight of his mother sitting on the edge of the bed in her nightdress and housecoat. She was not wearing her now customary headscarf.

And the reason was, she didn't need to: her long, dark hair fell in soft waves around her face, lightly touching her shoulders. Thick and glossy … and healthy.

Forty-one

'You *faked* a cancer diagnosis?'

There was a crack in Sebastian's voice as he spoke. Shock seemed to drench him like cold water. His mother froze, her eyes wide, her body language betraying panic, any explanation refusing to come to her lips. The air around Sebastian had an almost unreal quality, like he was trapped in some kind of strange dream or watching them both from above.

Then realisation flashed through his mind. 'You and Maxwell were in this together!' And as he said this, another connection fired in his brain. 'Denny never wet the bed at all, did he? Or went missing at the fête! This was all an elaborate ruse to bring Maxwell and Lily together again!'

Still his mother said nothing. She seemed less panicked now. In her nightgown, she lacked her usual gravitas. And there was still something about her that was shrunken, not her usual self. She looked like a woman at the end of her rope.

Sebastian leaned against the wardrobe behind him. He felt faint; his limbs did not seem strong enough to hold him up. 'I don't understand. Why?'

Fran ripped her gaze from Sebastian's. 'Maxwell made me.'

Whatever Sebastian was expecting, it was not this. He had never known anyone *make* his mother do anything. 'What do you mean?'

'He said he would tell you about…' His mother hid her face in her hands. 'Oh God, I can't bear to say it aloud!'

Fear hit Sebastian now, a dead weight in the pit of his stomach. 'Tell me, Mum.'

Still, she concealed her face. Sebastian crouched next to her, placing both palms on her knees, imploring her to look at him. 'Mum, you're scaring me.'

Finally, Fran took her hands from her face. Her eyes were closed, as if she couldn't bear to look at Sebastian. She took a deep gulp of air, her words rushing out:

'He … he raped me.'

A chain reaction of thoughts and emotions raced through Sebastian's mind. He felt like he'd been physically punched. Reeling, he grabbed his mother's hands, as much to anchor himself as show his support for her.

'When?'

'After the wedding.' She focused somewhere above Sebastian's head. She could not meet his gaze.

'On the actual day?'

Sebastian connected the dots straight away. 'Oh God … when you called me at the airport?'

Self-disgust hit him. He'd still been in the UK too; he could have come back, comforted her, called the police and averted all of this. But he'd rejected the call – when his mother had needed him most!

Fran wiped a tear away from her pale cheek. 'Yes, not long after you left. He called me, said Lily had left my number in case of emergencies, since I lived in Epsom too. He said Denny was ill, asked me if I could go to the pharmacy and bring round some Calpol for him. I was only too happy to oblige … I'm such an idiot!'

Tears tracked down Sebastian's face now too. 'Why didn't you tell me?'

'How could I?' Fran hid her face in her hands. 'You'd just got married. And Maxwell is Lily's ex! What if she'd sided with him? He is the boy's father…'

Disbelief flooded through Sebastian now. He couldn't believe Lily would have called Fran a liar. Not about something as huge as rape. But just as quickly, doubt crept in: Lily had known Maxwell for years. She'd known Fran for only a matter of months. Plus, Fran would never have wanted to charge Maxwell; take the stand against him; have her business paraded in front of strangers. Fran was too proud, too private, for that. It was what Maxwell had been banking on.

Sebastian threw his arms around his mother. 'Mum, I'm so sorry.'

But there was no recrimination on his mother's face. 'It's not your fault.'

Sebastian's sorrow now made way for anger; he could barely keep up with his emotions. His mother was right: there was only one person at fault.

Maxwell.

Sebastian staggered to his feet. Enough was enough.

'I'm going to kill him.'

Fran's eyes widened. 'Darling, no!'

But Sebastian turned his back, shame following him out onto the landing. As she shuffled after him, begging him to reconsider, Sebastian knew he should stay with his mother; try and get her to go to the police. But he realised her pride would never allow that. This was why she had let Maxwell bully her into this ridiculous charade. Maxwell had planned this all along, waiting until Sebastian and Lily were out the picture to launch his first attack. Fran had been a pawn from the beginning.

Sebastian made it to the front door. The house had a selection of deadbolts and a chain, which he had to stop and disengage. He did not turn around as his mother caught up. She clutched at his shoulders, trying to turn him back towards her.

'Sebastian, no. Please. I can't have everyone knowing…!'

Guilt slammed into Sebastian next; he'd already guessed she wouldn't like this, and he knew that he was going after Maxwell to satisfy his own sense of justice. He didn't allow himself to look at his mother, for fear he would falter in his mission.

He shrugged her off and finally got the door open, then staggered outside into the night. There was a fine mist of rain, the kind that deceives, pasting hair to forehead in minutes. Sebastian paused to gulp the cool air, trying to still his erratic heartbeat.

'Please, Sebastian!' His mother was outside too now, barefoot on the damp front lawn.

'He can't get away with this!' Sebastian bellowed.

His mother looked broken. The rain reduced her full hair to straggles around her thin face. 'You can't let him win!'

As Sebastian's mind cleared, he realised that they had attracted the neighbours' attention. Across the way, past the dead oak, lights were on. Curtains twitched. In the house next door, a young woman in a purple dressing gown watched openly from an upstairs window. When she caught Sebastian's eye, she gave him a glare and drew the curtains.

Sebastian opened his car door. 'I'm just going to talk to him.'

'We both know that's not true.'

He slid into the driving seat and turned the keys in the ignition. His mother was illuminated by the headlights, as she placed both her hands on the bonnet.

'Don't leave me … Stay. Let's talk about this!' she shrieked through the windscreen.

Unable to move forwards without running her over, Sebastian crunched the gearstick into reverse. He rocketed the car backwards, too fast.

His mother crumpled to her knees as Sebastian almost backed straight into the dead tree. He did a hasty three-point turn and left his mother collapsed there, outside her house, a wraith lost in the night.

Forty-two

Arriving at Maxwell's, Sebastian turned the engine off and breathed heavily, as if he'd been running. This was the house to which Maxwell had lured Fran – where he'd attacked her, presumably as Denny lay sleeping upstairs. Furious tears streamed down his face, his knuckles white as he gripped the steering wheel.

Grinding his teeth, he lurched up the pathway, focusing on his anger, so he might use it. He pressed one finger on the bell and left it there, grabbing the door knocker at the same time and slamming it hard.

Lights went on upstairs, then a voice called: 'All right, all right!'

Sebastian balled up his fist. The hallway light came on, then there was the clink of the chain and Maxwell pulled open his front door.

'What the *fu*—?'

Before Maxwell could finish, Sebastian landed his fist square on his chin.

It was a lucky blow. Shocking pain reverberated back through Sebastian's forearm towards his elbow, as his knuckles hit bone. Maxwell flew backwards, windmilling his arms. He grabbed Sebastian's shirt collar as he fell, and, dazed from the direct hit, Sebastian followed his adversary to the floor, landing square on top of Maxwell's bare chest.

'Wondered when you would turn up,' Maxwell snarled.

He recovered from the first blow in what felt like a microsecond. He bucked his hips and propelled Sebastian off him, easily, then drove his fist into one of Sebastian's kidneys.

'You're a cunt, Maxwell,' gasped Sebastian, trying to writhe away, as deep pain spread through his lower back.

He lay on the cold tiles gasping. Maxwell stood up, wobbly. He leaned against the doorframe.

'You're no match for me.' His breaths were laboured, but triumph was painted across his face.

'Too right.' Sebastian pushed against the floor tiles and with difficulty sat up. 'Fucking rapist!'

Maxwell raised an eyebrow. He seemed untroubled by Sebastian's accusation. Then realisation crossed his features: 'Good old Fran. Women will say literally anything to protect themselves. Too bad you never learned that. Besides, I didn't have to force myself on her, she was all too willing.'

'Liar!' Sebastian shifted into a crouching position, still puffing. 'I'll kill you!'

'No, you won't.' Maxwell enunciated his words like Sebastian would to one of the smaller children at school. 'Face it. You've already lost. There are bigger forces than you at play here.'

'Lily will never come back to you.'

Maxwell smirked. 'We'll see about that.'

'She hates you!'

Maxwell emitted that hearty chuckle of his as he turned to walk back inside. 'Well, you know what they say, bro ... There's a thin line between love and hate.'

With a roar, Sebastian launched himself at Maxwell's knees. They both crashed across the threshold and into the hallway. As they connected with the tiles, Sebastian's teeth crunched together. Blood filled his mouth as he bit his tongue.

But Maxwell was ready for Sebastian this time. He swiftly extricated his legs, then raised a fist and landed it on the back of Sebastian's skull. Sebastian made a woozy grab for him and they rolled through the living-room door, pitching head over shoulder.

Sebastian came out on top, but as he did, something connected with his face – a piece of furniture. Excruciating pain spread from the bridge of his nose and a fountain of blood spurted out. Sebastian cupped his hands to his face, but red spots hit the cream carpet, a crimson contrast. A low moan escaped his lips.

He had nothing left.

Maxwell stood over him, the victor, holding onto the living-room wall for support. 'You're really not very good at this, mummy's boy.'

Sebastian's ears rang, his head full of white noise. He stood carefully, determined not to faint, holding his sleeve to his nose.

'Fuck you!' His words sounded nasal, muffled.

Maxwell indicated the front door, still wide open to the night sky. 'Don't let the door hit you on the way out.'

Humiliated, and wracked with pain, Sebastian stumbled out of Maxwell's house and back towards his car.

Forty-three

In Sebastian's dream, he was at school, the only adult in a sea of children. They poured out of the doors of the gym. But there were far too many of them, surely? They jostled and pushed against one another, their faces indistinct. For some reason, Sebastian was the only teacher there. He was looking for Denny, but couldn't find him. He told the children not to run, but they ignored him. He grabbed at boys and girls as they ran, but they twisted out of his grip, falling back into the swarm.

A hand grabbed for his shoulders to turn him around. Before he saw her, he knew who it was: his mother. She looked up at him, smiling, but blood covered her hair and clothes.

'Sebastian, you left me alone.'

He could barely take in the horror of it: her eyeball perched on the ocular socket, her teeth and tongue exposed.

'What kind of son are you?' Half her face was missing. Her skull was caved in; fragments of bone tangled in her matted hair.

He stared at her, horrified. 'I'm sorry, Mum.'

'It's too late for that.'

The guilt enveloped him. His mother had told him her worst secret, the most shameful thing that could have happened to her, yet he'd left her alone. He'd been more intent on revenge than comforting her.

He awoke with a start. He was bent into an awkward shape behind the steering wheel of his car. He was parked in a layby on an anonymous side road, only hedgerows for company. He did not remember parking up, or falling asleep. He rubbed his shoulders, and stretched his neck. In a dopey stupor he stared at the darkness beyond the windscreen.

So, it was still night. He glanced at the red LED clock on the dashboard. It was just after half past one in the morning. He thought briefly about calling his mother, or Lily, but he'd left both of them on bad terms the previous evening. Surely both women were asleep by now? Even as these thoughts flickered through his mind, he knew what was really fuelling them: cowardice. He had no clue what to say to his wife or his mother. How the hell had it all got to this point?

As if in answer to his question, his phone started vibrating on the dashboard. Sebastian snatched it up eagerly, hoping Lily had decided to give him another chance. It was a text:

IF I CAN'T HAVE MY FAMILY, YOU DEFINITELY CAN'T.

The name on the screen: MAXWELL.

A sickening realisation hit Sebastian in the chest. This was a threat. And he had left Lily and Denny alone.

He had to get back to them, now.

Forty-four

I woke as the smoke alarm kicked in. I'd fallen asleep at the kitchen table. My brain was groggy, but it wasn't from alcohol: I'd only had a couple of glasses after Sebastian had left earlier.

My nostrils flared: smoke.

It hung over the kitchen-diner like a deadly fog, making me feel sleepy. Panic coursed through me; black smoke poured from the stairwell. Tendrils of flames had already made their way up from below, into the living area. There was a cracking of timber. Something – survival instinct, perhaps – flooded through me and I fell from the chair onto the floor, gratefully drawing the cleaner air into my lungs.

Denny! The hallway up to the second storey beyond was full of smoke. I could see nothing. But I knew I had to act fast; the more I dithered, the faster the fire would spread. Even though the maisonette was small and cramped, the distance between me and the upper-storey stairs felt like miles. My eyes streamed and my chest heaved as smoke cloyed in my throat. I crawled across the hallway tiles, trying to stay as low as I could. I moved forwards doggedly, elbows and knees up and down, fighting the urge to run, and moving into the heart of the fire. I couldn't leave my boy behind. It was unthinkable.

I stiffened as I crashed headfirst into something. Blind, I reached out and discovered carpet, steps. The stairs – I'd found them, thank God. The air was a little clearer here. I scrambled up on my hands and knees, coughing violently. Disorientated, I almost turned left into our bedroom. Then I grabbed for Denny's door and found him, sitting on his bed, awake and whimpering.

'Mummy!'

'It's okay, darling, I've got you. I've got you.' I made it up on to my knees, despite the pain in my chest. The air was still smoky in here, but the worst of the fire had not hit it yet. I tried to push Denny's window up. Locked. Frustrated, I whacked my palm against the glass. Where the hell where the keys? Even if I knew, I'd never find them downstairs in the smoke. Now what?

I grabbed Denny's hand and a towel he had abandoned on the floor the night before. We raced through into the bathroom, where I wetted it thoroughly under the cold tap. I grabbed another, this time for me, and did the same.

'You keep this over your head, no matter what, okay?' I blinked back tears, not just from the smoke, but fear for my child. 'Now, it's going to be very dark and scary down there. I need you to crawl with Mummy, on the floor, like a brave boy. You must stay with me. Do not stop. Do you understand?'

Denny looked up at me, his face stricken. He nodded hurriedly. Conscious of the fire gaining even more hold downstairs and marooning us on the second storey, I gave Denny a quick hug, sending up a silent prayer that we would get out alive … And if we both couldn't, that my little boy would.

'Let's go,' I said.

Forty-five

Sebastian left his car in the high street, parked at an angle. He was out of the car and running for the side alley to the Magdalene houses before the engine had stilled. He was not sure what he expected to find at the maisonette. On the way over, he'd imagined the worst-case scenario would be Maxwell, stalking through it with a knife.

The reality was far worse. The maisonette was on fire. The door to the side alley was consumed, driving him back. Even though he wanted to push through the flames, some kind of animal instinct wouldn't allow him to advance.

As he staggered backwards, he fell over something. He groped for it in the dim light, grabbing hold of a plastic handle and a hose as liquid fell on his jeans and hoody. He recognised the smell and feel immediately. A petrol canister. The realisation hit him. Maxwell had poured gas through the letterbox.

Suddenly a dark figure burst from the shadows. Tall, dressed in black, hood up, a scarf over his face. He struck out at Sebastian in his hurry to leave the alleyway.

'Maxwell!' Sebastian cried after the figure, and grabbed at his arm, but the tussle was short-lived. He was pushed against the brickwork, hard. Winded, the breath left Sebastian's lungs, replaced only with dark smoke cloying his throat. A combination of the increasing heat and his injuries from the earlier fight sent Sebastian into a paroxysm of coughing. The figure vanished into the night before he could stop him.

Sebastian scrabbled up, abandoning the can. He staggered as fast as he could back the way he'd come and around the outside of the building, so he could enter the small car park at the rear. He stood up straight and gulped down clean air. As he did so, he found he could see the large kitchen window from here and to his relief, saw Lily and Denny, very much alive, standing there and waving their arms.

Sebastian grasped his wife's logic immediately: from the kitchen window they could probably jump into the car park. A broken ankle would be the least of their problems. But why hadn't they gone out Denny's window? Guilt hit him: because he was the only one with the new window-lock keys and they were in his damned pocket!

'Fire!' Sebastian tried to holler, but coughed again. He ran over to the ice-cream parlour back door, where there was an intercom for the flat above. He jabbed at all the buttons. 'Fire! Fire!'

Looking back up at the kitchen window, he could see Lily trying in desperation to open it. It wouldn't budge. Sebastian looked on in horror: he had installed the locks to keep Maxwell out; now Lily and Denny would die before his eyes because of them. For a single, frozen moment he stared at Lily through the glass. He didn't know what to do. He couldn't save them.

Up at the window, he saw Lily pulling the rubber hose from the sink tap and wielding it like a club, throwing it against the glass. It bounced off, the window intact. At least she was still thinking straight.

'The corners!' Sebastian yelled and gestured. 'Not the middle, the corners!'

Lily must have understood him, or perhaps she'd thought of it too, because she threw the fat, metal end of the hose at the top corner of the window next. After five or six tries, the glass finally spidered, but it didn't break. Lily had the look of a cornered animal, a mama bear who would not let her child die. Eyes wide and teeth bared she ducked out of sight momentarily, picking something up. Then, with a wordless cry she hefted something at the window. A chunk of wood sailed straight through; it was the wooden knife block. It took the rest of the glass with it, showering down into the courtyard below. Sebastian had to duck and cover as shards of glass and the knife block fell onto the concrete.

Finally, now, people came running. A man and a woman and the gangly figure of a teenager rushed across the courtyard in their dressing gowns from the back door of the ice-cream parlour. Sebastian saw the woman make the sign of the cross and grab her mobile from her pocket.

The two men ran back inside. They reappeared with a large, thick blanket, enlisting the help of two other men who'd appeared in the courtyard. Having made the call, the woman took her place holding the blanket, as lights came on in the flats opposite. More people spilled out into the courtyard, now.

'Hurry!' someone shouted.

Sebastian took a corner of the blanket too now, looking up to see Lily seizing Denny by the elbows and pulling him up onto the counter with her. And before he could flinch or grab hold of her, she thrust him out the window. Denny dropped in the centre of the blanket and let out a sharp scream. The woman from the ice-cream parlour picked him up and pulled him to her.

Lily jumped next. She landed heavily, towards the edge of the blanket. Everyone on that side, including Sebastian, went down like dominoes. As Sebastian fell, he felt the back of his head crack against the ground. Stunned, he scrambled to his feet, blood roaring in his ears like the crackling of flames. But he seemed to feel no pain. All he could think was, *Thank God. Thank God!*

'Anyone else?' shouted ice-cream man.

'No.' Lily shook her head as she tended to a crying Denny. She ran her hands over him, checking for injuries. The little boy kept coughing, holding his arm. 'The downstairs flat is empty.'

Sebastian moved in, bending over to hug Lily and Denny. For a moment she seemed about to let him, but then she jerked away, untangling herself, pulling Denny to her. Her face was taut with horror.

'You … you smell of … of petrol!'

Everything seemed hyperreal to Sebastian, like he was watching himself in a movie.

He looked around him, aware now of the flashing of blue lights, the crunch of firemen's boots on the ground. He could hear Denny was just sniffing now, his head cradled in Lily's lap, both of them wrapped in crinkling foil blankets. Paramedics were checking people's grazes for glass. The fire engine was parked around the corner, its thick hose running down the narrow alleyway to the courtyard. The fire, which had seemed so serious and life threatening one moment, was extinguished just as quickly.

That's when Sebastian saw him, further down the alley.

Maxwell.

Lily's ex leaned against a wall, casual as ever, wearing that creased linen shirt over designer jeans. When he saw Sebastian spot him, he turned on his heel and ran back down the alleyway, out towards the high street.

Sebastian did not shout after him. He simply burst across the tarmac. Someone called his name, but he didn't turn in that direction. Only Maxwell was in his sights. He felt the urge to kill him, strangle the life from him, all over again.

But as Sebastian made it onto the high street, his breath was ragged in his throat. The back of his head throbbed now. Something was happening to his vision. The orange glare of the street lamps seemed to loom over him. A small queue of people, waiting for kebabs, turned to stare at him, their faces pale blurs.

Sebastian tried to focus as car headlights and buses thundered past, deafening. His chest, constricted by shock, the fight with Maxwell earlier, would not allow enough oxygen to his brain. The world spun as the blow to the back of his head seemed finally to have an effect. He gasped for air like a drowning man, then collapsed on the pavement, face down.

Everything went black.

PART THREE

September

'A thing is not necessarily true because a man dies for it.'
—Oscar Wilde

Forty-six

Sebastian woke with a pounding headache. As his surroundings shimmered into focus, he was able to discern where he was: the pale linoleum, the antiseptic smell, the crisp, clinical sheets. He was next to a window; it was daylight outside. There was a curtain around the bed; he could hear the hum of voices nearby, the hacking coughs and wracking sobs of other patients. It was a hospital, presumably the General. Not the Cromwell.

Sebastian turned his bruised hand over: there was a cannula in it, secured with tape. There was a tube in his tender nose; it stung but he left it there. He attempted to move and sit up, but sharp pain shot through his body, focusing on the back of his head. He stayed where he was. His tongue felt like sandpaper, too big for his mouth. He swallowed, but his throat was dry; it felt like he was gulping down razor blades. He blinked, then he was gone again, sliding back into oblivion.

When Sebastian came to once more, it was afternoon. He could hear the television playing the end credits of some lunchtime soap opera. This time, Lily was sitting next to his bed. Her face was no longer covered in soot and her hair was wet. She wore flip-flops, cut-off shorts and a T-shirt he didn't recognise, emblazoned with the slogan *BITCH*, in incongruous sequins.

Seeing that he was waking up, Lily proffered him a tight-lipped smile. He tried to return it, though it probably ended up looking more of a pained grimace.

'Hey,' Sebastian croaked. 'Where's Denny?'

He held his hand out to her, but Lily crossed her arms, her hands under her armpits, as if cold.

'Upstairs, in the children's ward. Just for observation. He's okay. We both are.' She sighed, rueful. 'Well, Denny landed badly. I broke his arm.'

'You saved his life!'

Sebastian recalled his panic outside the flat. How he'd just stood by, gawking first at the burning door and stairwell, then up at the kitchen window that wouldn't shift. He hadn't done anything. He'd shouted and gestured, but he should have tried to break in. He should have tried to save Lily and Denny – *his* family. But he'd been useless, just like he'd been when his mother had told him what Maxwell had done to her. Suddenly he wondered if anyone had thought to call Fran, or whether she was staying away on purpose. He couldn't blame her if she was.

'He's loving his cast,' Lily said, a little too brightly. Sebastian could see tears shining in her eyes as she gazed down at him. Her brow furrowed. 'What the hell were you thinking, running off like that?'

For a moment, Sebastian had no idea what his wife was talking about. But then his mind, so full of dark smoke and crackling flames, cleared. Sebastian was back in the courtyard. He'd turned and seen Maxwell, waiting up in the side alley. There could only be one reason Lily's ex was there.

'Maxwell started the fire.'

Lily scowled. Her manner was stiff, almost like she was a stranger. 'He wasn't even there, Sebastian.'

'He was. I saw him…'

Sebastian faltered as her eyes rose skywards, as if she was counting to ten. Why was it so hard to believe? They both knew how ruthless Maxwell was. He was a monster. Resentment coursed through Sebastian's veins that she should not believe him.

'You can't have.' Lily's voice was flat.

'I did!' Sebastian's pitch was too high. He knew he sounded juvenile, like Denny trying to evade the blame for some childish transgression. But he couldn't help himself. He had to make her see, make her realise the depths Maxwell would sink to. This was more serious than they could have ever imagined. He wasn't prepared just to attack Sebastian's mother, he would kill Lily and Denny if he couldn't have them.

'You have to get away – far from here.' Sebastian sat up and swore as pain hit him in the back of the head, spreading down his neck. 'Maxwell won't be satisfied until he's split us up for good. He'll kill us all if he has to. Last night proved that. He's gone mad.'

Lily shook her head. 'It's not like that.'

Sebastian tried another tack. 'I know it seems like he wouldn't hurt Denny, but you have to listen to me. Trust me, Lily…'

'How can I?'

Sebastian blinked, taking in Lily's demeanour with new insight. He regarded her, hurt rending him mute. She was not just wary of him, or the whole situation. Her gaze had a hard edge, her lips pursed.

She was suspicious … of *him*.

'Don't pretend you don't know, Sebastian.'

'Don't know what?' Sebastian couldn't think what she meant – what she was getting at; what was making her so harsh with him.

Lily gave a bitter little chuckle and a shake of the head, as if she resented him making her spell it out. Then she leaned closer to him, her face a picture of contempt.

'You can't have seen him at the fire, Sebastian, because Maxwell is dead.'

Forty-seven

I'd snuck out to see Sebastian while Denny was asleep. I was anxious to get back to him; I didn't want him waking in a strange hospital all alone. I ached all over from fatigue and stress. The doctors had checked me over too and apart from some smoke inhalation I was fine, they said. But I wouldn't be sleeping any time soon. The fire and the murder of my ex in the same night were going to keep me awake for weeks to come. Had Maxwell set the fire, then Sebastian killed him? But the police said Maxwell had died around midnight…

And Sebastian's clothes had smelled of petrol.

So, if Maxwell hadn't tried to kill us, what did that mean? Could Sebastian have tried to murder me and Denny in our beds? But why? Pain lodged in my throat, my heartbeat quickened with panic. He hadn't been himself lately, after all the stress with Maxwell and the stalking, and then with Fran. But why would he take it out on us? What the hell had happened to the gentle, dependable Sebastian I'd known?

As I returned to the children's ward from my visit to Sebastian, still prickling with rage, I rounded the corner, past a gigantic Disney mural, and through an internal window decorated with stickers saw Denny still fast asleep. Someone was standing beside his bed, head bowed, a large present in hand.

'Triss, you need to go.' I appeared next to her in the ward, grabbing her by the elbow. I steered her towards the door.

'Just let me leave him the present…?' Triss's voice cracked.

I folded my arms. 'We don't want anything from you.'

A mother opposite looked up from where she sat trying to distract a toddler who had a nasty burn from scalding water. The little girl was whinging, worrying at the bandages around her leg. Triss seemed to realise we were causing a scene and allowed me to escort her into the hallway.

She lowered her voice as a curious nurse passed by. 'I said I'm sorry, okay? There's a limit to how many times I can apologise.'

I'd flown out of Maxwell's place without waiting to hear any explanations or justifications from my oldest friend. If either of them had called after me, I hadn't heard. By the time I'd stopped walking I was on the common, at Webb's Folly. I'd wandered across the lush green, thinking about the last time Triss and I had been there. With a pang, I had recalled how insistent Triss was that we go to the common that day – the day Fran had collapsed. Had it all been a scheme? Had she called Maxwell when we'd found Fran? Had it been Triss's idea to pretend my mother-in-law had cancer?

Please, no.

'What now, then?' I asked.

Triss threw her hands up in the air. 'How about the truth?'

I sighed. I'd not even given her a chance to speak when she'd appeared at my door that night. There was still a part of me that wanted to give my oldest friend the benefit of the doubt. Another part of me was curious to know just how up to her neck in this she was; why she had crossed over to Maxwell's side from mine. Triss and I went way back. What could he have offered her? Or did he have some kind of hold over her? Could he have been blackmailing her into helping him somehow? I wouldn't have put it past him.

'I swear, it isn't what you think it is…' Triss sat down on one of the corridor benches, her expression earnest. She grimaced at my incredulous face. 'Well, obviously the sex is. That's exactly what you think it is. I'm weak. Pathetic. I hate myself. Okay…?'

I absorbed her diatribe against herself. 'A blind date, you said.'

'Yes, Lily, I swear. When I told you I was meeting a guy off that app, I meant it. I really was. But I got stood up. And Maxwell was there and he bought me a drink and said I looked beautiful and … Oh God!'

Triss dissolved into a fit of ugly crying, her shoulders heaving.

Even so, a tiny bud of hope opened inside me. One thing about being best friends since childhood was not only did you know each other's failings, but you tended to be able to detect when they were lying. Men had always been Triss's weakness. Her bad decisions involving the opposite gender were legendary. Maxwell wouldn't even be the worst of them.

I'd always sensed that Triss had been attracted to Maxwell. That was unsurprising – he *was* good-looking. And, frankly, she was welcome to him. My concerns were not about my best mate taking my sloppy seconds, or even her going out with Denny's father. It was more the thought that Triss could have been involved in Maxwell's campaign to destroy my marriage. Could Maxwell have been using Triss to make me jealous? Could she just be a victim in this Machiavellian plot, too?

I sat down next to her. 'So yesterday was the first day you had sex with Maxwell?'

Triss nodded hastily. She pulled a piece of tissue from her jacket sleeve and dabbed at her freckly nose.

'So, you haven't been coming round here, spying on us, reporting back to Maxwell?'

Triss's eyes widened. 'What? Of course not. I wouldn't—'

I held up a finger, like I did in my classroom when I wanted the kids to stop talking and let me speak. 'When Denny got lost at the fête, did you send him out to Maxwell? Is that why you had a go at Kelly, to divert attention from yourself?'

'No! I love Denny, I was really worried.' Triss shook her head, vehemently. 'I don't even have Maxwell's number. Look, it was just a weird coincidence, that's all. I never set out to hurt you...'

I laughed, shocking Triss. 'I don't care about that.' Then an idea germinated – I held out my hand. 'Show me who you went to meet yesterday.'

Triss grabbed her phone from her jacket pocket and handed it over, putting in her passcode first. I accepted it, swiped a finger across the screen, then tapped on the dating app and it opened.

The last picture Triss looked at sprang into life. A surfy, blond guy with a ready smile stared back at me from the screen. He looked vaguely familiar, like I'd seen him before, in a peripheral role in a soap opera, or maybe a TV advertisement. I tapped on his picture and his profile popped up next. I scrolled downwards until I found his mobile number. As I suspected.

I sighed. 'Triss, this is Maxwell's number. He catfished you.'

'You're kidding…' Triss clocked my expression, realising I had no reason to lie. 'Fuck. Ing. Hell!'

I placed a soothing hand on her back, relief washing through me. Triss was no actor. Maxwell was, though. He'd set Triss up with a fake date via the app, only too happy to provide the consolation prize at the bar, knowing Triss would have been despondent, having been stood up. What puzzled me was how he'd guessed I would go over there that afternoon; or perhaps that was just the icing on the cake. Maybe he'd planned to string Triss along, to make me jealous or create a rift between us. Whatever plan he'd had for that had been killed off as surely as he had. Perhaps he'd met his match in Sebastian. He'd pushed him too far, and Sebastian had snapped. I caught my breath. I could almost taste the petrol I'd smelled on Sebastian's clothes again. I shuddered.

I opened my arms and embraced Triss. She was all I had now. I felt her shuddering body against mine and I was transported back twenty-five years, when our situations had been reversed: when I was crying my eyes out in Triss's arms, after Mum had died.

My best friend did not betray me.

Forty-eight

'I didn't kill Maxwell.'

Sebastian had repeated this mantra on a loop to Lily, to no avail.

He couldn't have … could he? It was true he had a missing hour or so between leaving Maxwell's and arriving at the maisonette. But he knew Maxwell had been alive when he left him. Sebastian recalled the dark figure in the alleyway by the front door. And the petrol can. And the raw strength as he'd been pushed back against the brickwork. No, Maxwell had been there. The police must have been wrong about the timings. And then, after Lily and Denny had jumped from the window, he was sure he had seen Maxwell in the alleyway … hadn't he?

The more he thought about it, the more confident he became. Lily was jumping to conclusions. Sebastian was not a killer.

Lily's face had been like stone. 'How could you do this?' she said through gritted teeth. 'To Denny. To me! Maxwell had his faults, but kill him?'

'I did not kill him!'

'How can I believe you? Look at you: you admit you fought with him. And the fire … What the hell were you thinking? We were still inside!'

Sebastian blinked, unable to follow. Then it clicked. 'You're not suggesting I did that?'

Lily stared at him. 'Did you?'

Sebastian felt like she'd punched him in the gut. He gasped as the air left him; he could not believe she'd doubt him like this. 'Of course not! I love you. I love Denny! I came to rescue you. Maxwell sent me a text message…'

He groped for his clothes, his phone. They were not on his

nightstand, or anywhere nearby. His keys were gone too. On top of the nightstand sat his wallet, nothing else.

Lily's face was stony. 'The police must have taken them.'

The curtain fluttered behind her. A young nurse with vibrant purple hair appeared. In a low but firm voice, she asked Lily to leave. They were upsetting the other patients.

'Happy to.' Lily didn't look at the nurse, staring instead at Sebastian, as if cataloguing his face for the last time.

'Lily, let's not do this…' Sebastian began, but she was already standing. She shouldered past the nurse and through the curtain. It swung back after her.

Sebastian lay back down, his head spinning. Lily thought he'd tried to kill her and Denny. But it had to have been Maxwell; whoever had killed him, must have done so after he'd set the fire … He'd sent the text message after Sebastian had left him. And then he'd seen him, in the alleyway. But before he could puzzle this any more, he slipped back into unconsciousness.

Again, he dreamed of looking for Denny in school, but this time he saw that Maxwell had him. Sebastian found himself walking down corridor after corridor, Maxwell turning the corner with the little boy just ahead of him, every time he caught sight of them. It didn't matter how fast Sebastian ran, he was always five steps behind.

He woke in the early evening to find a doctor standing at his bedside. She was young, her face pulled in a perpetual frown, her shoulders tense with stress. She muttered something about someone to see him. On cue, the curtain parted again and two people, a man and a woman, entered his little enclosed space. Sebastian's gut twisted in apprehension as soon as he recognised them: Detective Inspector Su and Sergeant Meyer.

'In the wars again, Mr Adair?' Detective Su commented.

Sebastian nodded, his throat dry.

'We'd like to ask you a couple of questions, if you're up to it?' said Meyer, pulling a notebook and stubby pencil from his inside jacket pocket.

Su traced the end of the bed with long fingers, as if she was bored. 'So, Mr Adair, can you tell us what happened?'

'Err, yes, I got to the maisonette and the whole place was on fire—'

Detective Su raised a slender hand. 'Not at your flat, Mr Adair. At Mr Stevens' home. You went to see him last night, didn't you?'

Sebastian's thoughts clamoured through his brain. Had Lily called the police? Surely not. His mother definitely wouldn't have. But there would be evidence – Sebastian had been at Maxwell's; it was pointless to deny it. Sebastian opted for the truth.

'Yes. We fought.' He gestured to his swollen face.

Meyer scribbled something down.

Su raised a perfectly plucked eyebrow. 'About what?'

'You know that Maxwell – Mr Stevens – used to be married to my wife, Lily Adair…' He stopped, resentment blooming in his chest again, as he recalled his mother's tearful confession.

He forced it down. He could not tell the police about the rape. He knew he had to downplay anything that gave him motive to kill Maxwell; he was glad he'd not told Lily about what Maxwell had done to his mother. It was obvious now that Sebastian was a suspect. He could not be seen to be glad Maxwell was dead.

Su walked over to the window, her back to him now. 'I see. So, this was about you feeling Mr Stevens was encroaching on your territory?'

Sebastian ignored her jibe. 'He was alive when I left.'

Meyer sniffed loudly. 'We have a witness who says they saw a black Renault leaving Mr Stevens' property around midnight.'

Su turned. She picked an imaginary thread from her sleeve. 'You drive a black Renault, isn't that right, Mr Adair?'

Sebastian gritted his teeth. 'Yes. But, like I said, he was alive when I left. And I saw him after that … at the fire…'

But as Sebastian said these words, his memory shifted. The sight of Maxwell, hood up, scarf over his face, then again in the alleyway behind the maisonette, seemed to glitch, like bad reception on a TV screen. For the first time, doubt pierced Sebastian's psyche. Could Lily be right? Maybe he *had* imagined her ex being there. But who else could have started the fire?

'The pathologist estimates Mr Stevens' time of death as being around midnight. When was the fire, Sergeant Meyer?'

The other man flicked back a page. 'Approximately one-thirty a.m., ma'am.'

Maxwell *had* disappeared ridiculously quickly when Sebastian chased after him. Had the thump he received to the back of his head made him hallucinate? Sebastian recalled Lily's stiff posture by his bedside, her disbelief that Maxwell could have been at the scene.

'He was alive when I left,' Sebastian repeated, his fists clenched. He recalled the text message. 'I have proof! He sent me a message. That was why I went to the flat. You have my phone. Check it, you'll see.'

'I can assure you, we don't.' Su looked at Sebastian for the first time. Her dark-brown eyes were arresting; he felt like she could see into his soul.

Confusion pierced through Sebastian. If the police hadn't taken it from his bedside, who had? 'But my clothes … my phone … they were taken when I came in?'

Detective Su shook her head. 'Is there anything else you would like to tell us, Mr Adair?'

Sebastian averted his gaze, shook his head. Playing down his potential motive seemed his best option. He could not tell them about Maxwell's elaborate deception with his mother; or how he'd strong-armed her into it. First, he had to talk to Lily again, see if she had spoken to the police. Figure out what to do.

Su sighed and flicked a hand at Meyer. As she parted the curtain, Meyer moved towards Sebastian, a business card extended from his chubby fingers.

'If you remember anything else,' he muttered.

The curtain fell back into place behind him.

Still stiff and sore, Sebastian sat up and swung his legs over the edge of the bed. He winced as he pulled the oxygen tube carefully from his raw, bulbous nose.

He had to get out. Now.

Forty-nine

Sebastian rose and dressed carefully. There was a bag of clothes next to his bed now; items from a cheap outlet store with their labels still on. He presumed a nurse had left them for him, realising his clothes had been removed.

His ribs ached; just one of the legacies from his fight with Maxwell. Getting both legs into the boxers and then the tracksuit bottoms was excruciating. He picked up his wallet, checking inside. The money and cards were there; whoever had taken his clothes and phone had not been interested in robbery. For the first time, he wondered if Lily might have taken his clothes. It had been her suggestion it was the police, after all. But that was absurd. Why would she?

He pulled on the T-shirt with a hiss of pain, nostrils flaring from the stench of smoke coming off his hair. There was a pair of flip-flops too. He slipped them on, feeling the strange plastic between his toes.

Sebastian parted the curtain and looked around the room. It was a small side ward, just four beds. There was an internal window that looked directly onto the nurses' station. The ward sister sat there in her dark-blue uniform, staring at a computer screen and tapping keys. Another nurse appeared and reached over her, grabbing a sheaf of paper.

He was relieved to see no one appeared to be guarding him; there were no police nearby, as far as he could see. So that meant Su and Meyer must have been just making preliminary enquiries, as Sebastian was the last person to see Maxwell alive. They hadn't read him his rights, after all. It hadn't been an arrest – they hadn't interviewed him under caution.

But he was not stupid: Sebastian knew how bad it looked for him. They would be returning, and soon. He had to see Lily and find out what she was going to tell them. And he also had to find out who had killed Maxwell, because it sure as hell wasn't him.

The bed next to Sebastian was empty; opposite was an old man with sunken cheeks, asleep, the covers pulled up to his chin. Next to him, a young guy with a broad chest and bulging muscles lay with his leg in traction. He turned the pages of a bodybuilding magazine. He looked up as he perceived the swish of Sebastian's curtain and gave him a nod, before returning to his reading.

Sebastian did not want to have to go through the rigmarole of discharging himself. They would do everything they could to delay him, citing all kinds of concerns – some real, others just tactics. What really worried Sebastian was that they might notify Su and Meyer if he attempted to leave and he had to see Lily, immediately.

Sebastian strode towards the door of the ward. He was conscious of the *thwack-thwack-thwack* of the flip-flops under the soles of his feet, but he did not flinch. He held up his head and made it out into the corridor, willing the ward sister not to look up from her computer.

She didn't. But as Sebastian rounded the corner, another nurse coming in the opposite direction clocked him. She slowed. She flashed Sebastian a concerned smile, her visage saying, *Where do you think you're going?*

He tried to smile, but didn't break his stride. 'Just going down to the shop to buy some magazines. Getting a bit bored.'

The nurse nodded and continued on her way, but as she passed Sebastian he noted that she checked her watch, pinned to the front of her blue smock. He realised she was going to see how long it took him. Time really was of the essence, now.

First, Sebastian limped his way up to the children's ward. He was able to follow the signs through the labyrinthine building, but even if he'd not seen them, he couldn't fail to miss the gaudy cartoon characters on the walls to guide preoccupied parents in the right direction. He made it past the door and its codes by tagging along with a large family group who all seemed to be visiting the same child, carrying balloons and gifts. As siblings, cousins and grandparents filed past, Sebastian obligingly kept the door open for the father, who was carrying a large teddy bear, as well as a teen sister who was holding onto the biggest bunch of helium balloons Sebastian had ever seen.

He didn't get much further than reception, though. A burly male nurse, hands on his hips, blocked Sebastian's way and looked him up and down. 'You look like you been in the wars, mate.'

Sebastian touched his raw nose, self-conscious. 'I'm here to see Denny Stevens.'

The male nurse sighed. 'You a relative?'

'I'm his stepfather.'

The male nurse turned his back and huddled with a younger, female nurse who was passing by carrying dirty linen. Just as Sebastian was about to demand whether he could go through, the female nurse spoke, revealing a strong Eastern European accent.

'Denny gone. Discharged.' She indicated the bundle of bedclothes in her arms. 'I change his sheets, now.'

Thanking them, Sebastian turned on his heel as swiftly as his flip-flops would allow. Shuffling his way out of the ward, he made it into the lift and down to the ground floor without further incident. The big metal doors parted and he drifted out, hesitant now. In the hallway were a variety of people: a couple of doctors caught up near a vending machine; a male nurse tending to an old woman who trailed an IV stand after her; visitors cutting across the main reception, towards the small café.

A security guard floated near the entrance. He was a big bear of a man with a grey beard and a bald head; his radio was bursting with static. If he knew Sebastian was about to escape, he didn't show it.

Sebastian fixed his sights ahead and walked towards the big double doors of the entrance. He sailed straight past the burly security guard, into the bright sunlight of the ambulance bay beyond. No one called him back or shouted after him.

He was out.

Fifty

On autopilot, Sebastian managed to hop on a bus and make his way back to the town centre. He just wanted to be home. He'd not been back, not properly, in weeks; now he felt its pull like he was a sailor drawn to the Sirens. Like them, he fantasised about the embrace, the warmth he expected to find. In his confused mind, he felt sure he would get back and Lily and Denny would be waiting for him. Lily would tell him that everything had been a mistake; it had all been just a bad dream.

But as Sebastian rounded the corner of the car park behind the maisonette, he was shocked all over again by the broken glass, the yellow police tape and the scorch marks on the windowsills. There was a strong tang of burnt plastic in the air; it mixed with a more earthy, wood-and-ash smell. He appreciated for the first time just how bad the fire had been. His recollection had been like that of a nightmare: disjointed and perilous, but ultimately hazy.

In the cold light of day, Lily and Denny's lucky escape took his breath away. The alleyway that ran through to the front door and out towards the high street was impassable. It was black with soot, with much of the front of the building demolished by the heat as the brickwork ruptured outwards. But even if rubble hadn't littered the gangway, Sebastian realised he would never be able to make it up the stairs and into the flat. The stairwell was gone altogether. There was a strong undertone to the smoke and soot: he recognised the source as petrol, remembering the can he'd tripped over the night before. Could it have been pure bad luck – an unprovoked arson attack? No. With everything that had happened, lately, there was no way this was random. It had to have been Maxwell. But then he'd been killed. The police *must* have got when that happened wrong. Was the murder retribution for setting the fire? Lily couldn't have done anything like that … Could she? Sebastian felt cold. Had Maxwell finally pushed Lily too far…?

Sebastian took a quick look around. The family from the ice-cream parlour was nowhere in sight; neither were there any police – just their yellow tape blowing in the breeze. It was late in the evening now; the authorities would not be back until tomorrow. Even so, he did not want to linger.

He gritted his teeth and, stared at the flat roof just below Denny's bedroom. He could see the glass to the window was broken there, now; it was replaced with a yellow 'X' of tape. With some effort, he was sure he could make it up there. He abandoned the flip-flops, letting them fall from his feet, then he placed a bare foot against the sill of the window of the empty downstairs flat and pushed himself up.

His ribs protested, but Sebastian finally made it onto the flat roof. He collapsed onto gritty roofing felt, then rolled over and lay there a moment, breathing through the pain that wracked his entire body. Wobbly and light-headed, he stood, resting his palms on his knees. He felt a hundred years old and the back of his head throbbed. Very gingerly, he fed one leg and then the other through the broken window, anxious about cutting his bare feet on more glass. To his surprise, there was very little of it on the other side. Whoever had broken this window had done it carefully.

Inside the flat at last, he winced at the smell. It was like dozens of blackened bonfires, drowned by rain. He jumped down, his bare feet landing on the sodden carpet. Drenched soft toys sat limp and sad on the shelves. Posters and wallpaper hung in sodden ribbons from the wall, soaked by the firemen's hose. An involuntary shiver worked through Sebastian, both from the cold dampness under his soles and the close call his wife and stepchild had had.

Denny's room was smoke- and water-damaged, but more or less intact. Sebastian picked his way through the top storey with care. He was worried about floor joists, especially upstairs. He didn't need to plunge through to the lower floor, or worse, the empty flat under-neath. But, besides the odd creak underfoot, there were no worrying or ominous structural groans. After a few steps, Sebastian grew in confidence. He padded through to his and Lily's bedroom. Like Denny's room, it had escaped the worst of the fire. It was mostly dry too, the firemen having focused their jets of water up to the left side of the house where the fire had raged.

Sebastian went to the wardrobe and opened it: all their clothes smelled awful. Even so, he took a pair of socks from the chest of drawers, dried the soles of his feet off on the duvet and pulled them on. He needed shoes. He dropped to the floor and spotted his train-ers underneath the bed. He grabbed them and pulled them towards him, then shoved them onto his feet. That was better.

On top of the chest was Lily's handbag. Sebastian rooted through it, glad she hadn't hung it up downstairs. Inside was her phone. Perfect. He grabbed the bag, and took it with him.

If he was going to see Lily next, he still needed a key for the car. He had no idea who could have taken his from the hospital, but there was a spare. Since Lily didn't drive, he'd never given it to her. If he remembered correctly, he had left it in his bedside cabinet. He yanked out the drawer and tossed its contents on the bed. Mostly papers, a book he'd never finished, various odds and ends and … the key. He picked it up like a precious artefact and pocketed it.

The rain started pouring down as Sebastian left the maisonette the way he'd gone in: via the flat roof below Denny's room. As he jumped down onto the tarmac, he groaned loudly with pain.

From the corner of his eye he saw someone nearby start, then heard them laugh. 'Jesus! Where'd you come from?'

Sebastian froze. It was the teenage son of the couple from the ice-cream parlour; he was standing in his pink-and-white striped apron, his arms full of cardboard, heading for the big green bin at the back of the courtyard.

Sebastian raised a hand in greeting, and indicated Lily's bag. 'Stairs are out. And I had to get a few things.'

The youth nodded. 'Everybody okay, then?'

Sebastian smiled and gave him a thumbs-up. 'And thank you, again.'

The teen shrugged. 'No worries.' He went back to his recycling.

Sebastian unlocked the car and slid in behind the wheel. As he put the key in the ignition, something caught his eye. He turned and saw a plastic bag on the passenger seat.

The bag was wrapped around something. Heavy, hard and long – he realised with a thud of his heart what it was. Unable to help himself, almost in a trance, he unwrapped the plastic. The item fell out onto the passenger seat.

A knife, its blade dulled with dried blood.

Fifty-one

Sebastian left the little courtyard, and pulled out into the traffic, but, as he slowed for the lights at the junction, he spied a Community Support Officer in his wing mirror. He had to fight the urge to slump down in his seat. The CSO was just behind Sebastian's car, walking up the pavement on his side of the road in his yellow hi-vis jacket. Sebastian shouldn't have touched the knife, he knew that. But he had, so what could he have done about it? He'd dropped it in Lily's bag, as if it was burning his fingers.

Finally, the traffic moved on and Sebastian left the CSO in his wake. As he flicked the indicator to turn the corner, his tormented stare reflected back at him in the rear-view mirror. In his mind's eye he saw Lily by his hospital bedside again. Her rigid and severe manner, her accusations.

He had to see her.

Sebastian had a fairly good idea of where Lily would be. He pressed the name on Lily's phone.

It rang only once. 'Sebastian?'

Triss's voice on the end of the line was suspicious, cold. No doubt Lily had told her what he was supposed to have done – to Maxwell, to her and Denny. He closed his eyes, the betrayal still piercing through him.

'Is Lily with you?'

'No,' Triss replied instantly. But he knew her, she was a terrible liar. Sebastian gritted his teeth and rang off. Then headed for Triss's flat. When he parked outside Triss's home, it was growing dark. It was an ugly concrete nineties' low-rise block of flats, with hanging baskets placed around the main door to try to offset the grimness. It was opposite a small scrapyard, filled with the metal skeletons of crushed cars. Sebastian hovered on the front doorstep, then pushed at the door in the hope it would open. It did.

He wandered into yet more concrete; it looked more like a multistorey car park than a home. There was a bank of metal post-boxes opposite him, plus a noticeboard, the condensation on its Perspex cover almost rendering its posters for salsa classes and international phonecards unreadable. His nostrils wrinkled as he smelled the stale dregs of beer – and perhaps something worse – on the stairs. No wonder Triss had preferred it at the maisonette.

Fatigue and pain gnawed at Sebastian's bones, but he made it up the stairs to the top floor of the building. As he drifted past the open front door of one flat, a big Staffie launched itself at him, only to be arrested by a child's safety gate screwed into the wood of the doorframe. He flinched, giving the creature a wide berth as it continued to bark furiously. No one came to see to it, though he could hear the tones of a jeering chat show inside.

Triss's flat was next door. Sebastian pressed his finger on the doorbell. The door opened, the chain rattled and Triss peered through the gap.

'Oh, so you finally turned up, then.'

Irritation coursed through Sebastian, but he tamped it down. 'I need to see Lily.'

'Yeah, I bet you do.' Triss shut the door.

Sebastian was about to press the doorbell again when he heard the clatter of the chain as Triss unhooked it. She opened the door, her posture hostile, as if she'd rugby tackle him at any moment. She was taller than him, so she might just have managed it. He hesitated on the threshold. Was she going to stop him seeing Lily? Her body language was proprietorial, challenging.

'Well, I suppose you'd better come in, then!' Triss said at last, waving him in impatiently, like he was one of the kids in her class.

Sebastian skulked into the flat after her. The hallway was narrow and windowless; there was scarred lino underfoot. The walls were painted magnolia. Sebastian could smell damp in the air.

Triss bid him follow her into the room furthest away, at the end of the dingy corridor. Lily and Denny lounged on the sofa together, watching *Finding Nemo* on DVD. His head rested on her shoulder, thumb in his mouth as she tousled his hair. But as soon as Sebastian came in, Lily sat up, wary. Denny sat up too, eyes wide. Sebastian groaned inwardly. This was not going to be easy.

'C'mon mate, let's go to the shop, get some sweets.' Triss held a hand out to Denny. The little boy was noticeably thrilled at the thought of getting sweets after dark, but he looked from Sebastian to his mother for reassurance.

Lily nodded and smiled. 'It's fine, Denny. See you in ten minutes.' She shot Sebastian a warning glance; message received. She hadn't told Denny about Maxwell, yet.

Triss gave Sebastian a long stare, then took Denny's hand and led him from the room slamming the door closed after them.

Sebastian collapsed in a threadbare armchair opposite Lily. He looked around the small room. Triss had worked hard to make the place nice: there were throws on the sofa, black-and-white prints on the wall. A small television sat on an upcycled table in the corner, and there was a rag rug on the floor. But it was hard to conceal the cigarette burns on the cheap cord carpet, or the ominous wet patches on the ceiling. He could hear muffled voices from the other flats, the continued barking of the dog next door. It was a far cry from the life Sebastian had led at his mother's quiet, exclusive home out near the common, or even the imposing dormitories of his boarding school.

'They haven't arrested you yet, then,' said Lily.

Sebastian blinked. 'You thought they would?' He was hurt, but he couldn't go down that route right now. Instead he fixed her with what he imagined to be a sympathetic stare. 'I know, Lily.'

'Know what?' Lily's hostility faltered for the first time. She adopted a defensive pose, her arms crossed, her feet pulled up underneath her.

It was as if she couldn't bear even the possibility of her limbs crossing into his space. She looked even more confused and suspicious than she had before. 'Sebastian, what the hell are you talking about?'

Sebastian chose his words carefully. 'I'm saying I understand how you must have felt ... For him to have gone this far – endangered Denny's life. It had to be the straw that broke the camel's back. You thought you had no choice. You were protecting Denny. I understand that...'

'Whoa, whoa.' Lily put a hand in the air. 'You better not be saying what I think you're saying ... You think I could have killed Maxwell? Seriously!'

But Lily's outrage did not stop Sebastian in his tracks. 'I found the knife, Lily. In my car. I forgive you.'

'Shut up!' Lily was on her feet, as if she might move across the narrow room and strike Sebastian across the face. She flexed her hand, grabbing it with her other to stop herself. Then she seemed to register his last three words. 'Wait. Forgive me for what?'

'Trying to frame me. I understand. You can't be parted from Denny. You had to pin it on me – I'm the most likely suspect. But we can sort all of this—'

'For Christ's sake, Sebastian, will you listen to yourself?' She took another step back, like she didn't trust herself. She closed her eyes and inhaled, to calm down.

Sebastian could still see the anger in her stance, lurking below the surface, just waiting to peak again as she forced out the words. 'How the hell could I have killed Maxwell? He died around midnight, the police said. I was asleep. The fire started not long after! Or do you think I started that, too?'

Confusion swirled through Sebastian's mind. That seemed as nonsensical as him starting it. The police had to have been wrong...

Lily looked at him like DI Su had. She gave a pained, slightly weary shake of her head. 'You've been under a lot of pressure, for months—'

Sebastian cut in. 'No. No!'

'The wedding, the school inspection, Maxwell's meddling, the problems with Denny, the fake cancer diagnosis…' There were tears in Lily's eyes. 'It's no wonder … You were pushed too far. You're not bad, you just cracked.'

'I didn't kill him!' he bellowed suddenly.

But as Sebastian saw Lily's frightened eyes, for a microsecond he wondered. He *had* been the last person to see Maxwell alive. Even Sebastian could see how bad it looked for him. Maybe he had done the deed and then erased it from his mind? After all, who could have slipped in and killed Maxwell, if it wasn't him or Lily? And who could have set the fire?

Lily threw her hands in the air. 'Then who did all this, Sebastian? You tell me!'

You tell me. A vision hit his mind's eye: he saw Triss, sitting at his kitchen table, that smirk on her face. Like she owned the place. Like she had replaced him, made him extraneous. He recalled the figure in the dark hoody, the strength as they'd grabbed him and pushed him hard against the brickwork. Triss had always been tall, strong, lithe, like a gymnast. She'd always wanted Lily and Denny to herself. It was so obvious now. It hadn't been Maxwell, after all.

'Where was Triss at midnight last night, Lily?'

◉

I wait, biding my time. I look at my watch. The timing is absolutely crucial for the ultimate plan, the endgame I have spent all these months planning. A car roars away from Maxwell's house.

Now.

I have dressed all in black. My form is indiscernible from the shadows as I scamper across the lawn. I spy him through the open blinds as he lurches from his living room out into the bright, white hallway. The inner porch door is still open, though he ignores it. He ducks into the downstairs wet room. Perfect.

Full of purpose, I reach forwards and place a hand on the porch door, letting it creak loudly. This will bring him to the porch, where I want him.

Seconds later, he's there. He's bare-chested, wearing just a pair of jogging bottoms, bare feet. With an arrogant swagger, he's ready to land another fist and give the cocky little shit who just left another pounding. He wrenches open the front door again, just as I hide, camouflaged by a tall ornamental fern.

No one there.

Maxwell falters. Standing on the porch step, he doubts himself. He's so wired, perhaps the sound of the door was in his head? I feel a flicker of a smile pass across my face.

A slight breeze ruffles through the tall hedges that line his property. The dog barks somewhere inside the house. A bat flits across the black-and-purple sky.

Just as he's about to turn on his heel I clear my throat deliberately. His head snaps around. He narrows his eyes, trying to make out shapes in the darkness.

'Hello?'

Only the breeze answers him.

I fancy that a cold finger of fear works its way down his back now. Before it can hurry him back inside, I let out an unmistakable whimper. I allow it to escape, cutting through the night air.

'Who's there?'

Maxwell moves from the hall into the garden. A slash of light illuminates the bottom half of his face: a smirk tugs at his lips.

'It's okay, darling.' He's guessed it's me. He raises both his arms in my direction. In his mind, he fancies he must look like an all-forgiving angel. So predictable.

I rush towards him, like he wants me to. He braces himself to envelop me in his arms. Maxwell likes to hug crying women; it makes him feel manly, a protector. But I do not throw myself into his embrace.

I stop dead just a fist's distance from him. Before he can beckon me closer, I thrust forwards, feeling the deep connection between us. The blow is not the raw, red, heat of the punch he gave Sebastian earlier. This time, it feels deep, sharp and cold.

'Wha…?'

Then he realises. I've not hit him at all.

His gaze finds its way towards the knife buried deep in his stomach. He looks down, stupefied. I imagine the kaleidoscope of thoughts and images rushing through his mind, chased by thoughts of his impending death. Not now. Surely not now! And why?

He doesn't have time to puzzle this, because I pull the knife free again. He utters a strangled cry and falls to his knees, back across the threshold and into the porch. He can feel his life pouring from him, he is becoming more light-headed by the second. He can't raise his head; it's too heavy.

I pull a plastic carrier bag from my pocket and wrap the knife in it. Then I clamber over him, kicking his hand away as he grasps at my ankle. I push my way into the hall, making sure I close the front door after me, the sound of nails on the tiles wandering towards me. The dog sniffs around me – she knows me, after all – as I locate what I'm looking for. His mobile, plugged into a charger in the kitchen. I pocket it.

I slip back into the porch, shutting the dog in the house and Our Mutual Friend in the porch. Well, it's the kindest thing, really. I don't want her lapping up his blood.

I kneel and murmur. 'If there was any other way…'

He gargles something unintelligible. There's blood on his lips. Internal *haemorrhage. It does seem a waste, but Our Mutual Friend is now surplus to requirements. Besides, from the offset, his demise was inevitable, if I was to make sure my plan worked out. I leave, making sure the porch door clicks shut behind me.*

I'm sure he realises his predicament straight away. He is half-dressed, with no phone, badly wounded with unconsciousness rapidly approaching. And he is locked out of his home, yet also masked by the tall hedgerows outside. No one will see him, until it's too late.

Now, for the final phase.

Fifty-two

Lily collapsed back on the sofa, head in her hands, as if she couldn't hold her own body up any longer. 'Stop it.'

But it all slotted into place for Sebastian. It made perfect sense. Lily and Triss had been torn apart by Maxwell; she can't have been thinking clearly. Perhaps she'd only wanted to talk to him, yet it had got out of control. Or maybe she'd planned it. Whatever the case, she'd waited until Sebastian had left, then stabbed Maxwell. The front of Maxwell's home was surrounded by leylandii, so it was likely no one could have seen Triss butchering Maxwell just feet away.

'Think about it, Lily,' Sebastian entreated. 'Triss has always been so close to you. She probably thought she was protecting you from him. And she wants to protect you from me too! And the fire. That was her too … I fought with her; I thought she was Maxwell! Maybe she didn't mean to hurt you. She just wanted you here. With her. She—'

Lily sat up, her expression more exasperated than ever. 'Are you on drugs? Or is this what a breakdown looks like? Triss couldn't stamp on a bloody snail without giving it a matchbox funeral. Never mind kill Denny's dad. Whatever he'd done – to her or to me – he was still Denny's father.'

'She put the knife in my car! She's got Denny, this could all be a ruse!' Sebastian began.

'We're back!' Triss announced her presence in a sing-song voice as the front door slammed behind her.

Lily raised an eyebrow: *See?*

But Sebastian still wasn't sold. As Triss moved into the room ahead of Denny, Sebastian pounced. He grabbed her by both arms and slammed her against the wall like he was sure she had done to him the night before, taking advantage of surprise himself, this time. The back of her head hit the wall hard.

'You did it, didn't you?' he screamed. 'You killed Maxwell and tried to frame me! And the fire – you were there. It was you who put petrol through the letterbox, wasn't it?'

Stunned, Triss stared at Sebastian as he hollered in her face and shook her; behind him, Lily shrieked in both horror and rage. Denny burst into tears.

'Get. Off. Her!' Lily raced forwards and hooked her hands onto his shoulders, attempting to peel him off. Sebastian shook her off with ease as he choked Triss, who clawed at his hands with stubby fingernails.

An explosion of pain ricocheted off his shoulder. It made him let go of Triss and fall to one knee. Dazed now, he looked up at Lily. She was holding a tall floor lamp like a staff, her chest heaving with the exertion of hitting him with it.

Lily shook her head, tears pouring down her cheeks. 'And you ask why I think you did it?'

She threw the lamp down, holding out an arm for Denny who ran straight for her. He hid his face from the scene. Triss took a deep breath and sat down on the sofa, putting her head between her knees.

Shame flooded through Sebastian. He stood up and moved across the room towards his Lily, but she jerked away. He raised both hands, as if to try and grab at the imaginary silken thread that once bound them together. But it was gone. Lily only glared at him with hatred and distrust.

In that moment, Sebastian finally grasped that it was fruitless; the damage had been done. There could be no way back for them, even if he somehow managed to extricate himself from this mess.

'What's happened to us?' he whispered.

Sebastian reached out again towards her, wanting to caress her shoulder, her hair. One last time. But she raised her arm, a barrier against his touch. She brought Triss and Denny into her arms. Triss was shaking, burying her head in Lily's neck.

'You did,' she spat. 'You couldn't just trust in us, could you? If you'd just kept away from Maxwell, not let him mess with us … But you had to be the big man, didn't you?'

The words fell on Sebastian's ears. As he stared at Lily and Triss – Lily's dark skin pressed against Triss's pale face – he realised that Triss wasn't capable of hurting the woman who had been her sister, her protector … the love of her life. And it was as if a light turned on then. It was if Sebastian could see time through a tunnel: the past, present and future were no longer fragmented, but all lined up in a linear fashion. The whole situation, from the very beginning, was illuminated for him.

And it didn't just start with Maxwell. The seeds of this day had been sown much further back.

Of course.

Sebastian turned on his heel and ran out of the flat.

He could still fix this.

Fifty-three

Time compressed once again. Suddenly Sebastian was back at his mother's house. He screeched to a halt outside. He delved into the backseat of the car, grateful that he'd forgotten to hand Lily's bag back to her at Triss's. It meant he still had her phone.

He scrolled through the unfamiliar handset, looking for its record function. As he did so, it rang in his hand. He didn't recognise the number, but it was an Epsom landline, so he answered.

'Mr Adair.' It was the curt, unflappable tones of Detective Su. 'I hear you've left the hospital…'

Paranoia struck him, now. How had Su known he had Lily's phone, if she wasn't with Lily right now? But then he took a deep breath. He had to get a hold of himself. Su was a detective, after all. She could have been trying all their numbers for hours, for all he knew.

'I'm not on the run, if that's what you mean.'

'Your words, Sebastian,' Detective Su sighed. 'How about you come to the station, explain yourself?'

Sebastian gritted his teeth. 'I'll do that. I just have to sort something first.'

He rang off before she answered. Then he swiped through and found the voice memo app, pressed the red record button, and slipped the phone inside his jeans pocket.

Getting out of the car he let himself into his mother's house. Outside, dark had fallen. Was it really just twenty-four hours since he'd been here last? Since he'd discovered his mother in on the scam, he'd been beaten literally as well as figuratively by Maxwell; almost seen his wife and stepson killed in a fire; then felt the burn of Lily's suspicion – and even his own – over Maxwell's murder. Then he'd been accused of arson and the attempted murder of Lily and Denny. It felt like years, not just a single day. Yet at his mother's home, everything looked the same.

'Mum!' Sebastian strode through the tiled hall, into the living room.

The television was on, as usual. The patio windows were closed. He faltered as he took in the empty sofa. He ducked back out, calling as he went. She was not in the kitchen, either.

'Mum?'

He heard footsteps on the stairs behind him. He wheeled around as Fran appeared at the top. She peered down at him through the bannisters, her face a picture of maternal concern. She wore make-up now, her hair done, the headscarf abandoned. He noted she had a small bald patch at the back. That would be where she had pulled hair out, to present to him, evidence of her hair loss due to her imaginary chemo.

'Darling, are you all right?' She began her descent, one step at a time, still hiding behind the persona of the weak old woman, instead of the Lady Macbeth she really was.

'You look awful. Let me fix you some cocoa.' She appeared next to Sebastian in the hall, one hand still on the bannister.

'Mum, I *know*.'

His mother looked askance at him but did not reply. Sebastian followed her into the kitchen. He felt a nervous tremor ripple through him. Every inch of his body felt stressed: across his shoulders, down his spine and legs and into his feet. In his pocket, the phone was recording.

'Know what, darling?' She gave him an absent smile.

'It was you, all along. You didn't help Maxwell … Maxwell was the one helping you!'

*The first time I saw him, I was at the Cromwell for an appointment.
Such is the old boys' network, your dead father's reputation meant I got
first-class service, even thirty years later. That was why I got lead consultant Maxwell Stevens making an appearance when I'd only gone to have
a nasty cut seen to that I'd sustained gardening.*

*At least, that's what he'd said; he must have thought I was born yes-
terday. He was an oncologist. Why would he see me? He had worked
out I was related to you, of course. You and Lily had announced your
whirlwind engagement just a few weeks earlier, the date already set for
May the twenty-eighth, just a month away. I'd been knocked sideways by
the news, so Maxwell must have been too. Dealing with my cut, he was
very charming, but I realised straight away he was fishing for information about you both.*

*That's when I knew he would be perfect for my plan to split you up.
To end the ridiculous charade of your marriage.*

*'How about we continue this conversation over a drink, Frances?'
Maxwell flashed me his pearly white teeth.*

*'Fran, please.' I gave him my best girlish giggle; a man like Maxwell
would require it. 'But I'm a patient ... Isn't that against the Hippocratic
oath?'*

Maxwell smiled. 'Well, I won't do you any harm.'

Bless him, he thought he was the cat, not the mouse.

*We met in a delightful little country pub outside Epsom. Like me,
Maxwell was keen on ensuring we were not seen together. He was fash-
ionably late, as I expected, wandering into the dark bar dressed in an
expensive shirt and aviators. He looked like a catwalk model: high cheekbones, Roman nose, strong chin.*

*'Here you go,' Maxwell slid his body across the booth as he handed
me my drink. It was clear from the way he was touching me he found
me attractive – or perhaps he was the type of man willing to do whatever it took to get what he wanted. It made no difference to me. I*

felt an unfamiliar stirring in my abdomen looking at him: If I were twenty-five years younger … *Well, if I could have a little fun too, why not?*

After some small talk, we got down to business. I outlined my plan. He put up some predictable, minor resistance, especially when it came to the boy, Dennis.

'Nothing that hurts him in any way.' *Maxwell placed his fist on the table-top to show he meant business.*

I was unruffled. 'That goes without saying. Besides, what I have in mind means you'll be spending more time with Denny, not less.'

Maxwell leaned forwards.

I told him how I had already obtained and copied a key to your place and would be coming and going as I pleased for the next few weeks. I mentioned my existing plans for trashing the flat and causing various nuisances, in the hope the stress would set you at each other's throats. Then, with a flash of inspiration, I proposed we make it seem like Maxwell was Lily's stalker, to drive a wedge between you and her and put pressure on your new marriage.

Maxwell was predictably nonplussed. 'If I am a stalker, why would she want to come back to me?'

I was prepared. 'I've read about this. Many people go back to their stalkers, especially when they think they have no other option or escape. If you can't beat them, join them, and all that. But even if she won't come back to you, she will no longer be with Sebastian. You won't have to compete with another man for Denny's attention.'

Maxwell appeared to mull this over. Finally, he nodded, satisfied. 'So, what do you get out of this?'

I smiled. 'My own son back, of course.'

Maxwell grinned. I didn't tell him how this would really *end for him – he might have been less enthusiastic, then. Nor did I say what getting you back meant for me.*

As we continued our chat, we settled on the idea of Maxwell and Lily needing to bond over some vital parenting matter. I proposed that matter could be Denny wetting the bed over the supposed stress of his mother's remarriage. Maxwell was wary of this notion at first, but soon softened when I pointed out any anger Denny had would also be misconstrued as stress. Plus, it would be easy for me to pour small vials of urine on the boy's bed on my visits to your maisonette. Freshening up in the bathroom upstairs would give me the opportunity.

After that, Maxwell appeared to warm to the plan. He especially liked the idea of provoking you into hitting him and putting your job as a head teacher in jeopardy. It was also Maxwell who suggested cutting the electricity off. We needed a bill for the reference number, of course, so I promised to take a picture of one when I visited you. He also came up with the idea of sleeping with that common little harlot who clings so much to Lily. The betrayal would surely remind Lily who she really wanted to be with, he said. I was happy for him to work on this himself. I even gave him some direction about timings. He had so much promise did Maxwell.

He also threw in the idea he could fetch Denny unexpectedly from after-school club. Apparently, he and the club leader, Kelly, had a 'thing' once and she still had a soft spot for him, so would hand the boy over without incident.

Of course, the cancer diagnosis was my idea. It had been playing in the back of my mind from that first time I'd met Maxwell. With his role at the Cromwell, and my own powers of dissimulation, we were able to convince you – and everyone – that I truly was sick. Yes, it was hard work. I'm not a big eater, as you know, but even I struggled at times with starving myself for so many months to assume the required frailty.

But when have I ever shied away from hard work when I have a goal in mind? And Maxwell was more than happy to help me – with the fake drugs and scans and so on. He didn't need much persuading ... although I was happy to do some of that, of course...

Yes, it is sad Maxwell had to die. He was so creative. But no matter. He was disposable. I used him for what I wanted, then got rid of him – just like I did with Father.

So now here you are, in my kitchen. Expecting me to spill my guts?

Fifty-four

Sebastian was not sure what he'd expected. A confession would have been ideal, or perhaps a nod of assent. Anything.

But his mother did not react. Instead, Fran reached into a cupboard and pulled out a milk pan. She removed a pint of milk from the fridge and poured a mug's worth into the pan. She added two spoons of hot chocolate powder, plus a sprinkle of cinnamon. She turned the gas ring on and started to stir the milk with a small whisk, concentrating on her task as if Sebastian hadn't even spoken.

'I wondered how long it would take you to come in here, shouting the odds,' she said quietly, looking into the pan, a calm, peaceful look on her face.

'Maxwell never touched you, did he?'

'Oh, I don't know about *never*.' Fran closed her eyes, a beatific smile on her face. 'In fact, he was rather good. When I let him be.'

Sebastian felt nausea roil in his stomach. 'You won't get away with this.'

'With what?' Fran's sharp, beady gaze turned upon him now. 'I didn't make any false allegations about Maxwell to the police. As for trying to get between you and Lily? Well, you'll find that isn't a crime.'

Sebastian licked his dry lips. His whole mouth felt moisture-less. It was a surreal conversation. 'Murder is, though.'

Fran looked at Sebastian like he'd gone mad. 'You've lost me, darling.'

'You killed Maxwell, didn't you?'

Maxwell despatched, dying inside his locked porch, I cleaned myself up in the car. Hidden by the tall leylandii surrounding the property, I reflected on how this was not even my first murder. Father's death had been ruled an accident all those years ago when you were a baby. And, yes, he had been killed in a hit-and-run.

However, I was the one behind the wheel.

Nearly thirty years on and I've never forgotten the delicious thump of Father's body against the bonnet, nor the surprised 'o' of his mouth as he saw me, just a microsecond before I drove the vehicle into him. You slept through the whole thing.

I'd never planned on being married to Father for long, but I'd had to speed up the process of getting rid of him. One night, as I did my customary snoop through his office, I discovered he was planning on leaving me and taking you with him. He'd some tart on the go who was apparently going to fill in on Mummy duties. That wasn't ever going to happen. You were mine and so was the money Father had brought into the marriage with him. I'd worked hard to gain his interest and had allowed him access to every part of me … in return for everything I now possessed. I was not going to bow out gracefully and let him leave me penniless and alone.

Having to hurry meant I worried my plan would not come off. I hadn't needed to worry; it appeared I had a natural talent for covering all the bases. I'd bought a little car miles away; paying in cash. I'd even taken a train to go and fetch it, so as not to arouse suspicion. I'd had to take you with me, so I'd bought one of those new baby carry-cots, not that you minded. You were a lovely, placid little thing … back then, anyway. What a shame that children grow up.

Afterwards, I paid a man, some lowly criminal I found in a back-street pub, a few weeks earlier. He'd been surprised to see a young woman with a baby in a sling in such a place late at night, but when I told him how much I was willing to pay, he took on the job, no questions asked, *even when he saw the impression of your father's body on the bonnet that night. What he did with the car I still have no idea, but it never resurfaced.*

Next, I played the grieving widow to perfection. I never even came under suspicion. The hit–and-run was written off as a terrible tragedy and has stayed that way for the last twenty-nine years.

I told you Father's car had broken down that night, which is why he was by the payphone in the layby. The police told me they were not sure why he'd been using it, but I knew: he used them to contact that slut of his. In the week before his death, I would wait with you outside the Cromwell, hanging back so he would not see us. We saw him stop at those orange emergency payphones multiple times, before gunning his engine and driving off in the direction of her house. It was a veritable mansion, so she was probably married too: he was checking her husband wasn't in. A precaution that got him killed.

How ironic.

Now, the arson was possibly my most daring move. I first got the idea when I read about the case of a man who was convicted of the man-slaughter of his children. God, I love tabloids. A never-ending source of inspiration. This man burned down his home to avoid a custody hearing with their mother the next day. I suppose he also wanted to feel and look like a hero, Daddy sailing forth to the rescue. That was perfect for my endgame.

Things are a little more difficult these days, with such things as DNA in use, but I swiftly came to the conclusion that I'd be fairly safe. I've never been arrested, fingerprinted or profiled by the police. As long as I was wearing gloves and wasn't seen in the vicinity of the maisonette, no one would point any fingers at me. Even better, fire is dramatic, and destroys any potential evidence as well.

I'd already looked up online the best ways to set a house on fire; I discovered petrol through the letterbox might be predictable, but it was still effective. I bought a can and filled it to the brim, again miles away from Epsom, in a rural petrol station I was sure had no CCTV. I wore my hair tucked up in a baseball cap, as well as dark, shapeless clothes.

I waited an hour in my car, to make sure no one discovered Maxwell. He'd been bleeding heavily when I left him, so just after one o'clock in the morning I decided his number had to be up. I debated about double-checking, but I was eager to get going with part two of the final phase. I already knew you were miles away from the maisonette: probably sleeping off the fight with Maxwell in your car. I still had the tracker app on my phone, showing me where you were.

Ten minutes later and I parked up around the corner from your home. The alleyway to your front door protected me from prying eyes perfectly, especially as I was still dressed in black. I pumped the petrol through the letterbox with ease, sending a bunch of lit matches after it. I might have burned myself, but thankfully I was wearing your father's old leather gloves. Even from the other side of the front door, I could hear the flames crackle to life. I imagined them racing towards the wooden stairs, dancing from step to step. I grabbed Maxwell's phone from the pocket of my dark hoody and tapped out a text message for you:

IF I CAN'T HAVE MY FAMILY, YOU DEFINITELY CAN'T.

I pressed SEND. I smiled, knowing how you would react, receiving such a message from Maxwell's phone. You're so predictable! You would not be able to help yourself; you'd rush to Lily and Denny's rescue, the big hero.

I had to stay; it was the responsible thing to do. You might have been asleep in your car and it could be up to me to call the fire brigade. Denny is my grandchild, after all. I kept to the shadows and watched for your car. I'm not sure what happened, but I blinked and suddenly you were there, blocking my way. I hadn't even heard your car arrive or seen its headlights. It was as if the crackling of the flames inside the maisonette had hypnotised me.

Overpowering you wasn't difficult; you had already been in the wars enough for one night. As I ran from the alleyway and across the car park, I made sure I slowed down as I made it back towards the street and my car. It was a quiet night, clear and cloudless. As I walked, I shed my hoody and chucked it into a large red bin full of takeaway cartons. Another couple of streets later I pulled the scarf from my face and posted it down a grate on the road, into the watery depths below.

I still had part three to organise.

Fifty-five

'Why did you leave the knife in my car, Mum?'

Fran's face took on a curiously absent expression. As if Sebastian had just described some plans for an outing she didn't want to go on. He could feel the phone in his pocket, the seconds slipping away from him. He needed her to admit it. Then he could take the recording to the police.

It was his only chance of staying out of jail himself.

Sebastian sighed. 'Okay, let's try something else. Why did you try and kill Lily and Denny, last night?'

'Darling, you're really worrying me. This makes no sense.' Fran's voice was all maternal concern, though her face was still oddly vacant, like she was acting a part. 'You've been under so much stress, thank God Father's not here to see this.'

Father. That was what she'd always called him around Sebastian; never *your father.* Sebastian had always accepted this, but now it seemed strange, almost clinical. As if Jasper's only real contribution to Fran's life had been Sebastian – and of course all the money from his estate. It seemed so obvious now.

'You were never happy with Dad, were you? You got rid of him, back when I was a baby. You were the hit-and-run driver. You killed him!'

'Now you're being ridiculous.' Fran actually looked amused.

'You killed Maxwell, too.'

'Maxwell was a difficult man, intent on getting between you and Lily.' His mother said the words like she'd practised them. Maybe she had. 'It's not surprising you cracked, all the pressure you've been under.'

Cracked. The same word Lily had used. It sent a shudder through

Sebastian. Again, in that microsecond, he wondered if it could be true. Then he shook it off. No. That was mad. Sebastian could never kill a man, not even one as annoying and ruthless as Maxwell. And he would never, ever try to kill Lily and Denny.

'He was alive when I left him!' How many more times did he need to say it?

The cocoa frothed up in the pan, scalding hot. Fran turned the gas ring off and poured it carefully into a mug. She presented it to him with a tight-lipped smile.

'So, you didn't even try and rescue Lily and Denny?' Fran tutted. 'That is surprising.'

Shame coursed through him. 'The flames were too fierce.' He took the mug, but he made no move to take a sip. He wouldn't put it past her to have put something in it, even though he'd watched her make it. 'I did what I could.'

Fran crossed her arms. That maddening smirk still tugged at her lip. 'I'm sure you did.'

Sebastian stared into the cocoa, at the skin forming across the top. A dead man, a lost family, a fatherless little boy. Lily thought he'd tried to kill her and Denny. He'd assaulted Triss. Everything was ruined.

'Tell me why…' He had to understand what had motivated his mother.

Fran sighed, dropping her vacant look and now seeming a little irritated, like he was being fussy and spoiled. 'Something had to be done.'

Sebastian could not process what Fran was saying. 'Done? Done about what?'

She flicked a hand at him. 'You … You and that *tramp*.'

Sebastian was shocked at the venom in her voice. Her eyes glittered now.

'Lily?' he asked. 'She is not a tramp! For God's sake, Mum, how can you…? I thought you liked her.'

But once Fran started, vitriol poured from her lips: 'Liked her?

Don't be ridiculous. Single mother. Common background. Older than you. You deserve better, Sebastian.'

'Better, how? Someone more like you, you mean?'

She bristled. 'Maybe.'

Sebastian stepped closer, the air between them charged with white-hot fury. The anger burst out of him like invisible flames; the legacy of thirty years of keeping it all inside. He'd tried so desperately to have a quiet life; to keep the peace; to try and mediate between his mother and the rest of the world.

No more.

'Or maybe this is some sick Oedipal shit you've got going on!'

He felt the sting on his cheek as Fran's palm connected with his face. The mug fell from his hand and smashed on the floor, cocoa spilling across the tiles. He gaped at her. She'd never hit him before. He felt a stupid smirk rise to his face. That must have infuriated her, because Fran took another swipe at him. She just missed but caught his cheek with one of her long talons. Sebastian felt the scratch, the sting.

He roared – more with anger than pain – and pushed her, just wanting her away from him. She stumbled backwards, howling as she hit her lower back on the countertop then slipping and landing, hard on the kitchen tiles.

'Sebastian,' she whimpered from the floor at his feet.

Sebastian leaned down beside her, but he made no attempt to pick her up. He wanted to smash her head against the tiles. He managed to restrain himself. 'I'll ask you again. Why did you set the fire?'

But even in her vulnerable position on the floor, Fran would still not budge an inch. 'That must have been you. You've not been well, Sebastian. I've been so worried about you!'

Another cry of exasperation burst from him. He pushed her proffered hand away, as fear and panic consumed him. He could not believe how she was sticking to her story. What was he supposed to do? How could he catch her out?

Fran regarded him with sorrow in her eyes. 'You have to understand…'

Everything seemed to turn on its head again. For a single, blissful moment, Sebastian was sure that this was it: she was going to confess.

Then she beckoned him towards with her one finger, whispering in his ear: 'I'm sorry. This was the only way.'

I parked on a side street, beyond the General. Hospital car parks are extortionate and opportunistic for parking fees. I might have plenty of money, but I wasn't paying for the privilege of being just a few metres closer to the entrance. Besides, there are plenty of cameras in the car park. I needed to slip in and slip out, unnoticed.

I had agonised about when to come. It was early morning, not even six o'clock yet, so the hospital was fairly quiet. In the next couple of hours, receptionists and outpatients would arrive, meaning I could perhaps blend in with the crowds. But the more people there were, the more chance I had of being seen. What was more, if I left it too late, you might be awake when I arrived; my plan depended on you being dead to the world.

Accident and Emergency was the busiest department even at that early hour, though there were fewer patients and relatives waiting there than I thought there would be. Even so, I gave it a wide berth, going out of my way and down other corridors to your ward instead. On my way, I saw various doctors and nurses, all of them preoccupied and harassed. They didn't spare a glance for a woman dressed in black with bare arms; nor did the porter with the strained face pushing empty gurneys into an oversized lift.

I didn't have to worry about finding you. The tracker app I installed on your phone when I came to lunch at yours led me straight to your ward. I didn't have the ward code for the door, so I studied the posters and leaflets on the wall until a weary young man came along. I watched intently as, with his back to me, he presseed in the code: 1989. Easy. I waited for him to disappear inside, then stepped towards the door and let myself in.

Once inside, the rest was no problem at all. I had wondered if anyone at the nurses' station would tackle me, or even just ask who I was with; it didn't happen. There was only one nurse sitting there and she had her head in her hands, fighting sleep. It's alarming to think how security men and codes can make us think we're safe when they can be circumvented so easily.

I scanned the ward, and saw you in your bed. You were asleep like the other two men, so I pulled the curtain around you. I had a bag of clothes with me, in case anyone queried my being there. I placed them next to your bed. I needed your keys for the next part of my plan, plus I took your phone, so the text message sent after Maxwell's death could not be discovered. I left you your wallet. I'm not a complete sadist – you would need money to make your way back to the maisonette and your car.

Anxious to get out of there again, I nevertheless paused a moment. Maxwell really had done a number on you. Your nose looked bulbous and raw; dried blood was crusted around your nostrils and one of your eyes. You were bare-chested and there was blood still caked on your head. Tears sprang up in my eyes, but not from sorrow. The denouement of my plan was in sight! We could be together at last.

I reached out and brushed a tender hand against your forehead. 'Love you, son.'

I drove by the maisonette next and saw it was crawling with police and fire investigators, as you might expect after such an incident. I let them get on with putting up their yellow tape, making measurements and filling in forms before making my grand entrance. I returned home and changed my clothes. This time, I went full 'old lady'; I donned a twin set, a box-pleat skirt, flat shoes, even a string of pearls.

Later in the day, I returned to find most of the investigators had drifted away. There was only a single fireman and a couple of police making sure the property was safe. I'd read how fires sometimes reignite, especially in older properties, since wooden beams can retain heat deep inside them. Fascinating.

As the last three packed up for the day, I parked in the little car park behind the maisonette, partially blocking their way so they couldn't miss me.

'Oh, dear God! How awful!'

My eyes on the blackened building, I got out of my car, mouth open. I even managed to squeeze out a few tears for my audience: three tall young men in uniform. The smallest one came running immediately, a pale young thing with a bright ginger beard. He grasped my arm like I was made of china. I probably reminded him of his grandmother. He guided me towards his police car, letting me sit down in the passenger seat.

'Are you a relative?' the other policeman said, his expression grave. He was glad to tell me my family members had escaped harm and that they'd been taken to the General.

But I shook my head with vigour, one hand to my chest like I was trying to stop my erratic heartbeat. 'You misunderstand. I know. My son has sent me to get some things for them. I'm just … How could anyone do this? It's horrific.'

The three men all agreed with me. The fireman then told me no one would be able to go into the property for the foreseeable. This made me cry even harder: 'My grandchild needs his toy cars,' I wailed. 'He's just a little boy whose home has been destroyed!'

The men all looked at one another. I thought every single one of them would rather tackle a roaring blaze head-on than deal with a crying woman.

Eventually, the fireman said he would go and get Denny's box of Matchbox cars as I'd requested. Since his room was at the back of the house, it had seen some of the least damage; he could get in across down-stairs' flat-roof extension. He would unfortunately have to break the window though as it was locked … Is that okay?

I sniffed and dried my tears. 'That's absolutely fine.'

The box of cars was presented to me about fifteen minutes later, along with their commiserations. I promised to pass their regards on. Of course, the cars were not what I wanted at all. I wanted to make sure Denny's window was passable for you when – not if – you came back. I needed you to go and get your spare car key from the maisonette, as I had yours in my bag. I didn't want to risk going back to the hospital to replace them and I didn't want you to see the stairs and simply call a taxi.

When I'd watched them leave the car park, I walked over to your car, which you'd left at the back of the property. I pressed your key fob and the car unlocked. I opened the passenger door and placed the plastic bag containing the knife on the seat, in plain view. Then I shut the door and locked the car again. Everything was in play.

All bases covered.

Fifty-six

That's when Sebastian realised.

His mother had just been delaying him.

Maybe Fran had made the call upstairs, or perhaps Su had traced Lily's mobile. Whatever the case, there were shouts and loud voices. Men and women in black and white streaked past the windows.

The front door came crashing in.

Sebastian pre-empted the police by a nanosecond. He made it out of the kitchen and into the hall, then into the living room beyond. But he didn't get as far as the patio windows because someone made a grab for him, hooking meaty arms around his knees and bringing him to the ground.

Sebastian groaned in pain as he felt a knee pressed into his back and his hands yanked behind him. He felt the bite of steel handcuffs around his wrists as a raspy voice read him his rights.

It was Sergeant Meyer. 'Sebastian Adair, I am arresting you on suspicion of the murder of Maxwell Stevens and the attempted murder of Lily Adair and Dennis Stevens. You do not have to say anything…'

'It wasn't me. It was her. My mother!' Sebastian protested as Meyer hauled him to his feet like a five-year-old.

Sebastian found himself staring at Detective Su through the kitchen doorway. His mother had been helped up from the floor and was now sitting on one of the kitchen chairs, a grateful smile painted on her thin red lips. The detective stood next to her and patted her arm in sympathy. Su could only see the old-woman act, not the ruthless, manipulative harpy underneath. Fran would do anything – *anything* – to get her own way.

But there was one thing still Sebastian didn't understand: why would she want him, not Lily, put away? It didn't make any sense. Maybe it was a mistake. It had all got out of control? Sebastian fought against Meyer as he jostled him past both women.

'Mum! Mum … tell them. You didn't mean for all this to happen? Mum!' Through the open front door, Sebastian could see their unmarked police car at the end of his mother's driveway. Two patrol cars were parked at skewed angles by the old tree behind it.

But Fran was a consummate actress, as ever. Tears coursed down her made-up cheeks. Mascara left black trails.

'I just don't understand,' she wailed. 'He was brought up so well. I gave him everything. Thank God his father is not alive to see this!'

Su nodded, her face earnest. Meyer pushed Sebastian over the threshold and onto the driveway beyond, Su coming with them. Sebastian had left the doors to his car unlocked. Men and women in black and white crawled all over it. One uniformed officer, a young woman with an eager expression, held up the plastic bag like a trophy.

Su stalked over and peered inside, her expression grim. Sebastian knew what she was looking at: the knife. Su glanced over to Meyer, her eyes glinting.

'I found that, in my car. *She* must have planted it … Maxwell was alive when I left! I did not try to kill Lily and Denny, please … Listen!'

Though as the words left Sebastian's mouth, he knew how futile they were. He twisted around in Meyer's grip and looked back to the house and saw his mother on the doorstep, watching the proceedings. He was shocked to see now how detached she looked, her arms folded, like she was watching her guilty pleasure: *Deal or No Deal.*

It was then that Sebastian realised. Insight hit him with the force of a hammer blow.

There had been no mistake.

The ball had never been in his court. He'd thought he could outwit his mother, make her confess and record her doing it. Prove his innocence.

But she'd had Sebastian stitched up. It had never been a case of events running away with Fran. She had never wanted to frame Lily. She'd probably planned to murder Maxwell from the outset. It would not have been the first time she'd used a man.

Maxwell had just been Fran's marionette, but in real terms they'd all danced to her tune. This fucked-up sequence of events had pitched them all against one another. Fran had set them all up like skittles and watched them all fall down. It had been his mother's endgame the whole time.

But for what … Fun? Because she could?

She changed now, holding a hanky to her face, turning instantly into the grief-stricken mother. She held up her other hand in a plead-ing gesture. Meyer hesitated, allowing Fran to catch up. Sebastian tried to summon up more words, ask her why, what he'd done to deserve this fate, but they died on his tongue as she dipped forwards, as if to kiss his cheek. But she didn't. Instead, she whispered into Sebastian's left ear, a triumphant hiss, audible only to him:

'Just like Father … Let this be a lesson to you … for leaving me. No one does that to me.'

Comprehension stabbed through him, as shocking as a knife blade. It knocked his breath from his body.

He'd not walked straight into his mother's trap. He'd been born into it. He'd dared to defy her by trying to live his own life, so she'd taken action to ensure he did exactly what she wanted, for the rest of his doomed life.

'I hate you!' The vitriol burst forth from him. He surged forwards, only for Meyer and two other officers to grab him, holding him back from attacking his mother.

'I've always hated you! You've ruined my life! I should have killed you when I had the chance! You fucking bitch!'

But his mother simply regarded him with a woeful, puppy-dog expression, the fake black-mascara tears smudging her cheeks.

Su snapped her fingers at her colleagues: *Get him out of here.*

Meyer placed a brawny hand on the top of Sebastian's head and pushed him inside one of the patrol cars.

The uniformed officer shut the door.

To Sebastian, it sounded like the *clunk* of a closing coffin lid.

PART FOUR

Eighteen Months Later

'When a woman has lost her character, she will shrink from no crime.'
—Tacitus

Fifty-seven

'Bye, darling, have a lovely day!'

I offered my cheek up to Denny for a last kiss, but he snubbed me. Stung, I watch him wander into the before-school club with Kelly. He was nearly eight now. My boy was growing up. He wouldn't want to kiss me … Or was it because he was missing Maxwell. Was he still suffering after everything that'd happened? I couldn't bear to think of even a small piece of Denny being damaged forever because of what Sebastian did, or my own actions in marrying that bastard in the first place. I wanted to call Denny back, take him into my arms again and magic the pain and confusion away for him.

But my boy had already gone inside the classroom and I had no time. I raced to the staffroom for the daily morning meeting, arriving late; some things never changed. The head teacher obviously had, though. The school's reputation in tatters, parents had pulled their kids out left, right and centre – especially when I revealed I wasn't going anywhere. Why should I? I hadn't killed anyone and no one could shift me because of Sebastian's sins. Besides, I needed the money. Maxwell had left Denny a little cash, but it was all tied up in trust. The rest of it had mysteriously vanished, presumably in probate and debts.

'Decided to join us, Miss Okenodo?'

Awkward, I raised a hand in a 'sorry' gesture. Despite her tiny stature Miss Lipson, our new head, was a formidable figure. After the scandal of Sebastian's arrest and subsequent conviction, the governers announced they were bringing in one of those 'superheads' to kick some ass. Miss Lipson was actually a Miss Trunchball. But at least she remembered I had switched back to my maiden name. Hardly anyone else did.

As Miss Lipson continued in her dull monotone about learning targets, I plonked down in a chair next to Triss. She handed me a banana. I hadn't had breakfast and grabbed it eagerly. Triss had grown up considerably of late, looking out for me and Denny. Since we'd both sworn off men, it didn't make sense to live apart when Triss was at my place most of the time anyway. We'd pooled our resources and furniture, finding a house together with Denny. On two teachers' salaries, it was rather plain and boxy, but after the fire at the maisonette, I didn't want to live in a period property again. And we had a garden at last. Forty feet wasn't much, but it was a sun trap, with enough room for a barbeque, a trampoline and a garden bench. After everything we'd been through in the past year or so, I appreciated the simple things again.

The bell went. The meeting over, all the teachers scattered to their various classrooms. As usual, I found myself in my classroom seconds before the first children, inhaling the familiar scent of paint and PVA glue. There was an explosion of noise behind me as kids began to file in. Turning towards the window, I smiled as a variety of children bid me good morning.

There she was, again.

Though the morning sun was behind her, Fran's form was unmistakeable. Tall and willowy, she stood near to the playground fence, a few feet down from the gates. I could guess why she was there: she wanted to catch a glimpse of Denny, or maybe even of me. Sebastian had been her world and now he was locked away, we were a reminder of how it could have been for her.

Guilt and shame bloomed in my belly as I considered my *ex*-mother-in-law at the gates. I'd been the prosecution's star witness. I'd knocked down every one of the tactics that Sebastian's defence team had attempted to employ. Obviously I had corroborated his story about Maxwell trying to get between us both, but I'd also recounted how Sebastian had magically appeared the night of the fire, smelling of petrol. What else could I do? I had to tell the truth. Sebastian might not have been well, but he still tried to burn me and Denny in our beds. I could never forgive him for that … Or myself, for marrying someone so unstable and putting Denny in danger. It was all just so sad.

We'd hoped Sebastian would at least have the decency to plead guilty and spare everyone the trauma and hassle of a trial, but he couldn't even do that for us. The defence had been a mess, a logistical nightmare, no matter how much his poor barrister tried. Triss and I had gone to every day of the trial we could and just could not believe our ears. It was all so cut and dried: Sebastian had been the last one to see Maxwell alive, plus his own blood was found at the scene, with signs of a struggle. Fran's neighbours had confirmed Sebastian had left her home, yelling that he wanted to kill Maxwell.

We'd watched a psychologist come into the court. He told the jury he believed Sebastian had suffered a 'psychotic break', due to 'adverse life events', culminating in the murder of Maxwell and the attempted murder of me and Denny. In other words, Sebastian didn't remember either killing Maxwell, or setting the fire, which was why he was insisting he was innocent. Yet the ice-cream parlour boy also corroborated the fact Sebastian had been at the maisonette the day after the fire, which seemed highly suspicious now he thought about it … Maybe he'd been surveying his handiwork? Certainly sounded like it, to me.

I really couldn't swallow Sebastian's refusal to take responsibility for his crimes. I didn't buy the 'psychotic break'. But he never once admitted to anything, even trying to blame Fran for setting him up. Fran had been a victim of Maxwell's schemes every bit as much as us … She'd thought she was dying from cancer! The idea she had killed Maxwell herself, then sent Sebastian the text from the missing phone to draw him to the maisonette seemed fanciful. For him to insist Fran had set the maisonette on fire and planted the knife in his car afterwards? Utterly delusional. It didn't help his cause either when he tried to tell police Fran had killed his own father, Jasper, too. Sebastian came off looking crazier than ever.

I watched Fran move away from the fence, at last. I'd not visited

Sebastian in prison, either when he was on remand or after conviction. And of course, he was not allowed to contact me and Denny.

I didn't know if Sebastian's fractured mind still believed Fran was
evil and had plotted to put him away from the beginning, but I
felt sorry for her. I'd seen her a few times at the trial and each time
she'd been stoic, but I could see the pain in her eyes, always glassy
with tears. I'd seen her in town from time to time too, but always
accidentally. She'd told me she was visiting Sebastian, even though
he was still saying terrible things about her. I felt bad I hadn't been
there for her more, but at the time I had to concentrate on Denny.
He had just lost his father and he was just a child. And I was feeling
too fragile. But I felt much stronger now.

As Fran disappeared down the road and from my view, I made
a decision. I would take Denny to see his almost-grandmother that
weekend. None of it had been her fault and it would be good for
Denny to see her. Stabilising, even.

Fran was bound to like that.

◉

It's a pleasant enough drive, taking in just the right amount of greenery on the way. I've developed a taste for talking books recently. Give me a good romance any day; a little bit of escapism. None of those psychological thrillers about timid housewives with amnesia, whose husbands are involved in satanic rituals. Who buys such far-fetched nonsense I have no idea.

I pull up beside the prison. I had hoped you would be sent to Downview. It's only up the road and they reopened it recently as a male prison, according to the Epsom Guardian. *But it's only forty miles or so to Belmarsh, so I suppose I should be grateful you weren't housed further away. If I put my foot down, I can make it in fifty minutes. There's a fairly large car park beside the dour brown nineties' brick building. If one wasn't paying attention to the huge signage or the beady eyes of multiple security personnel, one might be forgiven for thinking it was a leisure centre.*

I make my way into the visitors' reception. I join a small queue of people, mostly women with scraped-back hair, piercings and over-plucked eyebrows. A couple of them slouch, their posture defensive, fists dug into their tracksuit pockets. Some are carrying babies, some accompanied by older children.

I don't catch anyone's eye. I slip my phone into my bag and draw out a selection of change. A pound for the lockers, some coins for the vending machine. Having visited you on remand all those months, then every week following the trial, I'm a dab hand at this now.

Before I zip up my bag, I whip out my powder compact and check my hair and make-up. There was a young male guard last time, a natural flirt. He reminded me of Maxwell: all white teeth and puffed-up bravado. Sometimes, in the dead of night, I do find myself hankering after Lily's ex, just a little. He was fun. And so easy to manoeuvre! Just like those digital soldiers and aliens on the games screen thing little Denny loves to play with so much.

The little queue surges forwards, towards two prison officers and a metal detector. If I close my eyes and ignore the institutional tang of disinfectant in the air, I can pretend I'm waiting at the airport. Maybe I'm going to Antigua, or Barbados this year? Perhaps I'll go for real. The last year has been so stressful; I've earned it.

I'm at the head of the queue at the prison, at last. I step forwards to allow a tall, chubby female officer to search me. I'm disappointed to see the young man I've taken such a fancy to is not here. Not to worry; I'll be visiting you in this place or another like it for a couple of decades or so yet … Even if you do manage to get out early on good behaviour.

But of course this is not likely, with your continued protestations of innocence and rantings and ravings about being fitted up. Parole boards like to hear expressions of remorse, culpability, responsibility. The idea that your own mother might have brought about your downfall is ludicrous.

As I move past the woman who has patted me down, I drift into the visitors' hall with the others. Greetings echo in my ears, with children squealing at the sight of their fathers. A woman is warned to stop kissing her tattooed beau within seconds of walking in, but I have eyes only for you.

My boy.

You are already seated at a Formica table, nearest a burly guard, who is sprawled on a plastic chair nearby, observing. This is because of the last time we met here with the others; you tried to throw a chair at me. I am the only person who visits you, so for the last couple of months, we've had closed visits, with you behind glass, like a monkey at the zoo. But those sanctions have finally been lifted and here we are.

As you look up, I see the light in your eyes, the abject fury, has gone out.

'Darling.' I sit down and grip your hand. It's limp in mine. 'How are you?'

You open your mouth to speak, but no sound comes. Your eyes look dazed, though whether it's because of the medication they've given you, or because you've finally accepted your predicament – or both – I'm not sure. Whatever the case, your shoulders are no longer hunched with resentment; your body is no longer sharp angles around me. It's like you've deflated. The fight has left you.

At last.

Your gaze meets mine. In here, you're isolated from the rest of the world, looking to me for news beyond your four walls. I feel a sense of deep satisfaction envelop me. It feels warm, all-encompassing, even sexual: a tingling sensation travels from my belly, through to my finger-tips. As your sole contact, only I can help you navigate this strange, cruel world. I'm reminded of you as a little boy again: lost, depending on me for everything.

Just the way it should be.

👁

Acknowledgements

So many people say parenthood is the best thing you can do with your life – and yet so few people admit it can also be the worst. When we say we're proud of our children, it's often because they delight us, since they have become just like us. It can challenge our egos as well as our own hopes and dreams for our kids when they do something we don't expect.

For this reason, I would like to thank my own parents, Ian and Jan Hay, for never putting me in that straitjacket of parental expectation. Even when I came home as a teenager with a pregnancy announcement, they never told me they were ashamed of me or worried I would not fulfil my 'potential'. Thanks for believing in me, even at such a young age with all the odds against me. I will ensure your legacy with my own daughters, Lilirose and Emmeline.

Since this is a book about control, thank you also to my husband David Cawsey, aka Mr C, who has NEVER been jealous or possessive. Mr C, you know I might have many friends, but you will always be my bestie! You realise I might need to roam, both literally and metaphorically, but I will always come back to you … Or if I can't, that I will call you to come and pick me up!

Thank you to my son Alfie, whose own route to adulthood has been plagued with confusion: I think sometimes you want me to sort it all out for you, but I will never do that. Not because I don't love you, but because I do. You've got this.

Thanks also to my fantastic agent, Hattie Grunewald, and all at Blake Friedmann: you guys have always had my back. Thanks as ever to my publisher Karen and editor West at Orenda Books, whose eagle eyes and discerning literary palates have made sure I dig deep and deliver. To the many beta readers for Do No Harm, especially

YOU, mega-reader Cheryl Brown, plus the unstoppable JK Amalou! JK, you read every single incarnation, just as you did for The Other Twin, and I'm so grateful for your friendship and support.

Last (but by no means least!), thank you to the book bloggers – you guys rock! Thanks for your endless support and I hope you enjoy reading Do No Harm as much as I enjoyed writing it.

L. V. Hay